"We need som... Sam."

Maggie's words tumbled from her lips in a nervous rush. "Some strategy to find what I'm looking for."

"I know exactly what *I'm* looking for." His voice husky and sure, Sam crowded her against the wall.

His touch was so warm, so startling, she could only stand there motionless. He hooked his thumbs beneath her chin and nudged her face upward. She caught the slight smile curving his mouth as his face lowered, pressing soft kisses along her neck. His breath lingered around her ear, doing crazy things to her insides.

This couldn't be happening. This was Sam. Her best friend, Sam.

Sam who was suddenly trailing a path of fire down her jaw with his warm velvet mouth. Sam who was suddenly kissing her. Sam whose mouth was hot, sweet...intense. And demanding.

"We're not going to pretend to be a couple," he whispered, that delectable mouth just a hairbreadth away. "We're going to be a real couple...sex and all." He brushed her lips with his. "And it's going to be incredible. Trust me."

Blaze™

Dear Reader,

Somehow it always works out that my family and friends jet-set around the globe while I remain at home, waiting to "ooh" and "aah" over the photographs of their trips. Just this thing happened—yet again!—when my cousin Marietta returned from Niagara Falls. I "oohed" over the magic of the falls—which even one-dimensional was pretty awesome—and "aahed" over her journey into the mist wearing a raincoat, and understood why so many lovers visit there. I wanted to visit, too.

Enter Maggie and Sam. Maggie's a woman who's not afraid to follow her instincts, no matter where they may lead—even if she winds up in Niagara Falls *observing* the effects of sensual games on lovers. Sam's a man who knows exactly what he wants, and *observing* sensual games isn't on his wish list. Not when he could be *playing* them with Maggie.

Blaze is the place to explore red-hot romance, and I'm excited to join the ranks of wonderful Harlequin authors who share their inspired journeys to happily ever after. I hope *Secret Games* brings you there, too. Let me know. Drop me a line in care of Harlequin Books, 225 Duncan Mill Road, Don Mills, Ontario M3B 3K9, Canada. Or visit my Web site at www.jeanielondon.com.

Very truly yours,

Jeanie London

P.S. Check out the special Blaze Web site at www.tryblaze.com!

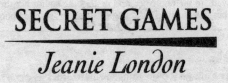

SECRET GAMES

Jeanie London

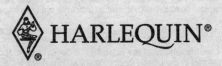

HARLEQUIN®

TORONTO • NEW YORK • LONDON
AMSTERDAM • PARIS • SYDNEY • HAMBURG
STOCKHOLM • ATHENS • TOKYO • MILAN • MADRID
PRAGUE • WARSAW • BUDAPEST • AUCKLAND

For my very own romance hero, Rick—*always*.

And a special thanks to Brenda Chin
for believing in my story, and me ;-)

ISBN 0-373-79032-5

SECRET GAMES

Copyright © 2002 by Jeanie LeGendre.

Visit us at www.eHarlequin.com

Printed in U.S.A.

1

SEX HAD CURED THEM?

The question played over and over again in Maggie James's mind as she left her office. She nodded at a passing colleague, plastered a smile on her face even though she knew the blush scorching her cheeks spoiled the effect.

Sex had really *cured them?*

Blushing was *not* a normal state of affairs for Maggie. First off, it was prickly, uncomfortable business. Second, she was a relationship counselor. As such, she spent her days listening to the most intimate details of her patients' lives and had long ago learned to school her reactions to unexpected revelations. This, coupled with her own rather…expansive relationship history, meant Maggie didn't blush easily.

But she was blushing now. No, not because she was embarrassed. She wasn't. Astonished, maybe. Perplexed, definitely. She'd thought the Weatherbys' relationship suffered from the result of too much stress, but apparently they'd been suffering from a lull in their sex life, instead.

How could she have misdiagnosed such an obvious problem?

Maggie didn't have a handy answer. She'd spent her three years in practice establishing herself as a competent therapist; in fact, her more experienced colleagues often consulted her about family counseling—dealing with blended families, divorce, children and the like.

Fanning her face with the brochure she clutched tightly in her fist, Maggie swept down the empty hallway, chanting, "Maintain, maintain, maintain."

Just because the Weatherbys had spent their abbreviated therapy session answering her questions while groping each other like two unsupervised teens was no reason to come unglued.

Maybe not, but Maggie sure felt the aftereffects of witnessing their passion at such close range.

The switchboard droned behind her, and the buzz of voices from the reception area suggested a busy night. With so many people working long hours nowadays, she and the other counselors who made up Baltimore Healthcare adjusted their schedules accordingly.

Thankfully, she wasn't pulling a late night. She honestly didn't know if she could regroup sufficiently to see patients right now.

A sharp rap on the door marked Lyn Milhausser, Ph.D., earned her a quick invitation inside, and Maggie found her friend and mentor seated behind the desk, poring over the contents of several manila file folders.

Lyn was intimately acquainted with the details of all Maggie's cases, not only because she'd been Baltimore Healthcare's program coordinator for well over a decade, but also because she'd supervised Maggie's college internship.

They'd grown close, becoming self-proclaimed sisters by love, if not by blood. Lyn had hired Maggie before the ink had dried on her diploma, and if anyone could help her sort through this mess, it was Lyn, whose years of counseling experience had always steered Maggie in the right direction.

"Sex cured them," Maggie said, and the explanation sounded absurd, even in the unbiased quiet of Lyn's office.

"Excuse me?" Lyn glanced up, but her welcoming smile quickly faded. "You look ruffled. Is everything all right?"

Maggie considered the question, then sank into the winged armchair before the desk. "No. Everything's not all right. I just finished my last session with the Weatherbys."

"They've resolved their issues, then. How wonderful."

"Not exactly."

"Not exactly?"

Meeting Lyn's confused stare, Maggie elaborated. "What was supposed to have been a normal session turned into a ten-minute explanation of why they no longer needed relationship counseling. Judging by how neither of them could keep their hands off each other for even that short time, I didn't bother trying to convince them otherwise."

"They claim sex is responsible for their recovery?"

"Not just sex—*incredible* sex. Apparently there's a big difference."

"I wouldn't argue, would you?"

Lyn grinned, but Maggie didn't appreciate the attempt at humor. She was too busy vacillating between disbelief over the Weatherbys' miraculous recovery and worry because she hadn't accurately recognized their symptoms. Now was not the time to ruminate on her own lackluster sex life.

"They claim that visiting a superclub has cured them of their problems handling emotional stresses. After a week at this, this *superclub*—" she waved the brochure wildly "—he's not shutting down when they try to talk and she has stopped feeling resentful."

"Wow. A superclub cured all that? A superclub is one of those resorts that cater to newlyweds and lovers, isn't it?"

"The very same."

Lyn stood, holding her glasses in place on the bridge of her nose. "Is that a brochure for the place? Let me see."

Maggie half sat on the edge of the desk and spread the brochure before them. She squinted at the blurb.

Fantasy, role-playing...titillating sex.

The words might have been illuminated in neon the way they leaped off the page, but as bold as the advertising was, she had to admit, the superclub looked, well...romantic.

Falling Inn Bed, and Breakfast.

Falling in bed, hmm. She could definitely see that happening. With its steep Mansard roofs and white gingerbread trim, Falling Inn Bed, and Breakfast was a place from another era, so picture-perfect it might have been a movie set designed to fire the imagination about what took place behind those sparkling paned windows.

Maggie could easily envision women garbed in bustled gowns, heels clicking over polished wooden floors, and men smiling debonair smiles, as they danced the candlelit nights away at grand balls and fetes. Lovers drifting into shadows for stolen moments, unconcerned as they gazed at each other with the sort of longing the Weatherbys had displayed in full view of her, Baltimore Healthcare's office staff and the waiting patients.

A place designed for lovers.

Men would whisper extravagant compliments and seduce their ladies with simple, but longing caresses. The graze of eager fingers against a smooth cheek. The intimate brush of knees while gliding effortlessly over a ballroom floor. Hushed breaths and lingering kisses and passion. Love. Romance.

Maggie smiled despite herself. Her entire career was built on the *reality* of relationships, not these whimsical imaginings of melodramatic avowals of devotion and happily-ever-afters.

Lyn must have been similarly affected, because she asked, "You don't believe a visit to this superclub and lots of good sex helped the Weatherbys overcome their issues?"

"I'm not saying sex didn't help, but it can't be that simple. You know as well as I do relationship issues aren't diseases to be eradicated with a round of antibiotics." Maggie glanced back at the picture of the romantic resort. "Or miracles, for that matter. Relationships require work. Men and women are different creatures, and if they don't respect those differences and keep the lines of communication open, their relationships run the risk of failure."

"That's all very true, Maggie, but sex plays an important part, too. Apparently, the Weatherbys were suffering from a lull. They've been married for years. It happens. If a superclub helped them put some passion back into their lives, I say good for them." She hesitated. "So what's the problem?"

Maggie let her eyes drift shut for the barest of instants, rallying the courage to force the awful truth past her suddenly tight throat. "I was working them through their differing reactions to stress. He'd become emotionally absent and she responded with anger. I didn't recognize that they needed intimacy to help them become available to each other again. I had them journaling, but they came up with sex to communicate."

"You've earned more of a highly regarded reputation in your three years of counseling than most therapists enjoy after decades in this business. But if you're expecting perfection from yourself, you're bound to be disappointed."

"Not perfection, Lyn." Maggie huffed, sinking back in the chair. "All right, *maybe* perfection. I believe in high expectations. Shoot for the stars and all that."

"There's something to be said for setting realistic, attainable goals, Maggie. You can't attain perfection."

"Apparently not this week, I can't. This episode with the Weatherbys has me thinking about Angie and Raymond."

After several years of living together, Angie Westlake and Raymond Mueller had been referred to Maggie for help sorting through some poor communication habits that were hindering them from making their relationship permanent. They professed to the same goals of a stable marriage and children and seemed to have love and dedication on their side.

Maggie had believed she could guide them through this rocky spot in their relationship, but after several months of counseling sessions—and practically every trick in her repertoire—she was forced to admit to an abysmal lack of progress. She genuinely liked the couple and worried they'd soon lose heart and decide to part ways.

"We all win some and lose some." Lyn correctly identified Maggie's dismay. "And you haven't lost Angie and Raymond yet."

"But I'm going to." She exhaled sharply. "Maybe I should refer them to you, or someone else with more experience in this area, since I obviously have a weak spot in my therapy."

"You've already suggested involving an associate to get another viewpoint on their problem. They're the ones uncomfortable with the idea."

"But I'm not helping them."

"You might not be able to keep them together," Lyn corrected. "But you are helping them discover whether or not they should undertake a marriage. Think of how complex their lives will be if they have to drag children through a divorce later on."

Maggie couldn't argue the point, but such a skinny ray

of sunlight couldn't penetrate the storm clouds gathering inside her. "I'm well aware I can't keep all my couples together, but I don't want to lose Angie and Raymond. They belong together."

"Then let's figure out how to strengthen your weakness with lulls in long-term relationships so you can help them."

Lyn's pragmatism propelled Maggie from her pity party. It was definitely time to reevaluate her strategy. She needed research into this topic and knew exactly where to get it.

"I'm going to Falling Inn Bed, and Breakfast."

Lyn blinked. "Exactly what are you planning to do there?"

"Research. Observation. Expand my knowledge base by getting ideas I can suggest to my patients. I'm going to research renewing passion in long-term relationships and I'm going to research it at the source."

Lyn emitted a very unladylike snort. "Research and observation? What do you think you're going to observe? These superclubs have doors on their rooms, don't they?"

Maggie opened her mouth to argue, but ended up staring as Lyn's words penetrated and understanding dawned. "But the foreplay should be enough to give me ideas, don't you think?"

"No. Foreplay isn't going to mean diddly to someone who has never uttered the words *long, term* and *relationship* in the same sentence when she's referring to herself."

"What does that mean?"

Lyn rolled her eyes. "Be real. You're talking about knowledge bases and you don't have one. When have you ever been involved in a relationship long enough to hit a lull?"

Maggie winced. Her immediate impulse was to defend herself, but Lyn's raised brows forced her to drop the pretense. After losing the Weatherbys, Maggie had no pride to be salvaged. Not tonight, at any rate.

"All right, so I haven't been involved in *many* long-term relationships. What can I say? I'm unlucky in love. That's why I kick yours and Charles's butts at poker every other Saturday night."

"Many, ha! Name one long-term relationship you've been in, and I'll up the ante from silver to bills the next game."

Maggie certainly wouldn't mind winning that pot. Finances had been tight all through school and didn't hold the promise of loosening up any time soon with all the college loans she had to repay. She mentally reviewed the list.

"And I don't count," Lyn said, as if Maggie needed the reminder. "I'm talking about a relationship with a male."

Maggie frowned, discarding name after name of the ex-boyfriends who'd contributed to her unfulfilling relationship experiences since her first ill-fated romance at seventeen.

Hmm. Not good. She couldn't come up with a single one who might plausibly qualify as a contender in the long-term department…. Then, with an inward sigh of relief, Maggie latched on to someone, the only someone she could think of.

His image sprang easily to mind. He was tall, dark and irresistible, judging by the way females had been throwing themselves at him ever since middle school. Not only was he athletic and charming, he was gallant, never casually availing himself of the multitude of feminine opportunities at hand.

"Sam," she said proudly.

Lyn tossed her glasses on the desk in obvious exasperation. "Cheater. Sam's just your friend. He doesn't count."

"Why not? I've known him since the fourth grade and we've been living together since my third semester in college."

"The only reason you live with him is because he had the second floor of his house renovated into an apartment after his parents died so your sorry butt wouldn't end up in the street. Unless you can tell me with a straight face that you've slept with Sam Masters, he doesn't count."

Argh! Maggie would have given their next poker game's entire pot of *real* money to wipe that look of superiority from Lyn's face with one emphatic yes, but not even for the sake of her pride could she tell such a whopper.

She'd never dream of sleeping with Sam.... Okay, she may have had a few dreams through the years, but they were very private dreams that would never see the light of day.

Sinking back in the chair, she avoided Lyn's smug smile. It was one thing to admit a deficiency in the long-term relationship department to herself, but entirely another to admit it aloud. She wasn't about to explain that most of her sexual encounters had been wanting.

Making impulsive decisions had gotten Maggie into more trouble during her life than she cared to recall, but there was one area where she was never impulsive—in bed. She *never* had sex with a man until taking the time to become acquainted and see if there was chemistry.

And all her uncharacteristic caution hadn't made one bit of difference. Sex was invariably the kiss of death for her relationships. The minute sex became involved, expectations followed, then the push for unrealistic promises, then the inevitable disappointments and hurt feelings....

"All right. All right," she finally said. "I concede the point, but this isn't my therapy session. What am I going to do to help Angie and Raymond?"

"Not observation and research." Lyn reached across the desk and flipped through the brochure.

"Then what?"

"If you're serious about visiting this superclub, you need practical application."

"Practical application? But how does that translate into—"

"Test out the theory behind the place. Look, they're talking about fantasy role-playing and other sexual fun stuff. Try this superclub out, then let me know what you think. Maybe I'll book a room, too."

"Lyn, I'm trying to increase my knowledge base here."

"There's no reason why I can't benefit, too. This place sounds great, and Charles has a thing for leather."

Envisioning the very dignified and well respected Dr. Charles Milhausser doing anything that involved leather proved too much for Maggie. "Stop! I don't want to hear this."

"But you need to. There's a whole world of sexual experiences you've been missing out on because you never keep a guy around long enough to get comfortable. Trust me, Maggie. Go to this superclub for practical application. You won't be sorry, and not only for your patients' sake, either."

"But I'm not involved in a long-term relationship, and if I wait until I cultivate one, I'll lose Angie and Raymond."

"Improvise."

"I'm not even dating at the moment."

"Anyone in the queue?"

"No."

Maggie wished Lyn didn't look quite so surprised. Sure, she'd had her share of casual relationships, but she really hadn't had that many.

"Well, what about Will Reynolds? If I remember correctly, you parted on decent terms."

Maggie shook her head, not quite certain where Lyn was going. Surely she wasn't suggesting that Maggie call up an ex-lover and invite him on vacation to act out sexual fantasies. "He met someone shortly after we broke up. Last I heard he was looking for groomsmen."

"Mike Jacobs?"

"He came out of the closet."

"Oh, honey. Why didn't you ever tell me?"

Maggie grimaced. That answer should be obvious.

"What about Troy Carver?"

"He found God. He's almost a preacher."

Lyn's eyes opened wide. "Ooooh, that good-looking man. Well, he won't work then, either."

Maggie leaned forward, propped her elbows on the desk, and stared hard at her friend. "Exactly what do you think I'm going to do with an old boyfriend? Say, 'Excuse me, would you mind dropping your drawers and hopping into bed, so I can test out some different positions?'"

Lyn chuckled. "Theory isn't the same as application. You need experience to identify the problem and talk the talk."

Maggie would be the first to admit there was a world of difference between reading about sex and actually participating, but this was therapy, for goodness sake. She didn't actually need to become depressed to know how to help someone who was suffering depression. "Observation will work fine. I've already figured out I'm misdiagnosing relationship lulls, so I'll read up on the subject and keep my eyes open for the symptoms. Now I need ideas to help my patients through their lulls. Especially Angie and Raymond."

When Lyn frowned, Maggie asked, "What's the option?

I'm not involved in any relationship right now, let alone a long-term one.''

"What about Sam, then?''

"What about him? Wait a minute....'' Maggie stared at Lyn. "You're not suggesting I invite Sam?''

"Why not? You're without a guy du jour, and Sam's perfect. He's the closest thing you've got to a long-term relationship. You're comfortable with him, and he cares about you. I'm sure he'd be happy to help.'' Lyn lifted her eyebrows suggestively.

After being forced to accept that her therapy needed help that her own extensive, but abysmal love life couldn't provide, Maggie couldn't handle this type of reasoning. Sex with Sam? This was *not* something she could tackle in the light of day.

Snatching the brochure off the desk, she shot to her feet. "Sam is my best friend. I can't have sex with my best friend.''

"Why ever not? I have sex with my best friend at least three times a week. Four, if you don't show up to play poker.''

"Oh, don't tell me that.'' Maggie beelined toward the door, knowing she'd never be able to step foot inside Lyn and Charles's town house again without feeling guilty for curtailing what might have otherwise been a steamy evening.

"Seriously, Maggie.'' The earnestness in Lyn's tone stopped her before she escaped. "Give Sam some thought. Sleeping with him might be the smartest thing you ever did. The minute you get close to a guy, you freak out and start finding reasons to dump him. You won't have a reason with Sam. You already know the good, the bad and the ugly about him.''

Maggie winced at hearing her behavior whittled down to

such unforgiving terms, but she didn't argue. Couldn't. "Even if I was attracted to Sam, which I'm not, he's totally not my type."

Fantasies didn't count while the sun was up.

"What type is that?"

Maggie waved her arms while she tried to find the right words to describe Sam. "He's stable, loyal, predictable."

Lyn stroked her chin, clearly considering. "Stable is good. Loyal is good. We could work on predictable, but that's no tragedy. He's a nice guy."

"Yes, he is."

"So what's wrong with nice? Last I heard we were recommending nice to our patients."

Nothing was wrong with nice guys, except it never seemed to matter whether they were nice or naughty—she always ended up by herself. Sinking back against the wall, Maggie blew a strand of hair from her eyes with an exasperated breath. Sam was definitely a nice guy, the nicest guy she'd ever known. That's what made him special. That's what made him off-limits. How could she possibly explain her feelings about him to Lyn?

They'd grown up together. Experienced so much. Both good and bad. Ever since Sam and his parents had moved into the house next door when she'd been in the fourth and he in fifth grade, they'd been connected.

They'd been there for each other through disappointing report cards and a host of parental punishments. She'd stuck by him when he'd broken his leg skateboarding and couldn't run with the neighborhood kids. Sam had cradled her and Hambone in his arms when her elderly Maltese had peacefully exited from life.

He'd proven himself the best of friends by helping her cope with the ugliness of her parents' divorce and the emotional fallout afterward. She'd led Sam through the process of funeral arrangements after his parents had died in a car accident and remained by his side during the long dark months while he'd dealt with his grief.

They'd survived her stint with vegetarianism and his fascination with home beer brewing. Sam was her friend, her anchor, her lifeline when life got crazy.

He was the only man in the world with whom Maggie could be herself. The only man she could count on not to turn his back when the going got tough. Through good times and bad, through changes of jobs, schools, friends and lovers, Sam was always there. Maggie trusted him in a way she'd never trusted another man. Not even her father. Especially not her father.

Sam was her ideal, the yardstick she held all other men to. Sex with Sam would mess things up completely.

"He's too important to me," she finally said. "Sex complicates things, and I won't risk ruining the special relationship we have, or risk losing him. Not to address the weak link in my therapy. Not for anything."

"Sex doesn't have to complicate things. It can add depth to a relationship and make it even stronger."

"With my track record? Please. The only reason my relationship with Sam works is because we stay out of bed."

Maggie clung to the doorjamb, longing to propel herself into the hallway, snuffing out the sound of Lyn and her too-close-for-comfort observations. All right. Maybe it was high time she took a long look at why she couldn't stay in a relationship past the time it took her guy du jour to memorize her phone number. Was her problem recognizing trouble in long-term relationships symbolic of her own inability to stay in one?

"I'll think about whom I might invite, Lyn. That's the best I can do."

"Ask Sam."

"Even if I was willing, Sam wouldn't be. He dates, but he doesn't do one-night stands. He's only had three long-term relationships in the entire time I've known him. And to my knowledge, he's never even had a quickie."

"Then you won't run the risk of catching anything."

How Lyn delivered that statement with a straight face, Maggie would never know. "Very funny."

"You need practical application, Maggie, my friend. Accept it and ask Sam. He's your best choice for the job. You can't go to this superclub alone and whoever you take is bound to have sex on the brain. At least you and Sam are long-term. Taking him will serve a purpose."

Lyn had a point. If Maggie spent most of her visit to Falling Inn Bed, and Breakfast circumventing sexual advances, she wouldn't have the time or the energy to observe the interplay between other couples.

Perhaps Sam was the best choice for the job. Sex didn't factor into their relationship, so he wouldn't be distracted by the sexual theme of the place.

"I think I will ask Sam to come with me," she said, taking an inordinate amount of satisfaction when she wiped the smile from Lyn's face by adding, "to *observe*."

"Now you're back to unrealistic expectations," she scoffed. "I've spent enough time with you and Sam to safely guess he isn't suffering from an inactive libido. If you take the guy to a sex club, he's going to want to have sex."

"Falling Inn Bed, and Breakfast is not a sex club—it's a romance superclub—and Sam won't want sex. He's my friend."

"Charles is my friend, too."

Maggie scowled. "Observation, Lyn. Not practical application. I'm going home now."

And *not* to ask Sam to have sex. *Observation, only.*

Though, if Maggie were completely honest with herself, Sam wasn't the one she should be worried about. Those late-night fantasies of hers didn't need any encouragement.

But she'd already had enough honesty today, thank you.

2

Tap-tap-tap-tap-tap, pause, _tap-tap_.

The sounds vibrated from Sam Masters's antiquated heater in a series of harsh taps that jarred the midnight quiet. Sam smiled. The crude, but familiar melody translated into a secret code. Though he never consciously hoped to hear it, he was always glad when he did.

Are you alone? Got time to talk?

He set down the mug of coffee he'd been nursing while reviewing a client's investment portfolio and made his way into the living room. A miniature replica of a judge's mallet hung by a leather loop from the side of the furnace heater.

Though Maggie always improvised with her own rendition of the Morse code he'd taught her when he was still in Boy Scouts, Sam adhered to the formal rules of the dots, dashes and spaces. Retrieving the mallet, he hammered out the word _yes_.

Tap-tap, tap-tap, pause, _tap_, pause, _tap-tap-tap_.

He waited.

Tap-tap. On my way.

Within seconds, Sam heard the tread of Maggie's footsteps loping lightly down the bare wooden stairs. He opened the door to their shared hallway just as she stepped off the last riser.

"Hi." Her bright-green gaze caught his, a welcoming smile clicking her expression to high beam. "Not too late, is it?"

"I was working."

Chuckling, she swept past him and through the door he held open. "You always are."

Though her laughter sounded silvery and light, Sam knew with one glance why she'd come for a visit.

Maggie had a problem.

Her gaze was a little too bright. Her creamy skin a shade too pale beneath the sprinkling of pale-gold freckles across her nose. Her smile rested easily on her pretty pink mouth, too easily. She seemed relieved to see him.

Throughout the years, Sam had experienced all sorts of Maggie melodrama. He'd survived nerves about dance recitals and ice-skating competitions. Worries about bum finances. Meltdowns about unfair grades. Angst about boyfriends. Way too much angst about boyfriends.

Sam recognized the symptoms, all right. She may sail into his living room with that breezy, devil-may-care attitude, but Maggie didn't fool him for an instant.

As always, that tough-it-out veneer she wore over her vulnerability did crazy things to him, made him want to wrestle her troubles to the mat. And her, too.

As always, Maggie didn't have a clue.

Sam pulled the door closed, before all the heat in his apartment could escape. Before Maggie could escape. She was his now. For a while, at least.

Though she was only of average height, her slim curves made her seem taller, almost lanky. The top of her red-gold head barely brushed his chin, and he was treated to a whiff of the scent he'd associated with Maggie for as long as he could remember, a scent that reminded him of orange blossoms.

There was a certain innocence about the fragrance that brought to mind a young Maggie, dabbing drops behind her ears from a girlish perfume bottle with ribbons. The years hadn't tarnished that innocence, but had made it a unique part of the woman standing before him.

To ward off the winter cold, she wore a white robe over gray jersey long johns and a pair of Gumby slippers that had seen the better part of a year's wear. Holding his glasses in place on the bridge of his nose, he noted that the green fuzz had been worn shiny in patches, and the protruding Gumby heads flopped limply with every step. Maggie didn't seem to notice their sorry condition. Or care.

"I owe you a new pair," he said.

"They're comfy."

"They're falling apart."

Giving Maggie a pair of cartoon character slippers was a tradition that began when Sam had been ten years old. He'd wanted to give a special Valentine to the young neighbor girl who'd been so instrumental in helping him make friends after his move to a new neighborhood.

The standard boxed fare had been too generic, and neither flowers nor candy had occurred to his fifth-grade brain. His mother had stepped in, deeming a pair of Bugs Bunny slippers—a character Maggie adored—perfect. She'd been right.

"Make yourself comfortable," he said, more out of reflexive civility than necessity, since Maggie had already deposited a folded sheath of papers on his end table and was situating a steaming mug onto a coaster.

"What's up?" he asked.

"Oh, nothing. Just wanted to say hi."

Maggie up at midnight? A cup of what he presumed to be herbal tea? Did she really think she was fooling him?

"Let me grab my coffee."

Sam nuked the dregs, parked his mug next to hers on the end table, and then settled himself in the recliner. Maggie, curled into a ball on the corner of his couch with her feet tucked neatly beneath her, watched him silently.

Even if he couldn't read the symptoms, Sam would have known Maggie was troubled simply because she wasn't chatting away about whatever was on her mind.

There was a high-strung sort of agitation about her that reminded him of the tense moments between a flash of summer lightning and the explosion of thunder.

"So how's it going?" He attempted to get her started.

"Fine, and you? Make lots of money on the stock market today?"

"My clients won't complain."

"Good." But a tiny frown creased her delicate brows. Work trouble, then.

"So, how was your day? Solve all your patients' problems?"

Her gaze pierced the distance between them, wide, worried, yet misty with recognition because she realized that Sam already suspected something was up. He held her gaze steadily, drew in an expectant breath, and waited.

This was all the urging Maggie needed. She exploded, just like a clap of thunder, launching into a jumbled and breathless account of losing patients to sex and split-ups, of nice guys and superclubs and observation versus practical application.

Sam watched as Maggie's cheeks reddened with agitation, or lack of oxygen, and her gesticulations grew wilder. He slid the mugs closer to his side of the table after she missed nailing one by mere inches.

He made a valiant effort to follow the threads of her disjointed tirade, but his own head was spinning by the time she'd braked hard on the emotions clearly racing inside her, stopped, and stared at him.

"So, what do you think?" she asked, winded.

He hesitated, unsure if she wanted his opinion about her choice in men or if she should take a research trip to some place called a superclub.

He must have hesitated too long because suddenly she was eyeing him accusingly, as though he hadn't been listening well enough to answer her question.

Latching on to the last thing she'd said, Sam gave his opinion. "I'm for the trip. You should go."

Jackpot.

Her narrowed gaze relented, and she said earnestly, "You really think so?"

"No doubt about it." But he did have doubts. He still wasn't clear on the correlation between sex and the so-called superclub. He'd stand a much better chance of getting her to clarify if he didn't come straight out and ask.

"If you can get the experience you need to help this couple and get away at the same time, the trip will be considered job training. You'll be able to write it off next year's taxes as a business expense."

She smiled, looking relieved. "Oh, Sam. You do have a gift for boiling things down to black and white."

He only inclined his head at her compliment, but was pleased he'd made her smile.

"You really think observation is the way to go?"

"Well, I think getting away will do you good, and with your crunched finances, you can use a write-off. Elaborate on this observation for me. I'm not clear on the details."

Staring into her mug, Maggie sipped before answering. "There's a couple I haven't been able to help, because I didn't recognize that they needed to put sparks back in their long-term relationship. I don't have much knowledge of long-term myself."

Now there was an understatement. With her pale red-gold hair and creamy skin, Maggie was gorgeous in a natural, unaffected way that made men trip over themselves for her attention. That none ever managed to keep her attention for longer than it took the Dow Jones Average to dip was an occurrence he couldn't entirely ascribe to her dates.

"How does a superclub translate into long-term experience?"

She huffed in obvious exasperation. "Think about it, Sam. I can't just snap my fingers and miraculously get experience, so I have to improvise. I'll visit one of these superclubs to observe the effects on couples. I'll get all sorts of ideas to help Angie and Raymond, and others, too."

Sam rubbed his temples beneath the arms of his glasses, certain it wasn't the late hour but Maggie's reasoning that encouraged this headache. She was infamous for her harebrained schemes and this one qualified as more harebrained than most. And who was she planning to take to this superclub? Last he'd heard, her current loser had already gotten his walking papers.

Man, this was exactly what he didn't want to think about tonight. Maggie running off to some hotel with another guy. When was she going to learn? Better yet, when was he?

He'd had years to reconcile himself to the reality that Maggie didn't think of him as anything more than a brother. By rights, the reconciling should be getting easier. No such luck.

"So your research trip is actually a visit to some sort of pleasure palace?" He was getting a clearer picture of what she was talking about and couldn't keep the disapproval from his voice. "Does that about sum it up?"

"No!" Maggie cried indignantly. "This isn't a pleasure palace. It's a romance superclub."

Which sounded like a classy name for a pleasure palace. Sam could tell by the way Maggie straightened her spine and lifted her chin that he was about to be treated to an in-depth explanation of the differences. Slipping the sheaf of papers from the end table, she sank to her knees beside him and spread what he recognized as printouts of a Web site over his lap.

Steeling himself against the brush of her fingers on his jean-clad thigh, he made a valiant effort to focus on the papers she brandished at him, tried to concentrate on her words rather than the wispy hairs fringing her cheeks.

"I went online and researched these tonight. Superclubs are the hottest travel destinations right now. They cater to newlyweds and lovers for weddings, honeymoons and vacations. Long-term couples go to get away from the daily grind and put romance back in their lives. I found one that's perfect."

With one casual graze of her fingers, she hooked the errant strands of hair behind her ear. She wasn't making this easy on him, but Sam knew Maggie had no idea she was providing him such distraction and undermining her own sales pitch in the process.

When she ran a painted pink fingertip over the page, he forced himself to follow its path, wrangled his unruly thoughts into compliance and read about the club's more unique features.

Fun, active and romantic, our superclub is unique, the perfect escape for energetic—and slightly wicked!—couples. After all, the point is to honeymoon or reignite the spark.

Romance-themed suites are also available, including the lush Roman Bagnio, Victorian Bordello, Sultan's Seraglio, Warlord's Tower, Wild West Brothel, Demimondaine's Boudoir, Roaring Twenty's Speakeasy,

Sixties' Lovenest, Red-light District and the Space Odyssey.

Specialty shops offer a variety of romance enhancements designed to drive your partner wild.

"Jeez, Mags. Perfect? Leave it to you to find this place. What's it called?" He scanned the page for a name. "'Falling Inn Bed, and Breakfast, the perfect place to experience love in the mist.' That fits. What's the mist? Some steamy sauna room with a water bed?"

Maggie rocked back on her haunches and exploded in laughter. "No, silly. The mist stands for Niagara Falls. There are superclubs everywhere—Vegas, Aspen, even in the Bahamas. The closest are in Niagara Falls and the Poconos. Since I've always wanted to see the Falls..."

Her voice trailed off, but Sam was only half listening. Visions of Maggie dressed in a harem girl's costume grabbed his attention. Her long, slim curves revealed through the sheerest whisper of silk. Flashes of firm breasts and smooth belly. She had an innate sense of movement, polished with years of dance lessons, and he could envision her dancing for him so vividly, the tinkle of finger cymbals rang in his ears.

Then another of the superclub's unique features caught his eye and snapped him from his fantasy.

Each superclub offers a variety of free services, including wedding coordination—let someone experienced in the ways of love help plan your special wedding.

Which led straight back to the question Sam didn't want to dwell on: who was Maggie taking on this erotic research trip? His head pounded harder, but he knew better than to ask. Knowing the bum-of-the-month's name would not make a difference.

Besides, Maggie wouldn't be planning a wedding on this

trip or any other, as near as he could tell. Given her inability to commit, he couldn't see her being persuaded to take the plunge.

Then again, Maggie was one of the most impulsive people Sam knew. What if this turned out to be the one time she let her heart rule her head?

"So, who's the lucky guy?" The question popped out, despite his determination not to ask. *Out of the frying pan,* he thought morosely, *and into the fire.* "Forget what I said about a tax write-off. Whoever he is, he should be paying."

To Sam's surprise, though, Maggie averted her gaze and hurriedly folded the superclub's printout, muttering something that sounded suspiciously like, "Well, actually, I've been giving some thought about who to take."

The uncertainty in her voice stopped him. The black temper responsible for this dull ache in his head receded. Miracle of miracles. Maggie didn't have a date.

Grabbing his mug, Sam slugged back the remains of cold coffee. Maggie retreated to the corner of the couch again, curled tight in her little ball, sipping tea that, like his coffee, had to be stone cold.

"What kind of thoughts?" he asked.

"About how to convince him. I'm not sure he'll go."

Sam found that hard to believe, but apparently not Maggie. She seemed fidgety and had an uneasy look in her eyes. He wondered if she was feeling the effects of discussing sex. Though they'd shared different aspects of their various relationships before, the details never included even vague references to the bedroom. What took place between lovers had, by mutual, unspoken consent, been off-limits.

Sam had always assumed Maggie needed to keep the stable parts of her life—mainly her home and their friendship—separate from the more transient aspects and wasn't comfortable blurring the boundaries. He knew she was no virgin, but in all the years she'd lived above him, she'd never had a date spend the night. She'd hosted plenty of dinners and get-togethers, but no man had ever walked down those stairs the morning after.

Sam knew because he'd been watching.

Maggie may need a push to think of him as more than a friend, but Sam had been thinking about it ever since he'd kissed her in their high school production of Rogers and Hammerstein's *Carousel.*

Not only had he been watching Maggie, he'd been watching closely, keeping her near at hand, and fitting into her life wherever he saw an opening.

He hadn't had a new opening in a long, long time.

"When are you taking this trip?" he asked to get her talking. Who was this guy who had Maggie so reluctant to talk?

"Valentine's Day, of course." She burst from her silence with a dramatic sigh. "The ancient celebration of amore. It's perfect." Then she grinned. "Besides, Lyn and Charles are closing the office on Monday for a long weekend, and I can't afford to miss much work. I don't know if there's availability, though. I couldn't find more information on the Web site."

"You've still got two weeks. You might luck out." He set his mug back on the table.

They lapsed back into silence, Maggie looking even twitchier than before. Then she drew a deep breath—steeling herself for the confession, Sam guessed.

She unfolded her legs, the ridiculous Gumby heads flopping wildly as she planted her feet on the floor and eagerly leaned toward him. "Sam, I'd like you to come with me. I can't go alone, so I want you to be my cover, help me observe how couples reignite their passion at this superclub."

Observe. He'd like to observe all right. Visions of harem girl Maggie flickered in his head again, earning a physical response from his body and kicking in his pride. A lethal combination. His instincts were up. And Sam had based his entire career on his instincts.

"You won't be distracted by the sexual atmosphere. Not to mention that I trust your judgment. And since you're familiar with long-term relationships, your input will be invaluable."

Sam didn't need a sexual atmosphere to be distracted by the idea of having sex with Maggie. He'd been preoccupied with that subject for years. He'd even tried to bridge the distance between friendship and romance before. One near miss in high school. Maggie had never put two and two together. What she'd dismissed as his temporary lapse of sanity had actually been his amateurish attempt to pursue her. Their friendship had emerged unscathed that go-around.

He hadn't been so lucky in college.

That time experience had been on his side, but good fortune hadn't. While he'd learned the nuances of seduction by then, Maggie had been horrified. His plans to woo her at the Fall Harvest Celebration had quickly become aborted plans, when she told him he was too good of a friend to risk losing with a romance that, given her track record, would end in disaster.

Maggie believed their relationship survived because sex wasn't involved. Here was an opportunity to change her mind.

She watched him breathlessly, hands clamped before her, perched so far on the edge of the couch she'd probably fall off if he touched her. Her eyes glowed with excitement, and she looked so alive, so totally beautiful that he almost didn't mind the possibility of making a fool of himself again.

"Sam?" she urged. "Come at this from the vacation angle. All you do is work. You're long overdue a break, and here's the perfect opportunity."

The perfect opportunity, all right, to convince her they could be much more than friends.

The bottom line was, Sam had devoted years to insinuating himself into Maggie's life, trying to prove he wasn't as erratic as her dad, who was far too preoccupied with his fourth wife to make time for his daughter. Time to risk another crash for a high-yield gain. He was damned tired of trying, and waiting. He wanted a return on his investment.

He wanted Maggie, not just as a friend, but as a lover.

"I'll go," he said, pointedly ignoring the icy feeling of déjà vu that made his heart kick harder.

"You don't mind pretending to be a couple? You won't have to do anything except be my escort, enjoy the facilities and watch people. Shouldn't be too hard."

"Not a problem." But he planned to be more than an escort.

"Then it's a deal." Her sweet pink mouth curved in a smile as she extended her hand.

Sam captured it, lifted it to his lips. He pressed his mouth to her skin. "It's a deal."

His words came out no more than a gravelly whisper against the silky flesh of her wrist. The faint hint of orange blossoms mingled with the fragrance that was Maggie's alone, and the moment became charged. His senses shot to life, his blood practically humming through his veins.

She tasted warm and sweet and feminine. Maggie. The woman he intended to make his own. And while his own needy reaction to their closeness didn't surprise him, Maggie's did.

She shivered. There was no denying that she recognized the connection between them. She couldn't hide the surprise in her wide eyes, the goose bumps that rippled along her skin.

He smiled, pleased. They'd be magic together, as good as lovers as they were everywhere else in their lives.

Maggie blinked, visibly coming to her senses, and Sam let her hand slip away. He would let her go. For now.

This would be his best Valentine yet, because by the time their weekend was over, Sam vowed to have discovered every creamy nook where Maggie dabbed that orange blossom perfume.

3

"WELCOME TO Falling Inn Bed, and Breakfast, ma'am."

Maggie handed the car keys to the valet, estimated him to be around eighteen or nineteen. He probably parked cars on holidays to pay his college tuition. Or maybe to afford one of the romance-themed suites inside.

Did he get an employee discount?

The less analytical part of her brain wondered if he thought she'd come to the superclub to have sex. She felt an absurd urge to explain she was here to *observe,* not *participate,* but suspected this young man couldn't have cared less. His mind was probably engaged elsewhere.

Like on what he might do inside one of those romance-themed suites with his own girlfriend.

As far as superclubs went, Falling Inn Bed, and Breakfast appeared as picturesque as the brochure had led her to believe. Clearly a tribute to the Northeast style of architecture with its steep roofs and canted bay windows, the superclub also had a wraparound veranda that would make gazing out over the park surrounding the Falls an incredible experience in any season.

Her original impression of the superclub had been right. The hotel and grounds combined looked like a movie set come to life. Or perhaps she'd stepped through the movie screen into another era. When the valet drove off in Sam's car, Maggie had the odd sensation that the twenty-first century had disappeared into an unseen parking garage right along with it. Or maybe it was her last link to reality that sped away.

A recent snowfall had enameled the grounds beneath a glaze of white and Maggie knew Sam would have insisted she fly if he'd suspected a storm. Luckily, she'd bypassed any difficult weather and her trip had been uneventful.

But Niagara was definitely a winter wonderland. Snow embossed the landscaping, creating glistening tiers of the frozen bushes and flower beds below. Lawn lights became icy rosettes that marked the walkway, and with the icicles hanging from the gingerbread trim along the eaves, Maggie thought the superclub looked like a giant wedding cake.

The air was filmy with moisture, the sky the color of pebbles, a combination, she supposed, of stormy weather and mist from the nearby Falls. Each exhalation formed smoky tendrils of breath, but it wasn't the cold that made her breathless. It was the atmosphere of the place. The aura of romance was tangible.

She made her way up the steps while a mature bellhop with grizzled hair wheeled her bags up a tastefully hidden access ramp. Bitter wind nipped at her cheeks, and somehow, the moment seemed symbolic, as if each step brought her closer to an unknown and uncertain future.

The doors ahead swung open, held wide by a smiling, well-bundled doorman. "Welcome to Falling Inn Bed, and Breakfast."

Sweeping across the veranda, Maggie inclined her head at the doorman, firmly tamping down any last-minute doubts that dared to surface. She'd just spent the past nine hours and five hundred miles driving to give herself a chance to come to grips with what she had to do.

She had couples to observe and a knowledge base to build. She would *not* be obsessing about sharing a romance-themed suite with Sam.

Though it would have made sense for her to fly into Niagara with him, Maggie had needed the long drive to formulate her game plan. Sam hadn't been thrilled with the idea of her making the trip alone and had offered to cancel his meetings and drive with her. But just the thought of sitting sandwiched together in the cramped interior of a car for so long was too much forced closeness for Maggie to deal with.

At least until she had a firm grip on her imagination.

Truth was, she'd had sex on the brain ever since Sam had agreed to help her. When she'd met him in their hall-way for a trip to the grocery store, their lovely polished-wood foyer had seemed to shrink to the dimensions of a peanut shell. Though she'd stood in that foyer with Sam a thousand times, Maggie never once remembered almost strangling from the lack of air.

When they'd bumped into each other at her twice weekly workout at the ice-skating rink, she couldn't help imagining what he would look like divested of all that bulky hockey gear. And when she'd glanced up to find him watching her from the bleachers, she'd been so rattled that she'd tripped on her toe pick and skidded across the ice.

While at work, her overactive imagination had been sufficiently occupied, but Maggie had spent the rest of her days staving off guilt for all the erotic images she'd conjured up during the nights.

Oh, the nights. They'd been the worst. Lying awake with Sam in the apartment below, imagining him in his bed, wondering what he was dreaming about.

Of course, she would never admit any of this to him, but after several barely lucid, and very lame excuses, he'd gotten the hint and backed off, giving her the time she needed to put all errant thoughts of sex out of her mind. His compromise had been that she drive his late-model, reliable car and allow him to make the return trip with her.

"I'll take your bags to your suite, ma'am," said a voice deep with the unmistakable burr of Scotland, when the bellhop reappeared by her side.

"Yes, thank you," she said, making eye contact with the man whose nose and cheeks had caught the bad end of the bitter cold, judging by their reddened tips.

The gold-trimmed sable uniform jacket sat stiffly on the bellhop's shoulders, as though he spent more time shrugging out of it than wearing it. A glance at his name badge revealed why—he was the maintenance supervisor. Why he was doubling as the bellhop, Maggie could only guess, but she smiled in greeting.

"I haven't checked in yet, Mr. Longmuir, but my..." How should she refer to Sam? Pretend lover, boyfriend, gigolo? "My *friend* should be here. Sam Masters. Just take them to his suite." She would head that way herself soon.

"Just call me Dougray, lassie," he said with a toothy grin that revealed a good bit of silver in those very same teeth. "I'm the jack-of-all-trades around here. If you have a trouble, with anything mind, press 19 on any house phone, and I'll be with you in a jiffy."

"Thank you, Dougray."

"Now, they're getting antsy for you at the front desk, lassie. You'd best get over before they accuse me of gibbering with the guests." Abundant gray brows dipped together in a scowl that bisected the older man's forehead and reminded Maggie of what Sam always jokingly referred to as a unibrow.

She followed Dougray's gaze to the front desk, where several clerks snapped to attention and quickly busied themselves with various tasks. Hiking her purse higher onto her shoulder, Maggie smoothed her skirt, wondered why she was attracting such an inordinate amount of attention.

She decided she really didn't want to know. "I, uh, think I'll look around a bit before I check in, Dougray."

"Press 19 on the house phone, lassie. Remember that."

"I got it—19."

With a respectful nod, Dougray retreated.

Maggie should let Sam know she'd arrived safely but decided the arrival of her bags would serve the same purpose. Taking off in the opposite direction of the front desk, she eagerly toured the lavishly appointed lobby. Falling Inn Bed, and Breakfast was nothing if not lavish.

The soft glow of light from a collection of cut-crystal chandeliers overhead enhanced the fabulous New England antiques arranged in welcoming, accessible clusters. The walls hosted several paintings of what appeared to be good-old-days scenes depicting the turn-of-the-century hotel and added to Maggie's impression that she'd stepped into another era.

While artful floral arrangements with wintry ivy and bright-red roses lent the room a charming Valentine's Day ambiance, the ten-foot tall Victorian topiary in the shape of three tiered hearts, immediately captured her interest.

She made her way toward it, passing a huge fireplace with a roaring fire that cast much appreciated warmth, and admired the unusual topiary, enjoying the sheer whimsy of the design. The hearts had been filled with huge white spider mums, then decorated with twinkling red lights, ribbons, hearts, and...

Maggie caught sight of a shiny ornament, a fragile glass likeness of a Rubenesque nude, one hand casually cupping a breast, the other positioned coyly between ample thighs. She inspected its neighbors with growing amazement.

Whoa.

Female nudes. Male nudes. Nude couples. While none was doing anything that might qualify for an entry in the Kama Sutra, all were clearly enjoying the effects of fondling themselves and each other. Maggie's surprise faded as suddenly as it had appeared.

Whoever had invented the name *Falling in Bed, and Breakfast* hadn't been kidding.

Time to move on. She glanced at the front desk again, but those clerks thought she was here to spend the weekend indulging in sex. *Incredible* sex, she remembered the Weatherbys' distinction, and decided there was no real hurry to check in.

Continuing her tour, she noticed for the first time grinning Cupids hanging everywhere. So many Cupids, in fact, she suspected management was encouraging the mischievous son of Venus to aim at guests the minute they walked through the door.

She kept walking the promenade of specialty stores, peering into shop fronts, not seeing much more than a blur. Until a display of lovely gift baskets caught her eye.

Arranged on platforms of all different heights and angles, the bright-colored baskets with festive ribbons contained what appeared to be bath and body items. Maggie paused, intent upon discerning the names on the assortment of jars and bottles, not surprised to identify champagne bubble bath in a replica of a champagne bottle and Treasure of the Sea bathing gels in a clever collection of seashell-shaped jars.

But Joy Jelly, Motion Lotion and *Peterbutter?* She leaned closer to inspect the silver-embossed labels which read, An Edible Lubricant with No Artificial Colors. Available in chocolate, espresso, butter rum or peanut butter.

Sexual props would be the first entry into her idea journal, and remembering Lyn's comments about practical application, Maggie swallowed back a bubble of laughter.

Observation was definitely the key here.

"I WANT YOU ALL to nap during the staff meeting," Mary Johnson, general manager and stockholder of Falling Inn Properties, Inc., explained to her crew of dogs. "I'll take you out for a walk as soon as I'm through with the meeting."

The dogs, a motley collection that included an English bull, a boxer and two teacup poodles, all made their way into the corner with a compliance honed by years of living in hotels. While they were usually relegated to the confines of her suite, the storm had made them restless. Mary had brought them into the offices today for a change of scenery.

Without a backward glance at her obedient crew, she pulled her agenda for the weekly five o'clock staff meeting from her organizer and glanced at the heading.

Worldwide Travel Association

The words figured in bold letters at the top of the page, emphasizing the importance of an arrival that needed no emphasis. The Worldwide Travel Association, better known as WTA, was the largest travel organization in the world, and they would be sending a representative to judge her property on how well they met the criteria for a prestigious industry award. An award her property desperately needed to win.

"Hey, hey, Ms. J." Dougray swaggered in, greeted her by the nickname she'd long ago acquired from her staff.

"Good afternoon, Dougray. I assume the heat pump in the west wing is cooperating now that you've worked your magic."

"'Twas the storm that pushed her past the edge, but she's purring like a kitty again."

Mary inclined her head in confirmation of a job well-done and recited a silent plea for any other mechanical or electrical failures to restrain themselves until after the WTA judge's departure. An unrealistic wish, given the size and age of the property, but she saw no harm in making the request.

After welcoming each of her department heads as they filed into the conference room, she watched from her seat at the head of the table as each settled into their respective places.

Silent for the most part, they acknowledged her before nodding casual greetings to each other. They all knew the drill because, with the exception of Laura, the special events coordinator freshly out of college, all of them had followed Mary to this property from the various hotels she'd managed during her thirty years in hospitality management.

They were her best staff ever. Not only were they competent in their positions, but they'd also willingly hocked their life savings and signed their futures away to leverage a buyout of this historical property when the previous management company had gone defunct.

Now Mary was in the unique position of overseeing a staff made up of corporate stockholders. Though a new company had partnered them in the endeavor, she and her staff held the majority shares. This circumstance had changed the gestalt of their situation considerably by placing a great deal of responsibility on her. She cared about every one of these people, and hoped to secure their futures.

"Has Cupid's Couple checked in?" she asked, beginning the meeting without preamble.

"Cupid's Couple," as Sam Masters and Maggie James had been nicknamed during one of the umpteen meetings in preparation for WTA's judging, was the only unmarried couple booked over the holiday. Their names had come to Mary's attention via the reservationist, who knew she was looking for some way of edging out the other nominees for the Most Romantic Getaway award.

Cupid's Couple had provided the perfect way.

Annabelle Simmons, the no-nonsense director of sales, gave a decided shake of her steel-gray curls. "He checked in shortly after three. The last I inquired, she hadn't arrived yet."

"The lassie's here," Dougray said. "About a quarter hour past. I took her bags to the Tower, but she went sightseeing on the promenade. Saw her peeping in windows just before I came to staff. I don't think the laddie will stay in his room long, now that he knows she's here. He seemed twitchy to see her." Dougray patted the black-encased radio fastened at his waist. "Front desk will call when he comes down or she heads up."

"Excellent. So we're prepared to get underway." Mary cut a glance around the table. "Are we ready?"

A few stoic nods of assent, a muttered "yes," and one very enthusiastic "as ready as we'll ever be," from an excited Laura.

"Have we heard from WTA's judge yet?" Mary asked.

"*He,* unfortunately, confirmed an early check-in tomorrow morning." Annabelle's possessive scowl compressed her stern features like a balled-up fist.

"Unfortunately?"

"I'd hoped for a woman." She impatiently rattled papers before her. "They're much easier to sell on romance."

Mary had hoped for a woman, too, but didn't disclose that tidbit. Annabelle was a crack salesperson. Her hardcore pragmatism ensured that guests' expectations were always enthusiastic and reasonable, but it could also have a sobering effect when the staff needed something to hope for. "Then we'll just have to work harder to sell him."

While an air of expectancy lingered over the table, Mary's staff appeared determined, and she felt certain her casual acceptance of their new judge had had the desired effect. No last-minute panicking. They'd come this far, and she wouldn't allow them to trip at the finish line.

"Think of this as the opportunity it is," Mary said. "We've been nominated as the most romantic getaway. This is the toughest industry award and the one carrying the biggest prize. We've earned this nomination. I want you all to keep that in mind, when the pressure is on."

Bruno, the former head chef and current restaurant supervisor, spread his hands in entreaty. "Five other properties have been nominated, too."

"But we're the only fully fledged romance superclub," Laura pointed out, with an enthusiasm Mary suspected was taught as a requirement in college hospitality management courses. "The other nominees are out of their league. They don't stand a chance, because we're owned and operated by our staff. We've got the edge. We're motivated. We're—"

"Desperate," Dougray said, cutting in.

Bruno issued a heavy sigh. "Yes, desperate."

"*Not* desperate." Mary halted the discussion. *Not exactly.*

While Falling Inn Bed, and Breakfast wasn't down-and-out, it wasn't far from it. Winning the prestigious Most Romantic Getaway award during this all-important first year as both a privately owned property and a romance superclub was essential for their continued existence.

The new management company hadn't thrown in with the employees to buy the 120-year-old property out of the goodness of their hearts. They'd done so to place themselves in a category that increased their credit limit to allow for both the buyout and a multimillion-dollar renovation of the historic property into a superclub.

There was an opportunity for substantial profit with the venture. There was also an opportunity for loss. While the management company could simply reorganize through bankruptcy in that eventuality, the staff would wind up losing everything down to and including the shirts on their backs.

Mary would do everything in her power to keep that from happening, starting with winning the million-dollar multimedia advertising campaign that was part of WTA's grand prize. The revenue generated by those promotions would effectively carry them all the way through next year's off-season.

"We have a unique opportunity here," she said. "We're off-season, yet we're close to running at full capacity. This isn't Florida, so we can't attribute those reservations to the weather. Our guests must have come to enjoy our amenities, and we're staffed to handle them. We're prepared, organized and completely capable of winning this award on our own merit." She steepled her hands before her and moved her gaze around the table. "And...we've got our ace in the hole."

Cupid's Couple.

The way Mary saw it, Ms. James and her escort were both successful businesspeople, young enough to be attracted to a superclub, yet old enough to know what to do with the unique services a superclub offered.

A few well-placed phone calls had revealed that this couple also had a long history between them and, as Mary—stepping into her role as Cupid—had summarily decided, a bright future.

Cupid's Couple didn't know it yet, but they were about

to be struck by one of Cupid's golden arrows. They would be bombarded with opportunities for romance this weekend, to fall completely in love and decide to get married, all under the guidance of her staff and the watchful gaze of WTA's judge.

Their path to love would personalize Falling Inn Bed, and Breakfast in a way that would give her property the edge it needed to win the Most Romantic Getaway award.

Or so the plan went.

"What do you say, Dougray?" Laura asked. "Think we can really pull this off?"

Dougray waved his hand in a gesture of dramatic impatience. "With this incredible superclub? With all of us playing matchmakers?" He rolled his gaze toward the ceiling and gave an exasperated snort. "Cupid's Couple doesn't stand a chance." He patted his hip reassuringly. "I've got me radio fixed tight to me belt, Ms. J. Front desk will call as soon as Cupid's Couple steps into the elevator."

Mary smiled. "Keep your eyes open for any opportunity to encourage romance. Phase one underway."

"Phase one underway," the staff chorused, a salutation.

Everyone knew the plan. Phase one would see Cupid's Couple exposed to every unusual amenity the superclub had to offer and ensure they were given a chance to avail themselves of those amenities fully.

Each member of her staff would handle his or her job competently. Luck would handle the rest.

And it just so happened that Mary had been born on Saint Valentine's Day, the luckiest day for love. The way she saw it, she had every right to play Cupid.

"MAGGIE!"

Sam's voice came at her out of nowhere. Getting caught with her nose pressed to the glass wasn't exactly the way

Maggie had hoped to greet Sam, but her disappointment scattered at the sight of him. Of course, she'd expected to see him, but something about him seemed so unexpected, so...*changed.*

Long-limbed and leanly muscled, he took each stride brisk and sure, smiling easily as he approached. His sooty black hair shone in the glow of the chandelier's light, the swoop in his bang that would grow into a full-fledged wave if he didn't keep up with his trims just beginning to show.

He still wore a suit, as if he'd headed straight to the airport from his last consultation and hadn't yet bothered to change. Though she'd seen him dressed for work practically every day since he graduated college, there was something different about his crisp white collar and butter-soft Italian leather shoes. So different that the breath tightened in her chest as he drew near.

Then the real disparity struck her. "Your glasses. You're not wearing them."

She tipped her head back to stare into his face, into dove-gray eyes that gazed so much more potently without the shield of clear lenses and wire frames.

He kissed her cheek in a casual greeting. "The arm snapped off. As fate would have it, glue wouldn't work."

"Your optometrist couldn't repair them?"

"Afraid not. The arm snapped below the joint. And I couldn't find my spare pair. I must have accidentally thrown them in with that last Goodwill trip."

"Oh, are you wearing contacts?"

Maggie knew he would have never seen her from across the lobby without some sort of corrective lenses. More likely he would have tripped over an ottoman.

"My optometrist had to order the frames I liked, but he was able to get these in a few hours. I suspect a conspiracy, though. He's been trying to sell me on disposable lenses for a while." Sam squinted myopically. "Have to admit they work. I can see fine."

She'd seen him without his glasses before, so Maggie couldn't figure out why his face—such a strong study of planes and angles that in themselves were not noteworthy but created a very striking whole—suddenly seemed so commanding and bold.

Or why catching her breath seemed to be a problem. She must be reacting to the pressure of the past few weeks. Wanting to help Angie and Raymond resolve their issues had weighed heavily on her, and now here she was, ready to implement her plan. She needed ideas, and she only had the weekend to fill up the blank pages of her journal. No wonder she was stressed.

Of course, Sam would notice. Understanding flickered deep in his gaze. He knew her well enough to know she was edgy.

"I checked in and went straight to our suite, so I haven't had a chance to look around," he said. "Mind if we do?"

Whew! "No problem." She wasn't ready to tackle the sleeping arrangements just yet.

"Here, let me take your coat." Circling in front of her in a fluid stride, he caught the strap of her purse when she slid it from her shoulder.

But the cold must have affected her more than she'd realized because unfastening the buttons of her pea jacket beneath Sam's steady gaze proved beyond her abilities. To her profound embarrassment, she seemed to have sprouted ten thumbs.

Of course, Sam would notice that, too. But like the gentleman he was, he took command of the situation. Sliding her purse into the crook of his elbow, he brushed aside her fingers and worked the button at her throat.

He didn't say a thing. Then again, he didn't have to. His sparkling eyes conveyed amusement loud and clear.

His eyes.

It wasn't stress or the cold that was unsettling her. His eyes were the problem. Without his glasses, Sam didn't seem at all like Sam. The omission had transformed him into a stranger. A very handsome stranger with soft gray bedroom eyes, who was further unraveling her already high-strung self.

Too taken aback to decide if this development would bode well or ill for the weekend ahead, Maggie simply avoided his gaze as she twirled around and let him tug her coat away.

"Thanks."

Returning her purse with a smile, he flipped her coat over his shoulder and inclined his head toward the shop front she'd been caught peering into. "Want to take a look in there? See something you liked?"

"Nothing especially." Although she should ask the salesclerk whether younger couples purchased Peterbutter or older couples, who'd had years to learn their partners' sexual preferences.

And what would Sam think about Peterbutter? Would the espresso flavor have a stimulating effect on him? Would the peanut butter flavor make him stick to the roof of her mouth?

Oh, my!

Maggie swallowed hard. She hadn't even been inside the romance-themed suite yet and she was already developing a serious case of naughty thoughts.

A fact that became increasingly obvious as they strolled along the promenade in silence. This moment was markedly different from any in memory. Sure, she and Sam had gone shopping together before. But pricing washing machines for the basement that doubled as their laundry room hadn't prepared her for walking so close beside him, so aware of their arms barely touching, staring into windows with the knowledge that somewhere above them a suite with one bed awaited.

Get a grip, Maggie.

Or she'd never survive this weekend. What she needed here was a firm hold on the reins. She always told her patients if they acted in control, they soon would be. Now it was the counselor's turn to test the theory behind the advice.

"So, how's our suite?" she asked.

"Medieval."

"The Warlord's Tower?"

"Our other choices were the Wild West Brothel or the Sultan's Seraglio. As much as I liked the idea of you dressed up as *I Dream of Jeannie,* I couldn't get past the fact that those romance novels you read all have knights on the covers."

He'd thought of her dressed up like a harem girl? Maggie wasn't sure what to make of this confession, and the only thing that saved the moment was the realization that here was classic Sam, thinking of her before himself. He wasn't her best friend and the most stabilizing influence in her life for no reason.

She actually managed to make her voice work. "*I Dream of Jeannie?* Really?"

"Really." A dimple flashed, and she couldn't find a shred of anything that even remotely resembled self-consciousness in his face.

Which was probably a good thing, considering she was experiencing enough self-consciousness for the two of them.

"Don't worry. Maggie, the warrior princess, works just

as well.'' His finger tapped the bottom of her chin, and the mouth she'd let fall open snapped shut. ''Or will I get to meet Maggie, the damsel in distress?''

Love-'em-and-leave-'em Maggie a damsel in distress? That wasn't how she wanted Sam to think of her, but by the time she'd rallied her thoughts enough to think of a reply, he'd arched a dark brow in a familiar expression that had never before made her stomach swoop.

''Maggie the damsel in distress, I think. You're the one who needs the favor, which means I'm coming to your rescue. So, Mags, am I your knight in shining armor?''

She stood there gawking at him, one small part of her brain cursing herself for not only letting go of the reins, but allowing them to be dragged beneath the horse.

Who was this man bantering about sex with her? Maggie had no idea. When she'd arrived in Niagara, she'd expected to meet nice, safe Sam. Where was he? And who was this man leading her into a store that looked like the embodiment of a designer lingerie magazine?

Sam's sexy twin?

He came to a stop so abruptly that Maggie ran into him. Absently, he steadied her with a hand on her shoulder, his gaze fixed above her head. ''Now that doesn't look comfortable.''

Following his gaze to the half mannequin on the wall, Maggie felt her heart stop in midbeat.

Fitted around the half mannequin's pelvis was a bright-red leather apparatus suggestive of a pair of medieval panties.

''Leather Chastity Belt,'' Sam read from the display card propped on the stump of the mannequin's thigh. '''Keep your treasures under lock and key. Supple high-quality leather harness with fully adjustable waist strap and T-back for a comfortable fit. Available in Valentine-red, shell-pink, lavender-purple, mint-green and canary-yellow.''' He paused, considering. ''Definitely not canary with your hair, but the shell or mint would work. What do you think?''

He glanced down at her, so obviously trying to contain his laughter that Maggie couldn't help but smile. Damsel in distress, indeed.

''Definitely shell,'' she said, and to her amazement, not only did her voice sound almost normal, she actually felt better. ''Pink's one of my better colors.''

Sam gave her hand a quick squeeze, before dragging her onto the next display, and then the next. By the time they reached the men's undergarments and saw the briefs that proudly proclaimed one double entendre after another, their wisecracks had grown so raucous and loud that they drew the saleswoman's attention.

''Can I help you with anything?'' she asked with a knowing smile, as though they weren't the first couple to come unglued in her establishment.

''We're just looking, thanks.'' Sam edged Maggie toward the door, while whispering, ''Candy condoms. Not good for protection—''

''But a very tasty treat,'' she finished.

They'd barely made it to the promenade and out of earshot before dissolving into gales of laughter.

The ice was broken. Maggie felt back in control again.

''Thanks,'' she said, gulping air and massaging the stitch in her side.

''You're welcome.''

He didn't even have to ask what she referred to, and that's how it always was between them, natural, relaxed. That was her strongest reason for asking Sam to come to Falling Inn Bed, and Breakfast—who else could make her feel comfortable while she observed sexual interaction between couples?

Only Sam.

"Ready to head upstairs?" he asked.

Her tummy did that crazy swooping thing again, but Maggie ignored it. "Let's go."

But once they were sealed inside the elevator and headed toward the fifth floor, their antics in the sex shop became a distant memory in the shadow of Sam's six-foot-plus presence, swallowing up all the air in the cramped space.

"We really should talk, Sam. Some sort of game plan. Don't you think? We should have an idea of how to go about everything, and you need to know exactly what I'm looking for." The words tumbled from her lips in a rush he couldn't possibly have understood.

But whether Sam understood her words or not seemed moot, because the elevator suddenly ground to a halt, somewhere between the third and fourth floors.

"Ohmigosh, what happened?"

"Looks like elevator trouble," he said unnecessarily. "Probably just a glitch. This is an old hotel. I'm sure we'll be moving in a minute, but in the meantime…"

Maggie's surprise died a swift death as Sam crowded her against the paneled wall.

The elevator's lights threw misty shadows across his face, made it appear changed, so very different from the man she'd known forever. He had her off center, and her impulse was to laugh and push him away, put things back to normal between them. But there was nothing normal about the boldness in his gray eyes. Her laughter dissolved in her throat.

"Sam, what—what are you doing?" she asked, a feeble attempt to regain control over this crazy moment, to side-step his unexpected move.

He arched a dark brow, visual confirmation that she should be able to guess what he had planned, even if she chose to deny it. He let her coat drop to the floor with a soft whoosh. It lay at their feet unheeded. Indeed, how could she heed anything but the strong fingers he slipped around her neck?

His touch was so warm, so startling, she could only stand there motionless. As far as touches went, this one should have been innocuous. They were standing in an elevator and he was only touching her neck, after all, but Maggie could feel the warmth of his fingers as though each had been dipped in hot wax.

When he hooked his thumbs beneath her chin and nudged her face upward, Maggie's breath shuddered audibly. She caught the slight smile curving Sam's mouth as his face lowered toward hers. Then dark silk hair and faint traces of aftershave kicked her senses into overdrive as his lips grazed her ear.

"I've got a good idea how to go about everything, and I know exactly what I'm looking for."

His voice was husky and sure, and she mouthed a silent, "Oh," while her knees turned to jelly.

She could only stare, waiting for him to back off now that he'd delivered his powerful message. He didn't. His breath lingered around her ear, doing crazy things to her insides, urging the breath to remain clamped tightly in her chest.

He traced her lips with his thumbs, deliberately, purposefully, as though he'd wanted to touch them forever and that alone gave him the right.

But that couldn't be. This was Sam. He may have tried to segue their friendship into romance once upon a time, but Maggie knew he'd only been experiencing a knee-jerk reaction to their closeness. They'd known each other for so long that testing out the romantic waters had seemed the next logical step.

And even if he had wanted to try sparks for a while, he'd been just as content to go back to their friendship. Hadn't he?

Yes!

He simply hadn't dated in a while and was caught up in the sensual atmosphere. That was all. She needed a favor, and as always, he'd been willing to help. He was also getting a weekend away in the mix. Though he'd insisted on making the reservation, Maggie fully intended to cover the cost of the suite at checkout. This wasn't a date; it was a *favor*.

And this was Sam, she reminded herself desperately. Sam her best friend. Sam who couldn't possibly know she'd entertained a few fantasies about him through the years. Sam who was suddenly trailing a path along her jaw with his warm velvet mouth. Sam who was suddenly kissing her.

The world as Maggie had known it swerved off-kilter.

His mouth was hot, sweet…intense.

And demanding. He deepened his kiss with a bold stroke of his tongue, and suddenly, without consciously willing it to happen, Maggie was kissing him back.

Their tongues tangled and teased, as effortless as getting wet in the rain. His warm breath caressed her mouth and that crazy swooping in her tummy rippled like a steamy wave downward, puddling between her legs. The ache, as unbidden as it was unexpected, made Maggie gasp.

Catching the sound with his kiss, Sam apparently considered her reaction an invitation to press on with his lusty assault, because he speared his fingers into her hair and tipped her head slightly, demanding even more.

Another gasp slipped from Maggie's lips, only this gasp sounded more like a sigh.

Suddenly, she was sliding her arms around his neck,

drawing their bodies close, until every muscle and ridge of his body pressed hard against hers. His legs braced wide, drew her into the cradle of his thighs, anchored her there, two bodies melting together, sharing the rhythm of sprinting heartbeats.

His hands traveled her neck in a downward path, unhurried, exploring, so intensely intimate for the way he savored their closeness, secured her against him. The shield of clothing proved a ridiculous barrier as his body heat warmed her, cajoled a responding warmth that weighted her breasts, drew her nipples tight, urged her to press even closer.

Maggie didn't resist the urge, *couldn't,* because each demanding stroke of his tongue chased away all thoughts, focused her on the fact that he was quite enjoying the moment, too. The rock-hard bulge pressed against her tummy only proved it....

When he drew away, his mouth lingering long enough to reveal his reluctance to go, Maggie just stood there, eyes closed and body vibrating, stunned by his kiss and by her own powerful reaction.

Wow.

Blinking open her eyes, she found him smiling down at her, his satisfaction unmistakable.

He'd leveled her with that kiss, and he knew it.

Pointing to an ornament of Cupid hanging from the rafter overhead, he smiled as though the mischievous son of Venus had been responsible for his crazy behavior.

But this was Sam, she grasped at the wispy thread of reason. Nice, safe, reliable Sam. Sam, who was always available with a listening ear and practical advice. Sam, who'd agreed to play her lover because she'd been in a pinch. Sam, the classic nice guy, who should have been safe to come to a romance superclub with.

There'd been nothing safe about his kiss.

This hadn't been an I'm-doing-you-a-favor type of kiss, but an I'm-hungry-for-you kiss.

Maggie knew the difference.

What she didn't know was why he'd kissed her that way. She didn't know this commanding side of him. Nor did she know why the need to press against him, to feel his heat fill the trembling hollows of her body, had grown so insistent.

The biggest puzzle of all was why his kiss had felt so completely…right.

"We do need some ground rules, Mags," he said, his voice husky and distressingly strong, when Maggie could barely catch a decent breath, let alone manage a sentence. "I'm all for research and observation, but practical application will work here, too. I'm uncomfortable with the fake couple thing. I want to give being a real couple a try."

A real couple?

No, wait, this wasn't right. This was *her* project, and she was supposed to be in control. "But—"

He held a fingertip to her lips. "Think Cupid and Psyche."

His gaze lifted to that stupid grinning Cupid, and her world canted wildly, though the elevator hadn't budged. What did he mean? Did he want to slip into her bed late at night and make love to her in the dark? Just the thought scrambled Maggie's thoughts, and she struggled to focus on his next words.

"You're looking for ideas about how to put sparks back into long-term relationships and I'm your perfect solution. We're long-term and I wouldn't mind sparks."

"Sparks?" She finally found her voice. "Since when?"

"Fall Harvest."

Sam didn't have to say another word. Fall Harvest during

Maggie's freshman year at college had been a weekend filled with events to celebrate a last fling with decent weather, before the snow came and the winter forced everyone indoors.

It had also been the weekend when Sam had tried to turn the corner on their friendship. He'd said he wanted... *sparks,* but she'd thought it nothing more than a whim.

Fall Harvest had been ten years ago.

"Oh." Maggie felt weak, suspected that if he hadn't been crowding her against the elevator wall, she'd have slid into a puddle on the floor.

"No pressure." He brushed his finger over her bottom lip, and to Maggie's shock, she trembled in reply. "Let's just go with it and see what happens." His smile deepened. "You won't be sorry."

One glance into his melting gray eyes revealed the promise of his admission. She supposed on some level she should have known he would still be amenable to sparks. She hadn't. "But sex will ruin everything, Sam. We'll never be the same."

"We can be even better. Trust me."

Her mouth still tingled with the aftereffects of his kiss, and for the first time since the fourth grade, Maggie questioned whether he was entirely trustworthy.

She'd certainly never seen any indication that such hot blood ran in a man who lived a nice orderly life.

Had she just never looked closely enough?

This was a question to consider...when she didn't have Sam staring at her with those bedroom eyes, awaiting an answer. Right now she needed to decide whether or not she could hand him the reins. Would he renege on their deal if she didn't?

She didn't think so, not because he didn't get his way.

Not Sam. He'd bailed her out too many times to abandon her now.

Trust me.

She did.

"What if it doesn't work out?"

"We've weathered worse."

No arguing that. "But—"

"No pressure, Mags. Let's just explore what's between us. There's something here. Something great." He traced her bottom lip, a gentle caress that held a world of sensual promise. "For the weekend."

"Just for the weekend?"

He inclined his head.

"And you swear that you won't get all weirded out and stop being my friend once we get home?"

A smile tugged at his lips, but he made a valiant effort not to make light of her need for reassurance. "I swear. No matter what happens, we'll still be best friends."

She searched his face and those unfamiliar bedroom eyes for some sign that he could be swayed from this reckless plan if she pushed hard enough. He looked disturbingly resolute.

The simple fact was she needed to be at this superclub, and she had to have an escort to be here. What could some practical application hurt?

Maggie couldn't come up with a single disadvantage. Research was good, but application could be even better.

If Sam wanted control, she'd give it to him. "Okay."

He smiled. "You won't be sorry."

She closed her eyes and whispered a silent plea that she wasn't making the biggest mistake in her life. Goodness knows she'd made some doozies.

Sam clearly didn't think this was one of them, though, and he'd been privy to them all. She found that in itself reassuring. When he moved toward the elevator's control panel, she found herself breathing a little easier.

He popped open the emergency panel and lifted the receiver from the cradle.

"Try 19," she suggested. This crazy turn of events qualified as trouble, didn't it?

He punched in the numbers and someone must have picked up on the other end on the first ring, because Sam was suddenly explaining their predicament and hanging up the phone before Maggie's racing heart had slowed its rhythm.

"Are they coming to rescue us?" she asked, trying to keep her voice casual and unaffected.

"That bellhop sounds just like Scotty from the Starship *Enterprise*. He said he'd have us moving in a minute."

"Dougray is the maintenance supervisor."

"I thought he was the bellhop."

"Jack-of-all-trades, he said."

Sam glanced askance, a look that clearly revealed his lack of surprise that she knew so much about one of the superclub's male department heads before she'd even checked in.

Love-'em-and-leave-'em Maggie. Damsel in distress. The relationship counselor who'd had loads of dates, but no long-term experience whatsoever. Except for Sam.

Maggie had some work to do on her image, but she didn't have time to consider ways to affect the necessary changes, because true to Dougray's word, the elevator lurched into motion almost immediately. Sam retrieved her coat from the floor and handed it to her, his strong fingers lingering on hers until she lifted her gaze to meet the promise in his.

"You won't be sorry, Mags." The lusty assurance in his voice sent a shiver through her.

''So you keep saying.''

Life as Maggie had known it had just taken the most incredible turn. Her friend Sam Masters had vanished, leaving behind this brazen, possessive and very intriguing man to take his place.

4

THE ELEVATOR FLOOR rumbled beneath Sam's feet, then lurched into motion, lifting them toward the fifth floor and the top of the superclub. He shifted uncomfortably, the seam of his slacks biting in exactly the wrong place as he subdued his firebolt response to kissing Maggie.

Beside him, she tried to look calm and unaffected, but to his eyes, she managed only pale and uncertain. Her chest rose and fell with sharp breaths, and she eyed him askance, as though the Swamp Thing had suddenly materialized by her side.

He resisted the urge to wrap an arm around her shoulders, draw her close, and reassure her that her long-term friend still resided inside the man who'd just kissed her.

But he couldn't let her in on that secret just yet. He needed her off balance and off guard, otherwise his plan to tear down her defenses would never get off the ground.

And he planned to go for broke this weekend.

Maggie thought she was an authority on relationships, both from her education and personal experience, and while she might be, she didn't know a thing about romance and intimacy. He'd convinced her to give him chance, because he intended to show her the difference.

Though he possessed no psychology credentials, Sam knew Maggie would never tackle a commitment until she was willing to acknowledge that she spent her life fixing relationships because she didn't believe they could work.

He'd witnessed the events leading to her family's breakup and wasn't surprised by her lack of faith, but it was high time she put the past in the past and got on with her future. A future that included him. But for Maggie to look squarely at her own behavior, she needed incentive. Serious incentive.

Sam had an invitation, a bed and a weekend to provide it. He would use seduction to wear down her defenses until she lost herself to passion. And to love.

That was the plan and he wouldn't entertain failure. Not when she'd melted in his arms as they'd kissed. Not when he wanted her so much that he feared taking it slow with her this weekend was going to resemble some form of medieval torture.

The elevator stopped. The doors hissed open.

The torture was about to begin.

"Well, we're here." Maggie sounded strangled.

"To the right. Suite 516."

Withdrawing the key from his pocket, Sam led her down the corridor, noting that she barely glanced at the antique portraits and gilded mirrors along the walls.

Good. He had her attention.

"Here we are. The Warlord's Tower."

Sam held the door wide, and Maggie swept past, coming to a skidding halt a few feet inside.

"Whoa," she said, gazing around like a kid on her first visit to a haunted house, not sure whether she actually believed what she was seeing, let alone whether to be thrilled or scared.

Sam swallowed a chuckle, remembering his similar reaction only a few hours earlier.

"Quite a place, huh?" He moved to the foyer closet, settled her coat on a hangar.

"Tell me I don't have to bathe in a horse trough."

"Nope. We've got medieval without the inconveniences."

"Thank goodness." Brushing red-gold waves from her face, Maggie pirouetted slowly. She took in the suite's semioctagonal layout and the vaulted ceiling bisected with wooden rafters, giving him a fine view of herself in the process.

While her wool turtleneck and long filmy skirt bore no resemblance to Sam's idea of medieval, the outfit was soft, feminine and perfect for inspiring visions of sinking into one of the massive chairs. Her long shapely legs would tangle around his as he maneuvered her naked onto his lap. Or perhaps the couch would be better. It was sort of a cross between bench and sofa, with thick cushions and a low back that would allow him to stretch out and explore her slim curves at his leisure.

The Warlord's Tower? More like the Warlord's Torture Chamber, since he'd barely tamped down his arousal, and his imagination was swiftly undermining his control.

"So, what do you think?" he asked, an attempt at distraction.

"Wow."

Sam appreciated the sentiment and feasted his gaze upon her as she feasted her gaze on the heavy wooden chairs and silk-draped footstools. With a sparkling glance, she strolled through the suite, pausing to touch the fringe of a canopied chair, to admire the wall hanging that, as he'd already discovered, lavishly depicted some of the more acrobatic sexual positions in the Kama Sutra.

Maggie quickly moved away without comment, avoiding his gaze, but her retreat gave her away. Sam squelched a smile. For a woman who was no stranger to sex, either in her own life or when advising couples on their relationships, she seemed unsettled. Must be the effect he was having on her.

This weekend would change everything between them, and Sam couldn't think of a better place to make the change.

The Warlord's Tower was a curious blend of historical accuracy and modern technology. Wall brackets and iron candelabra illuminated the suite, all medieval replicas adjustable from a dimmer switch.

Strategically arranged screens broke up the open floor plan, and Maggie ran a graceful hand over one tiled with bright designs and murmured, "Wow" again.

"The brochures explain that the suite isn't historically accurate, but rather historically themed."

"Works for me. I'm not much for straw on the floors." As if emphasizing her statement, she stepped off the woolen carpet onto the wooden floor, heels clicking as she walked toward the windows. "Where was the Warlord's Tower when I was in Mrs. Antoine's class?"

"I don't think a romance-themed suite would have done you much good in the sixth grade, Mags. Besides, wasn't the problem historical inaccuracy?"

"I put my heart and soul into that project."

"I remember, and who knew Mrs. Antoine would blast you for a little thing like medieval knights not wearing white cotton briefs under their armor?"

"Would have been comfy." Maggie waved a hand in a casual gesture of dismissal. "Well, I came out of the experience appreciating the importance of conducting thorough research."

Which explained her decision to come to this superclub. One of her finer schemes, if Sam said so himself. Though it didn't compare in scope to the time she'd rallied her sorority sisters to protest their living conditions by donning hard hats and tool belts and tackling the improvements themselves.

The repairs to the improvements had run into five digits, and Maggie had wound up living upstairs in his house.

"This suite isn't at all what I imagined, though," she said. "It's so light. I was envisioning a dark dungeon."

There was nothing dark and dungeonlike about the War-lord's Tower. Situated on the top floor of the superclub, it occupied an octagonal room on the west side of the building. Arch-topped windows overlooking the state park that surrounded the Falls and the Niagara River comprised one whole side of the suite.

Ice frosted the panes, and with the thin sections of bright stained glass separating each window, the winter sun streamed through to pattern kaleidoscope sparkles through half the room.

Sidling toward the suit of armor standing sentinel by the last panel of stained glass, Maggie flicked the bright-red plume on the helm and asked, "Who's this, the warlord?"

Sam joined her, moving so close their arms brushed and the top of her head almost touched his chin. She stiffened, in surprise, maybe, but she didn't move away. "That was my guess."

Standing side by side had taken on a whole new significance, and she smiled up at him, acknowledging the change. "How about you? Feeling like a warlord yourself yet?"

"Not quite." He brushed a stray hair from her cheek, pleased by the brightness in her green eyes. He recognized her excitement, if he could just get her past the nerves. "My damsel has spent her whole day driving. She must be tired."

"Even if I am, I'm so keyed up I can't tell."

He smiled. He'd wanted to invade her personal space for

so long that he was keyed up himself. "When did you last eat?"

"I had a chocolate bar and espresso break around three."

"Lunch?"

She shook her head.

"I know you didn't eat breakfast."

She shrugged.

"Hmm." He considered her thoughtfully. Maggie needed to eat, and he was hungry himself, but the idea of dinner in one of the superclub's restaurants didn't appeal. He didn't want to share her yet. Not even with strangers. But he knew that once a day spent in the car finally hit her, she'd be exhausted.

He could see the first signs of weariness in the slight slump of her shoulders as she stared through the window. Following her gaze, he admired the scene below. Winter-bare trees stabbed through the mist rolling off the river, and strings of red and white lights adorned their branches.

"You're calling the shots, Sam. What's next?"

He wondered if her acquiescence would last past tonight, especially once he put his plans for the perfect seduction into motion. Would she resist?

He hoped to keep her off balance enough not to have the chance. But tonight, their all-important first night, Maggie needed to relax and unwind. She needed to get used to the idea of him as a lover.

"Come on." Taking her hand, Sam led her back to the foyer to where he'd earlier directed the bellhop to put her bags in the closet. "Where did you pack your toiletries?"

"The overnighter." She pointed to the smaller of the two suitcases on the floor. "Why?"

"Just trust me." Sam slung the bag's strap over his shoulder and then, with Maggie still eyeing him curiously, he bent, slipped his arms beneath her, and scooped her up.

She wobbled precariously for a moment and with a gasp, flung her arms around his neck.

"What, oh...Sam!"

"Got you."

And he did. Every curvy inch cradled in his arms. The filmy material of her skirt may have hidden her shapely legs from view, but it did little to conceal the sleek length of firm thighs. Or the curve of warm backside that jounced against a very sensitive area with every step he took.

Their gazes met. Sam forced what he hoped was a reassuring smile and lifted Maggie a little higher. "I know exactly what you need."

She frowned when he maneuvered her through the bathroom door. "I need to brush my teeth? Are you telling me I have coffee breath or something?"

"Or something."

Sam suspected the knights and ladies of yore couldn't have imagined this bathroom in their wildest dreams. A hot tub occupied one corner, easily large enough for a couple to engage in a lot more than bathing, while the opposite corner boasted a shower stall with two walls of floor-to-ceiling showerjets.

Maggie obviously hadn't imagined this bathroom, either.

"Oh, my," she said with an expression of rapt anticipation. "This is my kind of bathroom. I'm going to keep this in mind for when my landlord finally decides to replace my chintzy porcelain enamel tub with the chip in it."

He didn't think Maggie was ready to hear that he'd like to do away with her apartment entirely, in favor of remodeling and expansion into a home where they might someday raise a family, so he simply said, "He might have to raise your rent."

She only harrumphed in reply, and after letting the overnight bag slide from his shoulder, Sam lowered her to the floor in a lingering motion that made them slide together. Her breasts molded his chest on the way down and his body jolted with the contact, a reaction his slacks didn't conceal.

Maggie's gaze shot up toward his.

Sam recognized her surprise, but she recovered quickly, schooling her expression, and saying offhandedly, "I hope not. He knows repaying loans is killing me."

"He just might be willing to work out something in trade."

"What could I possibly offer him that he'd want?"

Her words might have been flip, but her voice sounded breathless and trembly.

Sam let his hands slip down her back suggestively. "You've lived with him a long time. I'll bet you can think of something."

"Can't imagine what." She stepped away, laughing lightly, clearly trying to restore balance to the moment.

Sam let her go, not surprised by how the sudden rush of cool air between them jarred. He'd never had such a rapid-fire reaction to any woman in his life, not even when he'd been a kid exploring his libido with a high school girlfriend. He was in uncharted territory here and needed to move slowly.

"So exactly what is it that you think I need?" she asked.

"A bath or a shower." Recognizing her wary expression he added, "Alone. I thought you'd want to relax after the drive."

"Oh." She glanced at the tub. "I like that idea."

"What's it going to be, then?"

Maggie darted a gaze between the tub and the shower stall. "I don't have the patience to wait for that tub to fill."

"I'll order room service, then. We'll spend the night in."

"Works for me."

Thick round candles in several different sizes sat on the

ledge of the tub and along the vanity in replicas of medieval candleholders. A quick search revealed a lighter in the top drawer. Sam did the honors.

"If a shower in here doesn't relax me, nothing will."

Sam could think of a number of relaxation techniques he might apply on her to get the desired effect, but all involved roving hands and naked skin. "Are you hungry for anything in particular?"

A guy could hope, couldn't he?

"Nothing especially." Maggie grabbed her overnight bag and busied herself unpacking, and Sam had the distinct impression she would have agreed to anything that expedited his departure from the bathroom. "Whatever you want is fine with me."

Judging by her response, she wasn't ready for what he wanted. "Take your time and relax. Yell if you need anything."

Maggie turned to him, hands poised over her bag as she lifted out what he guessed to be a makeup case. A slow smile curved her mouth. "You'll help me scrub my back, is that it?"

It was a moment ripe with sexual innuendo and Sam had no fonder wish. Holding her gaze, he swept what he hoped was a courtly bow. "If that's milady's desire."

Departing to the sound of her laughter, he pulled the door closed behind him.

After ordering the kinds of light, finger foods he thought Maggie would enjoy after a day of inactivity in the car, Sam prowled the suite restlessly. When the sound of pulsing water emitted from beyond the bathroom door, he was barraged with images of a naked Maggie, red-gold waves piled on top of her head, stepping inside that killer shower.

Candlelight would spark her features, illuminate her

graceful shoulders and creamy breasts as they played hide-and-seek behind the clear glass....

Only activity would save him now. With renewed purpose, Sam lit candles in the bedroom, decided against opening the complimentary bottle of champagne. He'd never survive a trip into the bathroom to leave Maggie a glass without joining her in that shower, so he headed toward the closet instead. He unzipped her garment bag and smoothed the items. He lugged her suitcase into the bedroom, set the suitcase unopened on a luggage rack.

After changing into a pair of jeans and a sweater—more to avail himself of the jeans' confining features than from any real need to get out of his suit—he prowled the suite some more, looking for something to drag his thoughts away from the whir of pulsing shower jets and the images of Maggie's beautiful body slick with hot water and soapy lather.

"Sam?"

The last of his determination to take his seduction slow dissolved when he heard the sound he'd been waiting for—Maggie calling his name.

KNOCK-KNOCK.

Maggie heard the sound over the pulsing jets of water that had pounded the nerves, and most of the life, out of her body during a long hot shower.

At least until this nice little adrenaline rush.

"Damn, damn, and double damn!" She shrank back into the steamy spray and glared at the stupid shower door that had somehow jammed shut and locked her in.

She'd fiddled with the thing for as long as she could, unwilling to call for help with Sam the lusty stranger lurking around. But the darned thing had malfunctioned big-time, and she was about to turn into a prune. She should probably turn off the water, but the idea of freezing didn't appeal, either.

"Mayday!"

She watched the bathroom door crack open in some sort of bizarre slow motion, reminiscent of a scene from *The Twilight Zone*. Her heart thudded hard, whether from the effects of the hot water or adrenaline, she didn't know. Or care. Maggie only knew that she'd never felt more vulnerable in her life.

"Milady called?" Sam asked judiciously from the opposite side of the half-open door.

Under normal circumstances, she would have appreciated his gallantry. Right now it was just dragging out the suspense.

"The door's stuck. I can't get out of the shower."

Twisting from side to side, she searched for some way to stand without looking as if she were cringing before him, yet still maintain her dignity. What little was left of it.

On an up note though, debuting in front of Sam with nothing on but steam should certainly break the ice. Since she'd agreed to explore a sexual relationship with him, they'd be off to a bang of a start. She wouldn't feel nearly so discombobulated once they'd gotten past the clothing hurdle, would she?

He strode across the bathroom with long purposeful strides, so shockingly out of place in the intimate confines of the bathroom that she could hear *The Twilight Zone* theme song booming in her head.

Do-do do-do, do-do do-do.

He jiggled the shower door handle without meeting her gaze. "You're right. It's stuck."

Maggie could see his smile through the steamy glass. If she hadn't known better, she'd have believed Sam had engineered this predicament himself. Of course that was ridiculous—how could he have known she would take a shower instead of a bath?

"Can you open it?"

Soon, please?

His gaze lifted to hers then, but not before journeying leisurely all the way from her toes to her face. His eyes deepened from dove-gray to smoke on the trip and her entire body tingled beneath the potency of his stare.

His dimple flashed.

She forced herself to stand proud, praying the combination of steam and aggressive water provided some form of protection, telling herself it did, just because she needed to believe it.

"Hurry, please. The water is getting cold." As unlikely as it seemed in a hotel, the water was indeed dropping in temperature.

"Turn it off."

"I can't."

His gaze dipped downward again, and his smile widened, making him look like a grinning idiot. "I'd promise not to look, but that would be a promise I know I can't keep."

Her breath stalled in her throat, a string of broken gasps.

"And I'd offer you a towel, but..." He pointed to the top of the glass enclosure that reached clear to the ceiling.

"Sam!" She resisted the urge to slam her hand against the glass, not so much from restraint, but because she didn't want to treat him to a full frontal view. "You've got to get this door open. I'll die in here before I call maintenance."

Just the thought of dialing 19 and facing Dougray was enough to give her heart palpitations.

The thought seemed to sober him, too. Shaking his head, he blinked as if to clear his head and spun on his heel. "Let me get something to take apart the handle."

Maggie breathed deeply, trying to gain some semblance

of control over her runaway senses. She'd felt incredibly vulnerable beneath Sam's gaze, so totally naked before his broad, fully clothed self. But it was a titillating feeling, one that sent the blood slugging through her veins in pace with a deep, languid throb between her thighs.

There was no denying how the appreciation in his gaze affected her, no hiding from the tiny rush of feminine pride to have affected him similarly.

Of course, feminine pride wasn't enough to offset the effects of standing naked in this shower while he tried to dismantle the door handle with a pair of scissors.

"Ohmigosh, this—this water's like ice." Her teeth chattered, making ridiculous clicking sounds she hoped he couldn't hear.

"Turn it off."

"I—I can't." The water may be a thin, icy shield, but it was the only shield she had.

"Jeez, Mags. All right, I've almost got it." He ground out an expletive as he struggled with the scissors's blade, right before the handle came apart in his hands. "Got it."

With a clink and a tinkle, the inside of the handle fell and bounced along the stall floor.

"Get that water off, *now*." His voice was a command, and he strode quickly away, dropping the scissors and outer handle parts into a noisy heap on the vanity.

Maggie did as he bade, too cold now to find her pride in a body trembling so violently she could barely stand upright.

He reappeared, stretching a bath towel across the door and promising, "I won't look."

True to his word, he averted his gaze as she stepped into the towel, but he never gave her a chance to wrap it around herself before herding her across the tiled floor.

"Sit here." With a firm hand on her shoulder, he pushed

her down onto the lid of the toilet, then grabbed a stack of towels from a nearby linen rack.

Rather high-handedly, Maggie thought, he draped one over her knees and another around her shoulders. Wildly chattering teeth hindered her best attempts at an argument, and when he unceremoniously dumped another towel over her head, he effectively blocked any further attempts.

"Shh. Your blue lips are clashing with your hair. Now get it wrapped up."

With trembling hands, Maggie did.

A scowl etched hard across Sam's features, whether from her foolishness at running the icy water or because she'd been trapped inside the shower stall at all, she couldn't say. Maggie only knew she was bone cold straight through and didn't even think of resisting when Sam toweled her legs dry with perfunctory strokes.

She wasn't sure exactly when it happened—probably around the time her teeth stopped clicking together like dice in a Yahtzee cup—but she became aware of his hands on her skin.

He'd knelt back on his haunches and propped her feet in his lap, taking turns rubbing one, then the other in long firm strokes designed to force heat into her.

It worked. She suddenly warmed all over, and when his strong fingers encircled her ankle, lifted her leg higher along his thighs, she felt all remnants of her chill dissolve.

He massaged the towel upward. Behind her calf, her knee, and then raising her leg, he traveled to the sensitive skin behind her thigh. Flutters of desire, like silky hot ribbons, unfurled inside, twining around her senses until she became conscious of the individual heat of his fingers, the deepened pitch of his breathing, the way steam had misted his hair to a glossy black sheen.

And Sam recognized exactly when the change took

place, too. Maybe because he knew her so well. Maybe because he possessed some male sex radar. Perhaps a combination of both. But his expression altered from concern to awareness, a visible transformation that melted the hard angles of his face, eased the clenched jaw, softened the compressed lips.

His gaze met hers, smoky with intent, almost defiant with purpose. Lowering his head slowly, he brushed his mouth along her toes, and while still holding her gaze, he slipped his tongue between them.

Desire burst in a confetti of sensation that scattered her thoughts. She stared, unable to tear her gaze from his, unable to make sense of why his touch was so intense, why she reacted so strongly.

"I've wanted you for a long time, Mags. You want me, too."

To deny his assertion would have been a lie, when goose bumps rippled along her calf, like a breeze across the surface of a lake, in direct response to his touch.

"You're just better than I am at hiding it." His gaze captured hers, held her pinned with the desire she saw in their smoky depths. "There's nothing to hide from. Not from exploring this side of our relationship. Not from me."

Maybe. Maybe not. All Maggie knew for certain in that moment was that *her* Sam had disappeared, leaving behind a man who knew exactly how to affect her; a handsome, bold man who didn't ask permission to lavish the most erotic attention on her toes, drawing each slowly into his talented mouth in turn, lingering, hot pulls that made her gasp. The sound echoed in the steamy bathroom and brought a smile to his lips.

Then he moved on, licking the arch of her foot, trailing his lips up her ankle, raining kisses slowly upward, dipping his sensuous mouth to one calf, then the other in a sexy game of Follow the Leader.

Should she stop him? Maggie wondered, grasping at a wispy voice of reason, barely audible above the satisfied hum of blood in her ears. He'd taken her off guard in the elevator, but now she'd had time to think about his suggestion.

Let's just go with it and see what happens.

Should she?

Sam had wanted to explore this side of their relationship since Fall Harvest. That had been a very long time ago, and Maggie knew that frequently her patients would aggrandize their desires simply because they'd been denied so long. Would her smartest course of action be to indulge him and help him get her out of his system? Help *her* get *him* out of her system?

With his tongue tracing lazy circles on the back of her calf, she couldn't quite see what the harm was. One weekend. A chance to live out her fantasy. A chance for Sam to live out his. Anything beyond that would risk their friendship, and Sam had already promised not to weird out once they returned home. Maggie believed him. He wouldn't risk what they had together by pushing for a relationship if she didn't want to pursue one.

"This is the perfect place to explore," he whispered, his breaths ruffling in tiny warm bursts along her skin. "We're away from home, living out a fantasy. We don't have to deal with reality right now."

True. And neither she nor Sam had dated in a while. How realistic was it for them to stay in a romance superclub, surrounded by sexual innuendo and myriad ideas about putting passion into relationships, and not think about sex?

Not very.

His mouth suddenly found the sensitive fold behind her knee, and he sampled her skin in a way that made Maggie shudder in response to the moist caress of his lips and the rough velvet heat of his tongue.

She was attracted to him. They were at Falling Inn Bed, and Breakfast to explore passion. Could she resist one weekend with the man of her dreams?

Not when he nibbled his way along the inside of her knee, teasing, tasting, inching her legs apart to make room for his wide shoulders, demonstrating his eagerness to begin exploring.

And the more she thought about it, he'd rescued her from a painful hypothermic death and proved very inventive in warming her up. His distracting nibbles made her sex clench with tiny, rippling spasms that implored her to grab him by the ears and steer that magical mouth of his just a little higher....

It really all boiled down to the fact that this wasn't really Sam, anyway. When their fantasy weekend was over, they'd go home, he'd put on his glasses, and become her best friend again, leaving them both with some wonderful memories. Leaving them both sexually satisfied.

It was only a weekend, for goodness sake. She'd come to Falling Inn Bed, and Breakfast to gather ideas about putting sparks into a relationship, and Sam was doing exactly that. His ideas were rather clever. She'd jot this one down in her idea journal as *making the most of the moment* or maybe, *recognizing when opportunity knocks.*

5

INSISTENT KNOCKING from far off in the Warlord's Tower penetrated Sam's reality. Reality, hmm. This reality was far better than any fantasy he'd ever had, because in this reality, he explored the sweet, uncharted territory of Maggie's knees, plotted a course toward the beckoning hem of her bath towel.

The most charming sighs slipped from her pink lips, soft, melodious, breathless sounds that revealed how much she enjoyed his exploration.

These were the only sounds he wanted to hear right now.

The knocking grew louder. Sam resolutely ignored it, but some minuscule portion of his brain—the only portion that wasn't clinging to this fantastic reality with the tenacity of a sleepwalker—recognized room service had arrived.

If he didn't answer, the waiter would get the hint and leave. Why hadn't Sam thought to put up the Do Not Disturb sign?

He blocked out the questions, and the knocking, and the still-functioning part of his brain. Rubbing his cheek against Maggie's knee, he nipped her creamy skin, made her gasp.

That was the only sound he wanted to hear. That sound made his blood hammer. That sound galvanized his erection until only tight jeans spared him a premature end to this carnal torture.

Unfortunately that wasn't all he could hear. The knocking had grown insistent. Maggie heard it, too.

"What's that?"

Her voice was throaty with passion, a whisper he'd never heard before but found himself savoring. She was breathless with passion *for him.*

Not certain he'd be able to stand given his pounding erection, Sam clamped his hands on her thighs and carefully hoisted himself up. Confusion clouded her pleasure-dazed expression, and he planted a kiss on her ripe lips and said, "Room service."

On legs as stiff as if they'd been encased in plaster casts, Sam made his way from the bathroom, cursing the waiter's interruption and his own stupidity in placing the order.

How many years had he waited to coax those pleasure-drenched sighs from Maggie? Way too many to be dragged away now, for something as trivial as a meal.

Maybe someday he'd see the irony, but not anytime soon, no doubt. Grabbing his suit jacket from the back of a chair, Sam shrugged it on to cover his erection. With a scowl, he jerked open the door.

He hadn't even growled out a command to leave the damned food, when a brawny waiter with a balding head barreled through the doorway, almost knocking him down in his impatience to wheel the food cart inside.

"Mr. Masters," the man said in a booming voice. "Your food will taste like cardboard if you leave me standing in the hallway."

Sam blinked. Was that a reprimand?

The man didn't give Sam a backward glance as he brought the linen-draped cart to a stop beside the polished oak table occupying one corner of the suite. Only after he'd tipped up a lid to a silver platter and gave a laudatory sniff did he turn to acknowledge Sam.

"The name's Bruno, chef extraordinaire and restaurant manager. I'll be overseeing your menu during your stay at

Falling Inn Bed, and Breakfast. I want to discuss yours and Ms. James's preferences.''

Sam clasped the man's extended hand mechanically, not sure whether the pounding in his crotch or the man's totally unexpected conduct had shaken his brains loose.

''Judging from your order, I gather you and your lady enjoy seafood and Italian cuisine, and of course sweets. My raspberry cheesecake is my claim to fame. People come from all over to taste it. You must let me know what you think.''

The suspicion that this might be an exaggeration flashed in Sam's head, but only briefly, since he'd gotten stuck on the man's reference to him and Maggie.

You and your lady. That's exactly who Maggie was. For a weekend that wasn't going to last forever while this chef-restaurant manager was wasting precious seconds of it.

Since when did restaurant managers deliver room service to guests, anyway? Sam didn't ask. He didn't care. He wanted the man to do an about-face and march back through the door, so he could return to Maggie. *Before* she lost that passion-glazed expression. *Before* she did something foolish like get dressed.

Unfortunately, Bruno seemed determined to pick Sam's brain about his appetite. Just as unfortunately, the only appetite Sam could think of was hunger for the woman who awaited him in the next room. Judging by the chef's scowl, Sam guessed the man had noticed he didn't have Sam's complete attention.

''Excuse me?'' Sam asked, certain he'd missed a question.

''What about heartier fare?'' Bruno repeated. ''Do you enjoy good cuts of meat?''

''Uh, yeah. I do.''

''And Ms. James?''

"She likes vegetables."

"Vegetables, good." Bruno smiled broadly. "I've been playing with Oriental lately and make the most exquisite ginger-soy dressing over Chinese greens. And won ton shrimp. *Squisito!*" He smacked a kiss to his fingertips and sighed dramatically. "Does your lady like Chinese?"

His lady.

"She likes Chinese. So do I."

"Good. What about eggs for breakfast? Fruit?" He tipped a platter lid to reveal thin slices of lemon that served as the garnish for the shrimp dish. "The only fruits worthy of the name right now are the apples I have shipped in from an orchard outside of Poughkeepsie, some seasonal berries and citrus from a grove in central Florida. They've already had a cold snap down there, and the meat is sweet, sweet, sweet."

When Sam heard a door open and then close—presumably Maggie making her way to the bedroom—he couldn't care less if the citrus was sweet enough to sprout lips and give him a kiss.

"Eggs are good. Fruit is good." He eased away from the cart, hoping to lure Bruno toward the door. "But my lady doesn't eat breakfast." Sam savored the words as they flowed over his tongue.

Bruno's bushy black eyebrows raised up to where his hairline should have been had it not already receded back past his ears. "No breakfast? None?"

"Just coffee."

Maggie might have been guilty of a crime, judging by the horrified look on Bruno's face. "Surely she'll drink espresso?"

"As a matter of fact, she will. Just make sure it's as black as ink and as strong as jet fuel. And not just a swallow, either. Think large quantities."

"Good, good."

Clearly that revelation elevated Maggie a few notches in Bruno's estimation. Sam headed toward the foyer, brushing aside the superclub's promotional material to retrieve the room service menu from the desk, wondering irrelevantly if the customary bible was inside the drawer. Surely they wouldn't leave it in the bedroom?

"We'll visit the restaurant after we're settled in," he said. "Until then, room service should cover it. You've got pizza. She does mushrooms. I do pepperoni and sausage. She loves salads. Oh, and pancakes and waffles."

At Bruno's confused stare, he explained. "Not for breakfast, for dinner. And eggs. She likes to make scrambled egg sandwiches with toast and cheese and grape jelly." He spouted anything that came to mind about Maggie's eating quirks to lure Bruno toward the door. "Is it possible to order breakfast at dinner?"

"Anything for you and Ms. James," the chef said magnanimously, striding from the cart to confer over the menu.

It was a start.

"What about desserts?" Bruno peered at the menu Sam held open. "The cheesecake, of course, but what about chocolate? Or apple cobbler? Or tiramisu?"

"Absolutely. She likes biscotti, too."

Bruno rocked backward, clapping his hands excitedly, which served to move his bearlike self another two feet toward the door. "Wonderful. I have this recipe for a cranberry biscotti that's divine. She likes cranberries, of course?"

"Of course." At least Sam thought she did, but he didn't intend to worry about it now.

Clamping a hand on the chef's beefy arm, he maneuvered them around so they were facing the door. "It sounds as though you've covered everything. I didn't know the superclub had a five-star restaurant.''

"You make sure to tell the general manager that. She needs to tell marketing to promote us more." Bruno winked slyly. "There'll be a culinary reward in it for you, I promise."

"My stomach growls just thinking about it."

Sam glanced back at the bedroom when another door clicked shut, and Bruno followed his glance, eyes widening as though he'd just finally realized he was intruding. He didn't resist when Sam opened the door.

But then he paused in midstride, spun on his heel, and asked urgently, "What about allergies? Are you or Ms. James allergic to any foods, anything at all?"

A strange question, but Sam was so relieved to have gotten Bruno at least halfway through the door that he obliged. "No allergies at all."

"Good. Good. A chef needs to know these things. I make liberal use of many unique herbs and spices in my cuisine. I always send up extra so my guests can adjust the taste."

"You've thought of everything."

"I try—"

The rest of Bruno's statement ended abruptly when Sam shut the door.

"Jeez." He waited until Bruno had enough time to clear the hallway before putting out the Do Not Disturb sign.

"Sam, who was that?"

Maggie's voice came from the bedroom, and it lacked that misty, impassioned thickness that still echoed in his ears. He exhaled heavily in disappointment.

"The chef from hell." He wheeled the food cart to the bedroom, where the sight of Maggie sent all thoughts of disappointment scattering.

This was Maggie as he'd never seen her before.

She had indeed dressed, but in a whisper of peach silk that hadn't been designed to disappoint anyone short of a blind man. So pale it might have doubled as her skin, the lingerie flowed all around her, so sheer, the light from the flickering candles silhouetted her every curve.

She wasn't wearing anything underneath.

Blood descended from his head to his crotch in a dizzying rush. And if Sam had thought he ached before, it was nothing compared to the savage throbbing he felt right now. He'd already sampled the sweetness of her skin. The taste had only whetted his appetite.

His gaze feasted on the tangle of water-darkened hair that clung to the graceful arch of her neck, to the firm breasts and nipples that shone like burnished smudges through the almost invisible fabric.

He could make out the curve of her waist and the slope of her hips before being bombarded by the blur of dusky color forming a V at the juncture of her thighs.

He could barely breathe. The stock market could crash and Sam wouldn't have cared. He'd face financial devastation with this image of her burned into his eyelids and no thought in his head other than no woman could possibly be more beautiful.

Maggie was a vision. A vision he'd dreamed about. But his fantasies hadn't come close to this reality, though, and he was suddenly eager to explore all the intricacies of Maggie as his lover and discover how she meshed with Maggie his friend.

His gaze continued downward, along sleek thighs and shapely calves to slim ankles and peach-painted toes that played hide-and-seek beneath swirls of feather boa on her slippers.

"Wow. Look at those. They're so…elaborate." He managed to croak out. "Have you been humoring me with the

Gumby slippers? Do you only wear them when I'm around?''

"No!" She tipped her foot from side to side, so he could get a good look at the daintily heeled shoe. "I'm only wearing these because this is all I found in my suitcase. Everything I packed seems to have disappeared."

"Your clothes are missing?"

"Just my pajamas and my robe and the things I brought to lounge around in. My street clothes are still there." She scowled. "Did you take my things, Sam, and replace them with...stuff like this?"

She spread her arms in entreaty, giving him a breathtaking view of her slim curves beneath the filmy garment. The denial jammed in his throat and he managed only to shake his head. He hadn't tampered with her luggage, but he definitely wasn't complaining that someone had.

Her gaze narrowed. "If you didn't then who did? Surely not the bellhop."

Sam shrugged, though he didn't think that likely. Tampering with the guests' luggage would be lawsuit city for Falling Inn Bed, and Breakfast.

"If it wasn't Dougray when he brought my bags up, then the only other person it could be is Lyn." Annoyance crept into her voice. "I'm sure of it. She knew I had to squeeze Angie and Raymond in for a session at the crack of dawn this morning, because he's been out of town with work all week. I thought it was strange that she'd come in so early, but she said she was trying to get a jump on closing the office."

"You brought your bags into the office?"

"No. But she could have taken my car keys from my locker in the employee workroom." She folded her arms across her chest, effectively cutting off the view. "Don't look at me like that, Sam. Lyn's my friend. She's gone inside my locker quite a few times to help me out. And she was the one who suggested that I invite you, but she thought my idea about observation was way off. Said practical application was the ticket.''

"I'll have to thank her when we get back.''

"Sam,'' she snapped. "If I didn't know better, I'd think this was a setup. You wouldn't believe what she put in my suitcase. This is the most conservative of the bunch.''

Try though he might, he couldn't keep his attention fixed on her scowl. Instead, he darted his gaze downward for another awe-inspiring glimpse. "Trust me, Mags, I'm not complaining.''

"Sam!'' She stood her ground, tipping her chin up a notch defiantly. But Sam could see the uncertainty in her eyes, suspected she felt anxious about the reminder of their intimacy in the bathroom.

This was an opportunity if ever he saw one, a chance to forward his seduction. He covered the distance between them.

"Your slippers are sexy.'' He trailed a finger along the curve of her forehead and the silky arch of her brow. "Very, very sexy. And you're sexy. Whether you're wearing Gumby slippers or these. Or nothing at all.'' The sweet taste of her peach-painted toes was still wreaking havoc on his libido.

Maggie apparently remembered the moment, too, because she let her eyes flutter closed to hide from his gaze.

He brushed a fingertip across her gold-flecked lashes. "I almost tossed the restaurant manager out the door on his butt so I could get back to you. I was afraid you might change your mind and decide this whole thing wasn't going to work.''

The effect of his admission was twofold. When Maggie opened her eyes again, the doubt had gone, and she clearly felt comfortable enough not to back away. He trailed a finger along her cheek, then traced the shell of her ear. She shivered.

"I like when you respond to my touch," he said. "I haven't touched you enough to know how much I like it, but so far I like it a lot. I have a lot of seducing to do, Mags."

That full pink mouth curved up in a smile. "You don't have to seduce me. I promised you my undivided attention for the weekend, remember?"

"I remember. But trust me. I do have to seduce you, and you did promise to let nature take its course, remember?"

"I remember."

Her breath hitched, drawing his gaze to the sudden rise and fall of her chest. Her nipples had peaked into tight buds that strained against the filmy fabric. Sam swallowed back a groan.

Slipping his hand down to cup her breast, he reveled in its satin weight, the way it fit into the bend of his fingers as though fashioned specifically for his hand.

"This is a one-shot deal, and I want to do it right." He stroked his thumb across her nipple, his blood pounding so hard he grew light-headed.

Think slowly. Think seduction. Think *again.* Who was he kidding? Could he really expect himself not to crumble in the face of this kind of temptation?

The surprise in Maggie's expression answered his question. She clearly hadn't expected to be so aroused by him, either, and to be honest, Sam was a little surprised himself. She responded so naturally. In the bathroom, he'd warmed her from frozen to warm to on fire faster than he could rush into the stock trading pit during triple witching hour.

He'd always suspected Maggie was a sensual person, simply because she never did anything halfway. Her emotions ran the gamut. She was loyal and passionate, a live-wire who savored the moment, yet remained vulnerable to life's hurts.

She was also incredibly spontaneous. She'd gotten him into more scrapes through the years with her "brilliant" ideas. Like the time she'd kept him up all night stuffing condoms in the university's student welcome packets.

Administration hadn't appreciated her efforts to promote responsible sex, but the students had, nicknaming her Dr. Maggie, the campus conscience.

Sam had taken heat for his part in the scheme, but a dressing down by the dean hadn't distracted him from wanting to put one of those condoms to good use with Maggie.

He was still waiting to put one to good use with her.

But first he had to prove they were perfect for each other—not just for a weekend, but forever. He forced his hand away from her breast.

"Now, milady, let's satisfy your other appetite." He motioned toward the food cart parked beside the bed.

"A bed picnic?"

"A bed picnic. I thought it was appropriate."

"It is. Suddenly I'm starving." Kicking off her slippers, Maggie clambered up on the bed and tucked her legs beneath her, forming a graceful curl of beautiful woman who was uniquely Maggie. "This is one killer bed."

"That it is."

The bed stood so tall that sets of wooden steps had been placed on both sides. A thick quilt graced the king-size mattress, and heavily embroidered curtains in matching shades of gold and ocher had been pulled aside and fastened to the four posters with golden braids. Sam imagined pulling the curtains closed to create a tent to trap Maggie inside.

Like the rest of the suite, highly polished wooden furniture dominated the room, and the lighting was supplied by strategically placed sconces and a matching set of candelabra on the bedside tables.

Sam poured the champagne while Maggie unveiled their feast, platters of shrimp cocktail, ginger fruit salad and an appetizer of pizza rolls, stuffed with pepperoni, mushrooms and Italian cheeses.

"The chef uses lots of spices," Sam explained, gesturing to a bowl with a tiny spoon. "He usually sends along extra to adjust the taste."

"Thoughtful guy." She dabbed her pinky in the bowl, touched it to her tongue, while Sam watched, mesmerized. "That's tasty. For the fruit salad, I think."

Sam's appetite for food died a swift death as he watched Maggie gamely sprinkling Bruno's spices on different samples from each of the platters.

"Oh, everything is delicious." Scooping a shrimp through a crystal bowl of cocktail sauce, she brought it to her lips.

Sam realized he wouldn't last long watching the mesmerizing motion of her shiny pink lips as she chewed, swallowed then sighed her approval.

He needed a distraction.

Reaching for the comb she'd apparently been using before he'd come in, Sam grabbed it from the night table. "May I?"

She shrugged. "You aren't hungry?"

"I ate on the plane."

A lie. Settling behind her, Sam leaned back against the bed frame and positioned her between his knees, close enough to touch her yet still allow her access to their meal.

He lifted the damp waves from her shoulders, weighed the texture in his hands before running the comb through.

Heavy silk. Inhaling deeply, he tested the comb on a thin section and found it slid through easily.

She wore it well past her shoulders nowadays, in a layery sort of cut he liked much better than the waist-length style she'd been forced to wear as a kid. Maggie had rebelled in her freshman year of high school and cut it up to her chin. He hadn't been crazy about that style, either.

What she called flyaway, Sam called silky. The waves she complained gave her just enough curl to make nothing settle where it should gave him erotic visions of how it would feel draped across his skin.

The color she'd always called, "too pale to be a redhead and too brassy to be a blonde" he called perfect, though he did remember a time in sixth grade when he'd had a blast teasing her about her Nancy Drew-colored hair.

"Are you acting out some sort of fantasy here?" she asked, and he could hear the smile in her voice. "Have you always wanted to play with my hair?"

"I've never thought about combing your hair. Although, I've had a few fantasies about running my fingers through it." He wished he could see her face to read her reaction. "Oh."

He tried not to be disappointed when she fell silent and reminded himself that a chance to catch his breath was a good thing right now. Especially when he ached with wanting.

"Ever hit a lull in any of your relationships, Sam?"

He didn't really want to discuss lulls or former relationships, but recognized that Maggie had retreated into her analytical, relationship counselor mode. She would simply rephrase the question until she got an answer and Sam didn't have enough brain cells left to circumvent her questions with any intelligence.

And he had to admit, the intrusive thoughts of ex-girlfriends made great strides toward distracting him from his awareness of her rounded bottom tucked between his thighs.

"Definitely no lulls with Mara," he said.

"Ha! I knew she was putting out." Maggie swung around to shoot him a triumphant stare and Sam pulled the comb from her hair just in time to avoid tangling it. "Your parents thought she was Miss Goody Two-Shoes, but I knew better."

Sam suppressed a smile. Mara had been a cheerleader, a pretty, popular girl with bright-red hair, a color Maggie had deemed worthy of being called auburn, unlike her own pale-red shade. "You didn't like her."

"What makes you say that?" Avoiding his gaze, she settled back between his legs.

"I see right through your innocent routine. Why didn't you like her?"

"What innocent routine?"

"Tell me. You're the one who brought up the subject."

"I'm a therapist on a research mission, remember?"

"Tell me."

Maggie shook her head, sent waves tumbling over her shoulders, and Sam gathered the thickness between his fingers and gave a light tug.

"Oh, all right. She was threatened by our friendship. Let's just say she never missed an opportunity to remind me to keep my hands off you."

Sam frowned, guessed by her careful phrasing that she wasn't telling the half of it. "Why didn't you ever tell me?"

"I didn't want to spoil your fun. So, no lulls with the first steady girlfriend, none at all?" She segued neatly back to her questions before he could grill her further.

She'd clearly said all she was going to say, which was

a lot more than she'd intended if the edge to her voice was any indication. "You dated for two years in high school and the summer before college. That's a long time."

He ran the comb through her hair again, a soothing motion he wished would erase the disappointment he felt at having been so focused on sex he'd missed the antagonism between two people he'd cared about. "Raging teenage hormones. Scary things."

"What about Chrissy?"

"What about her? She wasn't threatened by our relationship, too, was she?"

"Miss I'm-single-handedly-going-to-convert-all-Americans-to-liberalism? I don't think she was threatened by anything."

Sam laughed at the description. Chrissy had been a crusader for one of the university's political clubs. She'd never been able to resist trying to sway Maggie to her views, and Maggie had never restrained herself from sharing her conservative arguments that had routinely sent Chrissy into emotional meltdowns.

"We did have a lull before we graduated. Things got…well, stressed. She'd been offered a position as a senator's aide and wanted to move to D.C. I wanted to stay in Baltimore."

He hadn't wanted to leave Maggie.

She turned to face him. "That was right before you broke up?"

"Mm-hmm."

"So a lull when the pressure was on. Very common. What about Emma? Your relationship with her was a pressure cooker."

"A pressure cooker? What does that mean?" Before he gave her a chance to answer though, another thought struck him. "You didn't like Emma, either."

She stared hard, and he could see the denial gathering in her expression. "I never said I didn't like Emma. It's just you always seemed either on or off when you were together."

"Now that I think about it, I remember we did experience a lull or two."

"You're surprised? Lulls are common among power couples."

"Power couples?"

"Be real, Sam. You were both on the fast track. When you weren't working, you were shmoozing, either with her law partners or with your bosses. And what about when she would go under to research a case? You wouldn't see her at all for weeks on end. You'd spend your free time with me and, trust me, there was precious little of that. I'm surprised the two of you even had time for sex."

He heard disapproval in her voice, but Sam wasn't sure whether she disapproved of Emma's ambition or his own. Setting the comb aside, he pulled her back into his arms, eager to stop her from counseling him on relationships that no longer mattered. If he had to be completely honest, not one of his relationships had ever mattered more than Maggie, but he didn't think she was ready to hear that.

"Done analyzing me, yet?"

She shook her head. "No lulls since Emma?"

"No one to have a lull with."

Sam had only dated casually over the past two years, and unlike Maggie's checkered history of whirlwind relationships, Sam's résumé seemed the epitome of stability and endurance.

Maybe even dull from Maggie's perspective. Now there was a thought to consider. Spontaneity and variety had certainly been the hallmark of her love life. From his angle, it looked as though the minute a guy tried to get close, she'd panic. She lived the self-fulfilling prophecy—expect the worst and get it.

Well, she wouldn't get the worst from him. He'd seduce his way past her expectations and prove that their relationship could succeed. Working as an investment advisor had taught him to weather any storm. He trusted his instincts and knew to strike when the time was right.

But he had to consider all the angles. If Maggie thought he was boring, he'd be facing an entirely different obstacle, than if she thought he lacked experience. Sam smiled. Either way, he'd have a very good time proving her wrong.

Another thought struck him, too. Maggie hadn't approved of any of his former girlfriends. Had there been more to her disapproval than personality clashes? Was it possible that she'd been jealous?

6

OPPORTUNITY KNOCKED, and Sam's long-range planning skills kicked in. "My turn, Dr. James."

"Your turn for what?"

Maggie nestled back against his chest, and he wrapped his arms around her, resting his chin on top of her head. He inhaled deeply of her freshly shampooed hair and the underlying scent of orange blossoms.

She'd dabbed the perfume behind her ears, definitely.

"You just picked my brain about ex-girlfriends, a topic I've avoided discussing with you for the past decade. I answered your questions. Now I want you to answer one for me."

"Shoot."

He hesitated, debating how to phrase his question so he wouldn't get her defenses up. "What's your idea of the perfect man? You obviously haven't met him yet."

With a silvery chuckle, Maggie pulled out of his arms and tipped her head back to meet his gaze. Amusement sparked green lights in her eyes. "How diplomatic."

"Always."

"So you want to know why I blow through dates like Mrs. Carr blows through rosebushes?" she asked, referring to their elderly neighbor, who, in her determination to raise award-winning roses, succeeded only in killing more bushes than the local nursery could supply.

"Yep."

"I don't suppose you'd believe that it's because I have the attention span of a gnat?"

"Nope."

The lights in her gaze flickered, but to her credit, she didn't try to evade his question. She settled back in his arms again. "This is nice."

"Yes."

Silence reigned for a time, broken only by the hushed sounds of their breathing and the whoosh of the central heat as it cycled on.

Sam didn't push Maggie to answer. He waited instead, allowed her time to gather her thoughts. He wondered if she'd bridge the distance from the analytical viewpoint of her work or if she'd shoot straight with him. While she decided, he enjoyed the feel of her warm curves molding against him.

"I've been so busy and satisfied in all the other areas of my life I think it's been very easy for me to make excuses about why my relationships never seem to last," she finally said.

She was shooting straight. There was a reason she shunned commitment like she shunned eating liver. She was scared of being hurt. And of hurting someone she loved. His greatest obstacle to winning Maggie was her fear of commitment.

"Are you going to be happy dating forever, Mags? Do you ever think about what you want for the future?"

"Sure, I think about it, but I know how much work is involved in making a relationship successful. I haven't yet met a man I thought capable of putting forth that much effort."

Sam would lay odds she hadn't met one because she hadn't kept one around long enough to scratch beneath the surface. Except for him. He definitely had the edge.

"Are you sure you're taking the time to look?"

"No, I'm not sure, Sam. What's your point?"

She sounded thoughtful, and Sam tightened his grip, a gesture he hoped would convey that he appreciated her honesty.

"My point is that I want you to be happy and I'm not convinced you're seeing relationships from a balanced perspective. You see all the problems with your work. I don't think you're paying enough attention to the good things."

"Like what?"

Like me.

"You know all the things you like about our relationship, Mags? Those are the positives."

"We're different than other relationships."

"Not really. We've just cared enough about each other to make the necessary changes as we grew and our relationship changed. How is what we're doing so different from what you advise your patients to do?"

Her continued silence told Sam that he'd made her think, and he didn't hesitate to keep her thinking. "Consider all the good stuff that only happens because we're comfortable with each other. Knowing we'll always be here no matter what. Trusting that I can put your needs before mine and vice versa. And what about crisis situations? Especially crisis situations. What would you do without me telling you what to do? You get so emotional, you run around in circles." He pressed a kiss to the top of her head, another gesture of reassurance.

Slipping her hand over his where it rested across her stomach, she squeezed gently. "You definitely win the award for a cool head in a crisis."

"I do," he agreed. "But I don't know what I would do without your emotion, Mags. Remember the first Christmas after my parents died? I couldn't think about anything except getting through the day at work. I didn't want to think about anything else. But you broke into my house, lugged that ten-foot Christmas tree in by yourself—I still can't figure how you got it into the stand—and decorated the place with all my mom's decorations. Do you have any idea how I felt when I walked in on that?''

"Like Santa had visited?" she asked hopefully.

"Like Maggie had visited. Like I was the luckiest person alive because you cared so much. You knew exactly what it would take to get me to face the most difficult times I've ever had. It was knowing that you cared enough to skip school, lug a ten-foot tree into my house and dig through a nightmare of an attic to find Christmas decorations that helped me get through the holidays. I knew you were there and that you would be, whether I made it through my rough spot that day or not.''

"Oh, Sam."

When he heard the tears in her voice, he knew he'd made his point.

"And let's not forget favors, Mags. Here I am freezing my butt off in Niagara Falls on Valentine's Day so you can expand your knowledge base. Tell me you can't see the benefits of long-term. Who else but your best friend, the most trustworthy man in the world, would subject himself to a weekend in a hotel called Falling Inn Bed, and Breakfast to observe *other* people falling into bed?''

Maggie huffed in mock indignation and sprang from his arms. "I'm just putting you out big-time, aren't I, Sam Masters? Of course I had no intention of sleeping with you. How was I supposed to know the thought of having sex with me has been on your mind since Fall Harvest?"

She was acting like a tough guy, but he saw the emotion in her face. Catching her just before her determined fingers poked him in the ribs, he pinned her arms beneath his and rolled her back on the bed, laughing.

"You can't imagine how the idea of having sex with you has been on my mind, Mags."

Because he'd thought he would never get the chance.

Just the mention of sex segued the moment from playful to intimate, and he became acutely aware of lying against Maggie, his chest pressed to her silk-veiled shoulder, the thickness in his groin brushing her hip.

"This is nice, isn't it?" She nestled close and purred, like a cat that had burrowed a cocoon of warmth in a comforter.

Her head rested perfectly into the crook of his neck, her fragrant hair teasing his senses as he scattered flyaway wisps with every exhalation.

"Who would have ever guessed snuggling would be so fun?"

He pressed a kiss to her hair. "I'm not surprised."

"You're not?"

"We're so good together everywhere else in our lives. Why not in bed, too?"

She seemed to have no ready answer and lapsed into silence, her cheek pressed to his chest, her hand draped casually across his waist. Their contact was relaxed, easy, the kind of closeness only people comfortable with each other could share.

"You really felt like you'd gotten the best Christmas present of all when you came home and found that I'd decorated your house?" Her voice was a whisper.

"I wouldn't have tackled Mom's decorations or the memories. Not so soon after their deaths. You helped me face them."

"I'm glad. I worried that I might be pushing you faster than you should go."

"Seeing the house decorated helped me remember all the good times and how lucky I'd been to have had them in my life for so long. How lucky I was to still have you."

They held each other, reveling in the close bonds they shared and the wonder at such a special gift. And as Sam pondered the softness of the woman in his arms, he noticed that her breathing had deepened....

"She sleeps," he murmured into the shadowed confines of the curtained bed, a smile curving his lips.

Putting Maggie to sleep on their first night alone wasn't an accomplishment he'd ever reveal to another living soul, but he didn't feel too bad. She'd driven five hundred miles in lousy weather today, and no matter how much espresso she'd consumed along the way, the trip had been bound to catch up with her. A good night's sleep and she'd be ready to go.

Besides, he couldn't lament Maggie's exhaustion, not when he'd had the opportunity to play knight to her distressed damsel in the bathroom, furthering his cause more than he could have hoped on their first night at Falling Inn Bed, and Breakfast. Especially not when she snuggled against him with a soft sigh that told him just how content she was to be here.

Holding Maggie while she slept was a fantasy in itself. With slow movements designed not to wake her, Sam maneuvered the bedcover from one side of the mattress and pulled it over her, effectively cutting off his view of her sleek curves beneath the tempting wisp of silk she wore.

He breathed deeply to dispel some of his own tension, but it didn't take Sam long to realize that he was wound so tight he'd never sleep. His mind raced with his plan for Maggie's seduction. In preparation for the trip, he'd dug through her old schoolwork and found a five-step strategy for building a solid relationship he believed would yield the desired results.

Step one had been to get Maggie to open up and express herself without fear of ridicule, and much to his surprise, he'd already achieved that goal without much effort.

Given that she'd been so receptive to his overtures in the bathroom and was currently sleeping contentedly wrapped around him, Sam thought he might have made a dent in step two, as well, which involved getting her interested in what their sex might be like. He was going to make her want him and he wasn't going to be had too easily.

Steps three through five would be much tougher.

Though he might get Maggie in bed to achieve step three's intimacy, Sam didn't fool himself for an instant that he could actually keep her there. Not past the time it took to check out of this superclub and drive back to Baltimore.

If Sam read her right, she was counting on their friendship to protect her from any threat of commitment. He could almost hear her wheedling her way out of a relationship once this weekend was over.

"You won't push me, Sam, will you? You wouldn't want to make things uncomfortable between us, right?"

Wrong.

The real trick would be convincing her they had a future. Once he managed that, he'd move on to step four and prove he'd support her while she sorted out her commitment issues, and then step five, which meant getting her to make a commitment.

He'd already spent most of his adult life insinuating himself into her life—everywhere but in her bed. Now his time had come and he planned to steal her heart.

He smiled, inhaling deeply of her freshly shampooed hair, enjoying the feel of her in his arms. As much as he'd like to continue his seduction, implementing his plans would have to wait until Maggie rested.

He wished he could utilize the opportunity to rest, too, but that was damned near impossible with Maggie curled softly around him. Every drop of blood in his body pumped hard and he could barely keep his hands off her, let alone sleep.

Fortunately, some conscientious superclub employee had left the perfect distraction on the night table. He reached for the television remote control with a channel selection guide.

The television sat in a huge antique armoire, positioned strategically in front of the bed. The doors had been left open, Sam supposed, so guests could actually find the modern equipment amid this display of medieval splendor.

Clicking on the power, Sam muted the sound and began to channel surf. Something should be on at nine o'clock on a Friday night, but he surfed one channel, then the next, then the next, skimming through a staggering satellite lineup before realizing with growing amazement that every program airing tonight had a very similar theme.

Sex.

MAGGIE AWOKE to the unfamiliar warmth of a strong body cradling her close. Knowing she couldn't possibly have slept long enough, she blinked drowsily, allowed her sketchy thoughts free rein, taking in the shadowy surroundings, the unfamiliar bed, the unknown arms anchoring her against very well-defined muscles…*Sam.*

With a sigh, she sank into the warmth of her memories, the long drive, the superclub's risqué shops, the locked shower stall…Sam's hands working magic on her body as he massaged warmth back into her frozen legs.

His mouth working a different kind of magic on her senses.

Hmm.

Though she was rooted in the drowsy haven of half sleep, she was more aware of her body than she'd ever been upon awakening. Blood slugged through her veins with every beat of her heart. Her pulse ached low in her tummy, each throb a moist heated ache that had nothing to do with the food she'd eaten.

Falling asleep so soon after eating usually caused her to have nightmares. This was no nightmare. This was…an awakening, an unusual one, because Maggie couldn't remember ever being so aware of *everything,* as if each sense was heightened.

The shifting shadows and achromatic glow of a silent television. The faint scent of their meal on the heated air and the taste of the chef's special spices still lingering on her tongue. The warm strength of the man who held her. The hush of his even breathing. The peignoir grazing her nipples in slow, teasing sweeps with every rise and fall of her chest.

Maggie let her eyes drift closed, recognizing the problem.

She had a very bad case of lust. For Sam. Each breath trembled with anticipation. Excitement hissed and fizzed through her veins much like the bubbles in a glass of champagne.

Sam lay silently beside her, but in Maggie's mind he loomed large and mysterious, no longer the man she'd known. His bold kiss in the elevator and his rescue from the cold shower had revealed facets of him she'd simply never anticipated.

Long-term with a twist, she supposed, wondering if other long-term couples experienced this same sense of the unknown with their partners. The sensation definitely came from out of the blue, yet it was mingled with a certain freedom. She had an entire weekend to explore this astonishing side of him, with no risk to their friendship. No muddling their perfect relationship with all the complications that arose when fantasy weekends segued into reality, into expectations that would invariably be unrealized, leading to disappointment and the kind of disenchantment she saw in so many of her patients.

If she could just help those patients rediscover *this* feeling...

When Sam emitted a low, frustrated groan that rumbled deep in his chest, Maggie forced her eyes open. His profile was dark against the haze of glow and shadow, set in hard glowering lines. One quick tensing of his muscles and she realized that he held the remote control clutched tightly in one hand.

He stared fixedly at the screen and she followed his gaze, eyes widening at the tangle of bare flesh there, the erotic twisting of limbs, the flashes of pale body parts as a couple rubbed, gyrated and thrusted for public viewing.

That pulsing ache low in her tummy, momentarily forgotten, began to throb in force. "What are you watching?"

Sam glanced down at her and blinked, as if only just realizing she'd awakened. A forced smile twisted his lips.

"Torture T.V., the twenty-first century equivalent of being stretched on a medieval rack. It's got to be called something like that. Or programming for the man who enjoys suffering."

"Why don't you change the channel?" she suggested, still unable to drag her gaze from the screen as a blonde actress shimmied down her lover's model-toned body and began to issue her own brand of torture. The *mouth* torture.

"Trust me, I've spent half the night trying. Watch this."

With a touch of his thumb on the remote, the channel changed, revealing a flip-flop of the previous couple—this woman sable-haired and the man blond—engaged in what appeared to be quite earth-shattering orgasms.

"Whoa."

Sam nodded his agreement and kept clicking. A slim woman scantily clad in Indian feathers, doing a slow bump and grind for an appreciative male audience. A uniformed man treating a naked and well-oiled woman to a full body massage that gave new meaning to Maggie's interpretation of the term *full body*.

Sam paused on a channel with a group of men, all gleaming muscles and radiating testosterone.

"Here's one you might enjoy," he suggested.

A doctor pranced across a stage, parts jiggling, not wearing much more than a surgical mask over his mouth and the stethoscope around his neck. A construction worker, wearing a tool belt and a helmet, and a police officer, wearing a weapon holster and a whistle, flanked him on both sides.

"They remind me of the Village People," she said. "This isn't doing a thing for me. How about you?"

Sam arched a dark brow and scowled, effectively halting even the thought that he could enjoy this program. He clicked again, and the screen filled with yet another couple, this one appearing to have sex in midair, the man standing, and the woman suspended from some sort of black leather swing, attached to the ceiling.

There was a more documentary-type look to this program, but before Maggie had a chance to assess the differences, Sam surfed to the next channel.

"Ohmigosh! Sam, go back." When he obliged, she asked, "Do you recognize that?"

"It's a Bungee Swing for weightless sex. There was a

commercial on a while ago with a post office box and a toll-free number, so we can order with our credit card.''

"We don't have to order one. We've already got one.''

Sam frowned, and Maggie rolled out of his arms and off the edge of the bed.

"Honestly, Sam. Maybe those contacts aren't working so well, after all.'' Covering the few feet to the corner of the room, she lifted the black leather harness from its perch on the wall. "I can't believe you didn't see this. I noticed it the minute I came in to dress. I just didn't know what it was.''

"I saw it,'' Sam said, not a little defensively. "I just thought it was some sort of medieval artwork. You know, display the warhorse's harness beside the warlord's bloody battle-ax.''

Giggling, Maggie resettled the soft leather apparatus back on the wall. "At least now we'll know what to do with it.''

Sam darted his gaze from her to the television and then back again. He grimaced, as though the idea of strapping her into that swing was one he'd have to spend more time considering before actually attempting, which made Maggie wonder whether he was the type of man who would appreciate using sex toys.

She knew some men didn't care for them at all, while others did only if they initiated the sex play. Both were common occurrences, Maggie knew, having encountered several in her practice. Where would Sam fit in? What new side of him was she about to discover?

And there was a whole other side to discover, because Maggie suspected most men would be thrilled with a television that aired only sex programs. But not Sam. He was still scowling at the screen.

"Forty channels from all over the world and not one of them airs CNN," he complained. "Or at least ESPN."

"Must be a new package. Basic satellite, movie satellite and sex satellite."

He rolled his eyes at her attempt at humor. "Not exactly. The signal has been locked into a favorite channels mode. I tried to unlock it, but the superclub controls the settings."

"You should have turned it off, then."

"I tried that, but then I had nothing to pay attention to except you and that wispy little thing you're barely wearing."

Oh. Maggie recognized the frustration in his expression. Twirling around, she gave him the full effect of the silk swirling around her and experienced a tingle at the abject misery in his groan.

"You like," she asked, very pleased at his reaction. "It had to be Lyn. She tried to drag me out of the office during lunch one day to brave the noon traffic and hit Harborplace for some new goodies for the trip."

Stop being such a wimp, Maggie, Lyn had said. *You can't afford denial right now. Denial isn't going to get you experience. Sexy lingerie will.*

"You didn't go?"

"Trust me, Lyn only shops upscale. My credit cards couldn't take it. Besides, I wasn't planning on having sex."

Had she been, Maggie wouldn't have minded the hefty minimum payment to her credit card company to earn this appreciation on Sam's face.

Sidling onto the bed beside him, she folded her hands primly in her lap. "I'm sorry I fell asleep. I had planned to spend our first night together checking out this place."

His gaze sliced through the shadows between them, skeptical, yet so powerful as he searched her face. "You didn't think you'd be tired after the drive?"

Maggie shrugged, then exhaled an unsteady breath, deciding to shoot straight. Given the changed dynamics of their situation, she knew Sam would respect nothing less. "Actually no. I've been so nerved out by the thought of coming here with you that I haven't slept much at all."

Spanning the distance, he swept an errant curl behind her shoulder, and though he hadn't actually touched her, the warmth of his fingers seeped into her skin like hot water.

"Why nerved up, Mags? We've gone away together before. We went camping that summer before my parents died—"

"Separate tents."

"What did you do when you couldn't sleep? Did you get up and organize your closets, or did you lie awake in bed, thinking about us sharing a room?"

His dusky tone brought to mind images of the nights, not so different from this one, when she lay awake, trying not to think about him asleep in the apartment below. Something deep inside Maggie shivered and she recognized from the gleam in Sam's eyes that he sensed how deeply his words had affected her.

"Me, organize?" she said lightly. "I wish. I'd lie in bed and obsess about how I was going to lose all my patients to separation and divorce if I didn't fill this gap in my therapy."

Sam frowned, looking so disappointed that Maggie quickly added, "I did wonder how comfortable we'd feel observing sexual interaction between couples, when we've never talked about it."

He brightened slightly. "We seem to be doing okay so far."

"But you've changed all the rules, Sam. I'd be lying if I said that I'm not worried about whether or not we can really go back to being friends without things changing forever.''

"We're not going back, Maggie.'' Sam trailed a fingertip down her arm, then slipped his strong fingers over the hands she clasped in her lap. "We're going forward.''

Forward? Did that mean they'd move past the sex and get on with their lives? Did she dare ask him to clarify?

No. Quite simply, Maggie didn't want to hear anything that conflicted with her idea of where they'd end up after this weekend was over. They'd be friends just like they'd always been—sexually satisfied friends. She was too emotionally edgy right now to handle anything else.

But she had the sneaky suspicion that pretending this weekend had never happened would be out of the question. Heck, she couldn't even get Sam out of her mind before he'd kissed her, when she'd only anticipated sharing a romance-themed suite. Now that he'd kissed her on the mouth, on her knees…

This on-and-off-again feeling was driving her crazy. One minute she felt confident, the next hesitant. One moment she was aching for him, then the next she felt absurdly shy beneath that dove-gray stare that saw right through her. If this is what she'd been missing with long-term, Maggie considered herself lucky she'd managed to avoid it.

His fingers squeezed hers, a gesture she was sure he meant to reassure, but one that did little but to emphasize the closeness between them.

"Don't worry about next week,'' he said. "We've been through a lot together, Mags, and always come through the better for it. Think you can just kick back and enjoy our vacation and let whatever's meant to happen just happen?''

Her gaze flicked to the television, where the weightless sex couple was demonstrating how to mount their Bungee

Swing, a task involving a lot of strength on the man's part and a good deal of flexibility on the woman's.

Sam followed her gaze and winced. "How about we both just enjoy the good stuff? Not just the sex, but everything leading up to the sex."

"I thought the sex *was* the good stuff."

He shifted his gaze from the screen and shot her a roguish grin. "Sex is only part of the good stuff."

"What's the other part—being unable to sleep and feeling edgy and vulnerable?"

"Of course. That's anticipation. Tell me you don't find it stimulating."

Just hearing the word *stimulating* tumble from his lips in such a blatantly sexual way made her blood tingle in that oh-so-sensitive region between her legs. Even if she'd been of a mind to deny it, Sam would only laugh. She was so excited and breathless, hyperventilation was a very real threat.

Besides, not only was he clearly enjoying the fact that he had such an affect on her, but he was right. The anticipation was stimulating. It was also killing her. Maybe if she just did the deed, then she wouldn't have anything to anticipate, because she'd finally *know*.

It was a plan.

Without giving herself time to consider the consequences, Maggie unfolded beside him and pressed close, seeking out the hard, warm angles of his body. "I find *you* stimulating."

Sam stared and she laughed at his surprise, a sultry sound that surprised her because it sounded like temptation itself.

Twining her fingers around his waist, she explored the sinewy firmness of his waist beneath the soft cotton, slipped her hands over the waistband of his jeans to follow the line of trim hips. Only Sam's clothing provided any shelter—

her peignoir might have been invisible for all it concealed—but even through his jeans, she could feel the hard length of his erection against her abdomen. She pressed greedily against him.

The effect upon Sam was startling.

Threading his fingers into her hair, he tipped her face toward his. "Oh, Maggie."

His words were warm breathy puffs against her lips, erotic, exciting, and spiking a yearning inside her that was unlike anything she'd felt before. She could only moan softly in reply and he apparently took that as a yes for whatever he had in mind, because suddenly his mouth was on hers.

She shivered at the taste of him, bold, hot, sweet, then melted with the enticing motion of his lips tracing hers, sending the blood rolling through her veins like breakers during a summer storm.

Obliging his efforts, she opened her mouth, sighed when he rewarded her with the warm caress of his velvet tongue. In a daze, she ran her hands along his arms to the exposed skin of his neck, not daring to touch him anywhere else. Not yet. Not when his kiss was a feast in itself and their weekend spread before her like a new millennium.

He sighed against her lips. The simple sound of need in his voice matched the ache inside her so completely that she smiled. Longing sizzled between them. Her body felt hot and heavy all over, and she wanted him, wanted to discover what would make him come apart in her arms.

Desire guided her fingers to the hem of his sweater. "May I help you out of these?"

Her whisper hung between them for a breathless moment. Then, to her profound disappointment, Sam rolled away and was on his feet before she'd even raised the hem an inch.

"I've got it," he said, whipping the sweater over his head.

Maggie opened her mouth to complain—after all, while he might be able to undress himself more quickly than she, the undressing was half the fun—but the sight of his bare chest made the protest catch in her throat.

Sam was beautiful. There was no other word to describe him. Black hairs nestled in the ridges of his firmly muscled chest, veeing down to a trim tummy, hairs that shifted and gleamed like black silk as he leaned down to unbutton his fly, to tug his jeans down those lean hips.

Sam was a briefs man, but in the winter he was a sexy *long* briefs man. White cotton glowed in the TV-drenched darkness of the bedroom, molded his shapely backside and clung to the muscles of his hockey-playing hard thighs. The briefs ended barely at midthigh and her gaze dipped to his strong, straight legs as he kicked off his shoes and shed his jeans.

Though she'd seen him often in swimming trunks and shorts, and even once she'd caught him sneaking out to get the newspaper at five in the morning dressed in nothing but his underwear, watching him undress gave her a new perspective. There was just something about the way that white cotton molded his tight backside that made her swallow hard.

Or maybe knowing she'd soon have free rein to explore all those hard ridges was what made it difficult to breath. The bulge in the front of those briefs was nothing short of impressive.

"I take it you like what you see," he said.

Maggie's gaze shot upward. He was smiling as he watched her stare at his crotch.

She ignored the sudden warmth in her cheeks and smiled back. "Very much."

"Glad to hear it. Now scoot up." He pulled the covers from beneath her. "Get under."

To her surprise, he climbed in bed with his briefs on.

"Cold?" she asked.

"Hardly." He rustled around for a moment, tugging pillows from beneath her, fluffing them, stacking two for her and then two for himself.

Propped up on an elbow, Maggie watched this ritual with silent interest, waiting until he settled back with a sigh.

And closed his eyes.

She frowned.

He cracked an eye open and gave her a sidelong glance. "Which side do you sleep on? I want to do spoons."

Spoons? Sleep? The man wanted to wrap himself around her and *go to sleep?*

"Am I missing something here, Sam?"

Now it was his turn to frown.

"Sleep?" she said by way of explanation. "Did I misunderstand you or did you say you wanted to…you know, do a little more than sleep?"

Maggie could tell when understanding dawned in his thick head, because he looked amused at her terminology.

Reaching out, Sam forced her to roll over, before tugging her into his arms, filling all her hollows with the hard heat of his body, nestling his erection square in her bottom.

"We've got a lot of ground to cover before we engage in more than sleep. I told you that already."

She could hear laughter in his voice, but couldn't summon a decent angry response when his warm breath tickled her ear.

"Now close your eyes and go to sleep. Trust me, you're going to need it."

Trust him? A man who'd obviously lost his mind, if he expected her to close her eyes and sleep when every nerve ending in her body hummed as though she'd just stuck her finger in an electrical socket.

She opened her mouth to let him know exactly what she thought of his high-handedness, but he chose that exact moment to slip a hand around her waist. He scavenged around a bit before settling his fingers around her breast, and in the process scattered her thoughts so completely Maggie forgot what to complain about.

Desire shot through her as if she'd been struck through the head by a lightning bolt. A fierce sizzle of sensation that made her quiver from head to toe. Made Sam tighten his grip just enough to let her know he'd noticed.

"Trust me, Mags," he said again, reminding her of what she'd meant to protest. "Give my way a shot. It'll be worth it, you'll see."

His way? Did the man think she was one of his stocks that he could buy and sell whenever he thought the time was right? She had feelings. And needs. So many needs right now she felt a single hard throb between her legs just thinking about them.

Then several of the comments he'd made since her arrival clicked into place in her brain. *Seduction. Ground to cover.* Why was Sam so intent on building up the anticipation before they had sex? Was he giving her another entry for her idea journal, or was this some sort of guy power thing, where he wanted her to want him so bad that she begged for it?

If he kept up playing with her breast, she just might.

Maggie was very well aware that some men got off on power, and under normal circumstances, she'd have dismissed the notion as crazy. Her friend Sam was a decent guy, who'd put her needs before his own so often that she'd never question his motives.

But her friend Sam hadn't kissed her in the elevator. Her

friend Sam hadn't blazed a searing path up her legs with that incredible mouth of his in the bathroom. Her friend Sam wasn't currently playing with her nipples and lighting fires inside her that he had no intention of satisfying. Her *friend* Sam would never completely disregard her needs and insist she play games.

This Sam was a stranger, one who had another thing coming if he thought she was going to meekly give in without a fight.

She'd give him the fight of her life.

Squeezing her eyes tightly shut, Maggie instructed herself to relax, because Sam was right about one thing: it was time to get some sleep. He would seriously need the rest if he planned to keep playing games with her, because she'd show him exactly which one of them would soon be down on his knees.

She'd play the game his way and see if he could resist her.

7

HALF-CONVINCED the previous night's events had been no more than an invention of his passion-starved brain, Sam emerged from the steamy bathroom, expecting to find himself back in the familiar confines of his house, the memory of Maggie's smooth skin the remnant of a very erotic fantasy.

When the steam cleared his vision, Sam felt a thrill that the Warlord's Tower hadn't been a figment of his imagination, after all. The bedroom, with its heavy medieval furnishings, still surrounded him like a scene from a 3-D history book.

Even the fair princess slept peacefully beneath the bed's canopy. Her hair tumbled over the white linen pillows in a riot of waves, and sleep softened her profile in a way that made Sam want to trace the creamy curve of her cheek, just to make sure she was real.

The hunger that still gnawed at him, served to remind him that Maggie was very real. Her eager responses to his kisses last night had been enough to prove that to a dead man.

Sam wasn't dead. Not even close.

Though how he'd actually managed to close his eyes and doze throughout the night was a mystery, unless exhaustion from trying to keep his hands off her had been responsible. Not that he felt rested at all. Not by a long shot. He remembered Maggie's claims of feeling "edgy" and could relate in a big way.

Yawning, he toweled his hair dry, mentally reviewed his game plan. Rescuing Maggie from the shower had not only sped them over the first hurdle of getting naked together— or at least one of them getting naked—but also had the added benefit of achieving an intimacy that had allowed them to talk freely.

While Sam hadn't been thrilled about rehashing his own former relationships, he'd seen an opportunity to show Maggie that by sharing his past, he was willing to share hers, too. And more importantly, to accept it.

Step two—interest. He wanted Maggie to know he was interested in everything about her, not just sex. He was going to make her want him, but he wasn't going to be had too easily.

However, he also suspected that conducting this seduction on his terms wasn't going to be easy. Once Maggie had agreed to allow nature to take its course this weekend, she would want to do the thing and be done with it. Never one to dwell on her doubts, she preferred dealing with the consequences of her actions rather than fears of what those consequences might be.

Knowing this, Sam had just engaged her in a classic power struggle. He only hoped she'd back down eventually, because he wouldn't. This was a struggle he intended to win.

Sam called room service, then dressed while the pale winter sunrise brightened the suite by slow degrees. He knew Maggie was typically a morning person and the fact that she hadn't awakened yet spoke volumes. Moving around quietly, he hoped she'd sleep off the effects of yesterday's drive and their late-night escapades and wake up ready to face the day.

When the espresso arrived, he carried the tray into the bedroom, then poured himself a cup, sipping appreciatively as he watched Maggie sleep, fascinated by the way the rising sun threw splinters of light through the windows, bathing her in a watercolor glow of crystal-and-jewel-toned sparkles.

The image of her as she'd been last night, sleek shapely legs and smooth thighs, beautiful body revealed beneath a thin veil of silk, was still clear in his mind. The sounds of her pleasured sighs chimed in his memory, filling him with a sense of well-being he'd never felt before. Maybe it was knowing that while Maggie usually slept alone, she'd felt comfortable enough to spend the night with him. Or maybe it was simply the added intimacy to a friendship that was full already. Whatever the reason, Sam knew that he and Maggie were right. Not just for a weekend, but for the week after and the week after that.

He only had to convince Maggie.

"Morning," she said in a voice velvety with sleep.

Her gold-flecked lashes fluttered open and her green eyes focused on him. Sam stood rooted to the spot, mug poised at his mouth, transfixed by the gentle smile curving her lips.

Sleep may handle some with harsh fingers, but it touched Maggie with a dreamy softness that made him want to stand here and watch her forever.

"Good morning yourself," he finally said.

"Is it late?"

"Almost eight."

Rubbing her cheek against the pillow, she let her eyes drift closed again.

Sam forced his feet to move. He poured a mug of espresso from a carafe on the tray, and then sat beside her on the bed. "Caffeine, milady?"

"Mmm." She cracked a lid and eyed him warily. "Almost eight o'clock? Espresso without having to get out of this warm bed? Is this a dream?''

He held the mug where she could see it. "Nope. Not a dream. This is the reality of waking up with me."

He wondered if she caught the promise in his words, and when she reached up to stroke his cheek, Sam knew she had.

"You're much too good to me."

Awareness made his mouth go dry, but he managed to reply, "You haven't seen anything yet."

Her silvery laughter chimed through the air, sent a shiver through him. She let her hand trail away and eased into a sitting position.

"Be careful, Sam, or you'll spoil me. I may never want to go back to being friends."

If she only knew.

Carefully balancing the mug with one hand, he helped her arrange the pillows with the other, swallowing hard when the comforter slipped down to reveal a glimpse of her breasts swaying gently with her movements.

Accepting the mug, she sipped enthusiastically, while he marveled at what the wisp of silk she wore looked like in daylight. Next to nothing, yet far more enticing, the sheer lingerie reminded him of the morning mist that veiled the park outside.

"Sleep well?" she asked softly.

He heard the innuendo in her voice, the reminder of their night spent wrapped around each other. Sliding off the bed, he sought refuge with the room service tray, knowing he wouldn't last long this close, with her smiling like a seductress.

"I slept fine." A lie. He capped his espresso and tried to collect his thoughts.

"But you must be hungry. You didn't eat much last night."

Her double entendre spurred him to replace the mug on the tray with a rattle, before retreating a few more feet from the bed. Unfortunately, distance only made Maggie turn on the high beams to make sure she covered the distance.

"How about breakfast?" She settled the mug on the night table beside her.

"You're not hungry, are you?"

"Not for food." Slipping from the bed in a fluid motion, she reached her arms above her head and stretched languorously.

Sam watched openmouthed as she stood silhouetted in profile, slowly swiveling her neck so red-gold waves tumbled over her shoulders and framed the supple arc of her breast. Peach silk slid upward, treating him to a view of the slim curves beneath, smooth skin he'd barely tasted the night before.

He hadn't lost his wits enough yet not to recognize a performance when he saw one. This was a show, plain and simple. Was Maggie tempting him to pick up the pace of his seduction or was she seeking vengeance because he did not make love to her last night?

With Maggie, he couldn't say for certain either way. Not that he was thinking clearly right now anyway. His groin pounded. He could barely swallow past the lump in his throat. With the few brain cells that hadn't yet suffocated for lack of oxygen, Sam decided he didn't care. He'd never imagined this bold side of Maggie and wouldn't look a gift horse in the mouth.

Think long-term, he reminded himself.

Maggie slowly lowered her arms, sent silk swirling as she turned to face him. Sam could distinguish the deep coral color of her nipples and the auburn V between her thighs. He sucked in a ragged gulp of air before making a complete fool of himself by tackling her onto the bed.

What had made him think she'd be any easier to resist in the daytime?

"Breakfast," he forced the word out, sounding as though he might need the Heimlich maneuver. "Great."

Her gaze captured his, and Sam could tell in that one glance that Maggie knew, she *absolutely* knew, while she may have given him control, she still had the upper hand.

"I'll get ready." With a light laugh, she twirled on the balls of her feet and swept toward the bathroom.

To Sam's utter amazement, she let the lingerie trail off her shoulders as she walked, letting it slide past her waist, over the pale curves of her bottom, and down long, long legs, before she disappeared in a sleek blur behind the closed door.

Her laughter echoed in Sam's ears, and he felt a...*tingle*—there was just no other word for it—shoot straight to his toes. Dropping onto the edge of the bed, he cradled his face in his hands and tried to gauge the long-term effect of moving up his timetable. He was in trouble here.

MAGGIE FELT a shiver of pure feminine satisfaction when Sam anchored his hand possessively around her waist as the male host led them into Bruno's Place for breakfast. She hadn't been awake a full hour yet, and she'd already made a dent in Sam's determination to take things slowly. A very promising dent.

The waiter seated them, provided menus, then departed. Opening the menu, more to occupy her hands than with any real intention of considering the fare, Maggie watched Sam over the top, tried to reconcile the Sam she knew with the Sam who'd kissed her so deliciously last night. Was he really only comfortable being in control? And if that was so, how had she missed such a pertinent little fact all these years?

Maggie also considered that she might be interpreting Sam's actions wrong, but couldn't figure out why else he'd be so determined to conduct this whole seduction scene. Was this something he needed in order to feel as though he weren't taking advantage of her?

Perhaps she needed to reassure him that while she hadn't initiated the idea of a fantasy weekend, she'd benefit by experiencing passion in their long-term relationship, not to mention enjoying sex that promised to be more fulfilling than any she'd ever had before.

Practical application. Just like Lyn had suggested. Lyn had also said that sleeping with Sam might be the smartest thing Maggie had ever done. She'd have to make the most of this opportunity and hope the esteemed Dr. Lyn Milhausser was right.

"Well," Sam said, catching her gaze over the menu.

"Espresso."

"No surprises there."

He was very wrong about that. She may not be hungry for food before caffeine, but she was hungry. And she was definitely full of surprises. "What about you?"

"The Western omelet."

"Found your appetite?"

"Just curbing it for a while."

She set her menu on the table with a deliberate motion. "A very little while."

He set his menu on top of hers with a thump, the cutting gray gaze he shot her conveying that he knew exactly what she was doing. "Longer than you might think."

Those were fighting words and Maggie thrilled at the challenge rising between them, an almost tangible sensation that seriously undermined all the headway she'd made in the privacy of their suite this morning.

The moment brought to mind another powerplay from long ago. "Remember your fifth-grade banquet, Sam?"

Maggie had been a year behind him in school and determined to claim the honor of being the only fourth grader to attend that banquet. Sam had been equally determined not to escort her, or anyone else. In fact, he'd planned to skip school.

She'd won that round through sheer relentlessness.

He arched a dark brow. "I'm not in fifth grade anymore."

True. She had testosterone on her side now. "We'll see."

He only smiled with infuriating calm. "Anything special on the agenda today?"

"I'd planned to spend the day checking out the place and observing the guests, but now that you've introduced practical application into the mix, perhaps you'd better tell me."

Sam opened his mouth to reply, when a deep-throated greeting boomed, "Welcome, Ms. James, Mr. Masters."

"Good morning," she said, ignoring Sam and his scowl. This bearlike man approaching their table could only be Bruno whom Sam had described as the chef from hell.

The brawny man extended his hand. She accepted it, but to her surprise, instead of issuing a friendly shake, he bent low, giving her a prime shot of his balding head, and then grazed her knuckles lightly with his mouth. "Ms. James, welcome, welcome. This is such an honor."

"Maggie, this is Bruno. The superclub's chef and restaurant manager." Sam performed the introduction with less enthusiasm than he managed for the biannual replanting of Mrs. Carr's rose bushes.

"A pleasure."

"Trust me, Ms. James. The pleasure is all mine." Bruno let her hand trail away and straightened, whipping out an order pad from the pocket of his uniform jacket. "What will you have this morning?"

Maggie deferred to Sam, who ordered, and watched as Bruno nodded approval at his choice.

"Sure I can't tempt you into something more than espresso, Ms. James?"

"I'm still stuffed from last night," Maggie admitted. "Dinner was delicious."

"All your dishes were seasoned just right?"

"Perfect."

Plucking the menus from Sam's hand, Bruno beamed down at her. "Wonderful, wonderful. Good food is the key to good living, and a good chef is worth triple his weight in gold."

Maggie assumed must be a quote from a very hearty eater, or another chef. She bit back a smile when he patted his ample belly and chuckled. "I'm worth a fortune, and just to prove it, I spoke with Mr. Masters last night about your preferences, so I can personally oversee your menu."

"That's very kind."

"Not at all. It's my job to make sure you enjoy your stay at Falling Inn Bed, and Breakfast so you'll come back. Repeat business, word of mouth and all that, you know."

Remembering Dougray's similar affability, Maggie ignored Sam's scowl and encouraged the conversation further. "Everyone I've met here seems to take that part of their job seriously."

"They should." Bruno tucked the order pad back in his pocket and winked conspiratorially. "All the department supervisors are stockholders in the company."

"So satisfying the guests has a whole new meaning around here," Sam said dryly.

Bruno nodded. "Exactly."

"I think it's charming." Maggie shot Sam her own disapproving glance. "And so is the superclub. What I've seen of it so far, anyway."

"You must make it a point to see it all. The building, the grounds. In fact—" he paused, glancing through the restaurant's lace-draped windows overlooking the front lobby "—Laura, our special events coordinator, should be on duty by now. I'll find her. She'll set up your schedule."

"Great, more attention." Sam frowned.

Bruno clearly didn't catch Sam's sarcasm as he assured them he'd only make a pit stop in the kitchen to turn in their order before hunting down Laura.

Maggie watched Bruno disappear, noting how the restaurant, named Bruno's Place, was as opposite in appearance to its namesake as a snowstorm in July. While Bruno was brawny and gruff in both appearance and manner, his restaurant kept accord with the turn-of-the-century charm unique to the Falling Inn Bed, and Breakfast.

Soft light from the crystal-cut chandeliers twinkled on walls busily papered with florals and pinstripes. Decorative shelves displayed beautiful china and ornamental glassware. The dark wood tables were draped with lace-trimmed linens and delicate glass epergnes that held fresh long-stemmed flowers in wintry colors. The effect was both quaint and romantic, but also made Bruno look like a bull in a china shop as he maneuvered a winding path through the tables.

"You weren't very polite," she said to Sam.

"He doesn't need encouragement."

"He was just being nice. I think."

"Any nicer and he'd have invited himself upstairs for a slumber party."

"Sam!" she said, surprised by his utter lack of amusement.

Where was her good-natured and usually laid-back friend who could find humor in the stupidest of situations? Noting the way his jaw worked tensely, Maggie decided there was nothing laid-back about Sam right now. Despite his declaration that he could easily control his appetite, Maggie got the distinct impression he was starving.

For food and for her.

"You might have to up your pace with the seduction." She cast a gaze around the restaurant at the other diners, all of whom appeared to be enjoying unusually hearty breakfast fare. "I think I'm going to need the exercise."

"Afraid you'll leave the superclub weighing more than you did when you got here?"

"I'm sure I would if it was up to Bruno."

"A little more of Maggie to love doesn't sound bad."

A smile erased the edge on Sam's features, signaling the return of his good humor. But humor didn't erase that hungry look in his expression, a look that made her feel as if he would swallow her whole given the chance. The crazy zing that raced through her in reply to that thought told Maggie she wouldn't mind being swallowed whole, either.

Espresso arrived, and after the waiter departed with an assurance Sam's meal would come shortly, Maggie cradled the warm cup in her palms, took a sip and contemplated Sam over the rim.

He rifled through the newspaper the waiter had left, toward the business section, Maggie guessed, to make certain the stock market hadn't crashed since he'd last been in touch with his office. When he settled back in his chair, looking content, Maggie assumed he'd found the market safe and sound.

She only wished she felt quite so content.

Samuel Patrick Masters was certainly proving to be full of surprises. Everything inside her melted when she thought about the way his hands and mouth had felt on her legs last night. The way he'd kissed her so possessively in the elevator. And the way he'd so arrogantly declared that they would cover a lot more ground before he'd sleep with her.

Perhaps the biggest surprise of all was the way Maggie found herself responding to him. Yes, she was very physically attracted to him, but she also felt something more. Edgy and energized, she wanted to push Sam to move quicker, wanted to see how he'd respond to being pushed, wanted to see if she could make him lose control.

She wanted Sam to want her.

This was definitely a new experience for Maggie, one she needed to analyze, so she could help her patients rediscover a similar enthusiasm with their partners. So she could discover it herself. She'd never felt this way about any man but Sam, both preoccupied and eager, and in moderated doses the feeling was, well…exciting.

Was the excitement what made him seem so different?

Though he was only sitting across the table, exactly as he'd done a thousand times before, he didn't seem like Sam at all. What was it about today that made her notice how strong his blunt-tipped fingers looked as he held the newspaper? Or the way his inky black hair shone in the chandelier light? Or how his gray eyes slid over her as he reached for his coffee?

What was it about Sam today that made her go weak when he smiled distractedly before dropping his gaze back to the stock market? What was it that made her want him to glance back?

The contacts? His kisses? The way he'd nibbled his way up her calves last night? The way he'd touched her almost reverently through her see-through peignoir?

There was no denying her anticipation at this new and unexplored intimacy between them. She felt like a child with an unopened gift.

"I'm being rude." He folded the newspaper and placed it on the table.

Maggie shook her head, deciding to cut him a break, since he genuinely looked abashed. "You're being Sam."

"Meaning?"

"Work factors high on your priority list."

"Too high?"

"Sometimes," she said honestly. "When was the last time you kicked back and had fun?"

"I play hockey twice a week—"

"I know—Thursday and Sunday nights from seven until ten. That's scheduled fun. It doesn't count. When was the last time you did something just because you felt like doing it?" At Sam's blank look, she elaborated. "I've got the perfect example. Last Saturday night was poker night with Lyn and Charles, but I didn't feel like playing poker. Instead, I dragged them out for a moonlit sleigh ride. We had fun."

Of course, Maggie hadn't felt like playing poker because she couldn't sit in Lyn and Charles's condo, thinking that if she hadn't have been there, they would have been in their bedroom doing something involving leather.

"Fun, Sam. And I don't mean toddling outside to rake leaves because you've got cabin fever."

Sam frowned, looking more stumped than he had the last time he'd gone under the hood of her car to figure out what was causing the radiator to overheat.

"I told you."

"You're telling me I'm a boring workaholic."

At the hurt in his expression, Maggie backpedaled. "I never said that."

"You did."

"I only said you don't make enough time for fun." She reached across the table and slipped her fingers through his. "I worry about you sometimes. You're so career focused life passes you by. That's why I didn't think Emma was good for you. She was exactly the same and you didn't need encouragement."

"All work and no play makes Sam a dull boy." The lightness in his tone didn't match the intensity of his expression.

Maggie held his gaze, knowing she'd given him something to consider, but before she had a chance to expound on her remark, a chipper voice asked, "Ms. James, Mr. Masters?"

Maggie and Sam sprang apart as quickly as they had on a night long ago when Sam's father had caught them igniting a toilet paper bonfire with Sam's motorized car gasoline. They turned in unison to face a spiffily dressed young woman, wearing a superclub uniform jacket. She was pretty, with a cloud of soft blond hair.

"I'm sorry to interrupt, but I wanted to catch you before your meal arrived. Bruno said you wanted to see the grounds."

"You must be Laura." Sam extended his hand in a welcoming gesture. "We've heard about you."

After greeting Maggie, Laura glanced down at the name badge on her collar. "I'm the special events coordinator, which is just an upscale title for a concierge who plans weddings."

She launched into a breathless commentary about the superclub's unique features, including an indoor heated lap pool, a whirlpool, sauna, top-of-the-line exercise equipment in a newly remodeled health club, walking paths, a hill perfect for tobogganing and even a nondenominational wedding chapel.

During the summer, Laura informed them that Falling Inn Bed, and Breakfast offered beautiful waterfront bungalows, tennis courts and a marina with canoes for trips onto the river.

"So you like to ice-skate?" she asked in response to Sam's query. "Well, it just so happens we have a pond that's frozen right now. Perfect for skating. Did you bring skates or should I make arrangements with the front desk?"

"My hockey bag is in my car. What about you, Mags?"

"I brought them."

"Great." Laura nodded enthusiastically. "Let me give you this then, since you're planning to head out today. It'll save you a trip to the front desk." Slipping a radio from her pocket, she handed it to Sam.

He shot Maggie an amused gaze before glancing back at Laura. "And a radio is necessary because..."

"A standard precaution for our guests who venture outside in the winter. Think of it as an outdoor house phone. You can radio the front desk if you get lost or run into trouble."

"Good idea." Though the idea of snuggling close with Sam in one of the giant snow tunnels they'd made together with the neighborhood kids on snow days sounded even better.

"If you'll just sign here, Mr. Masters..." Laura flipped the clipboard and handed Sam a pen.

Maggie watched as Sam penned his name along the paperwork with quick, no-nonsense strokes. Why had she never noticed how attractive his hands were before now?

Long-fingered with well-maintained nails, his hands had boldly explored her skin last night. But she must have seen

Sam's hands a thousand times, so why was Maggie suddenly noticing how tapered and sensual they were?

The answer seemed so obvious that Maggie bit back a smile.

She was learning all sorts of new things about him, things that were altering her comfortable perceptions. She'd read about this phenomenon, where infusing a relationship with passion helped couples uncover new facets in each partner's personality by creating an intimacy that gained momentum the more attention a couple gave one another.

Remembering Anna and George Weatherby and how they'd sat in her office, gazing at each other like two newlyweds on their wedding night, Maggie suspected she was experiencing the phenomenon firsthand. How else could this bold and sexy Sam come as such a complete surprise?

Reaching for her purse, she pulled out her idea journal and a pen. She definitely needed to add this trick to her repertoire. Her patients would surely thank her.

When Sam's meal arrived, Laura took her cue to disappear, leaving Maggie and Sam to marvel over the attentiveness of the superclub's staff. Bruno stopped by again to make sure Sam had enjoyed his breakfast, and before he'd let them escape, he'd wrangled Maggie's promise to come for dinner.

"I've never seen anything like this before," Sam commented as they departed the restaurant and made their way through the lobby. "Look at that poor guy. He's trying to check in, and the superclub staff is conducting an honor guard."

Sure enough, Maggie saw a man around Sam's age, standing at the front desk. His long brown hair had been pulled back into a careless ponytail, revealing silver hoops that glittered in both ears. A matching stud adorned his right eyebrow, and with his black leather motorcycle jacket and scruffy jeans, he looked positively bohemian compared to clean-cut and professional Sam.

"Maybe he's someone important," she suggested.

"Must be. Look, there's Laura, three desk clerks and that Scottish guy who brought up your luggage last night."

"Dougray."

"Dougray." Sam nodded. "I haven't met that woman, though. She obviously works for the hotel."

Maggie inclined her head in agreement, noting the familiar gold-trimmed uniform jacket layered over the woman's dark slacks. With her crown of steely gray curls and no-nonsense expression, she might have been a den mother leading her troops.

"The general manager, do you suppose?" she asked.

Sam shrugged. "But here comes Bruno to join the party. What do you say about heading out to the pond before we get cornered by the superclub brigade?"

"Works for me. I'm stiff from the long car trip."

Sam let his gaze slide suggestively from her head to her toes, a hot-blooded look though Maggie couldn't imagine she made a very fetching sight, since she'd just bundled up in her coat and scarf to head outside. But the appreciation warming Sam's expression suggested otherwise. "I'll be happy to give you a massage to ease that stiffness."

"A massage sounds great." She flashed him her brightest smile, very much enjoying the challenge of getting to know this new side of Sam and testing the boundaries of his control. "But I'd rather give you one. To make something stiff, if you know what I mean?"

Judging by the smoke gathering in his eyes, he did.

8

"DO YOU WANT the good news or the bad news?"

Mary glanced up from the columns of numbers that indicated the percentages of the superclub's occupancy for the past two weeks to find Annabelle and Laura poking their heads through the open door of her office.

"Good news, always." That way, she'd end up emotionally back where she started after she'd heard the bad.

They filed into her office. Laura pulled the door closed behind them, and the fact that she wasn't talking their ears off was a sure sign of impending doom.

Mary had an open-door policy, which kept her accessible to her staff at any time. The ivory tower style of management had never suited her, and though she was definitely much more of a delegator than a hands-on GM, she'd established accessibility as the hallmark of her career.

Shuffling the reports aside, she steepled her fingers and steeled herself for whatever news had earned this closed door. When Laura glanced expectantly at Annabelle, respectfully deferring to the older woman's experience and rank, Mary had to pull in hard on her nerves.

"What's up?" she asked.

Annabelle fixed her with a sober stare. "The WTA judge checked in. He didn't have any problems because of the storm."

"This is the good news?"

"I'm afraid so."

Unfortunately this good news wasn't lifting Mary's spirits in a way that might offset the bad news yet to come. Never one to dodge the inevitable, she asked, "And the bad?"

"He's not the judge we expected. The WTA board member who booked the reservation had an allergic reaction to some Valentine's candy. He'll be in the hospital until Monday at least. WTA sent a photojournalist, instead."

"A photojournalist," Mary repeated, staving off any reaction until she had the facts. But an inescapable question formed in her mind: how could a photojournalist have the same wide-ranging view of what made up the most romantic getaway as a board member who'd actually operated or owned a property? "I take it you don't believe the change will work in our favor."

Annabelle shook her steely cap of curls. "He's awfully young, Mary."

"Ugh! You should see him, Ms. J." Laura flounced down in a chair and exhaled dramatically. "He's got…earrings. In his ears, in his eyebrow. He looks like he hangs out on a street corner. Or someplace they don't have shower facilities."

"How young?"

"Thirtyish," Annabelle replied stoically.

Okay. Definitely not a hotel owner who'd spent years working in, operating and owning his own property, but not a tragedy, either. "I'm not concerned with the fact that he's scroungy. That's WTA's problem, not ours. But the fact that he's not established in this industry like the other judges could be a problem, if they don't take him or his opinion seriously." She settled her gaze on Annabelle, not liking at all the strain on the older woman's features. "Any ideas on how we're going to sell him?"

"Forget the marriage angle. He's not married. I asked."

"Like who would marry him?" Laura grimaced. "Though I suppose in all fairness, he isn't unattractive, if you can see past the ponytail. Some women like those scruffy-around-the-edges artist types."

Mary leaned back in her chair, racked her brain for some angle to turn this unexpected twist to their benefit and infuse her staff with the confidence they needed for the judging.

"Consider this," she said. "He's a photojournalist, so he's bound to have a creative slant on things. We're nothing if not creative around here. Perhaps he'll see that if we sell him on the romance we provide our guests."

"Romance?" Annabelle asked. "I think we'd do better to focus on the sex angle."

Mary nodded. "Falling Inn Bed, and Breakfast does sex, and we do it well. Let's focus on the whole package. Romance, sex, and yes, even marriage. He may not look the type to settle down, but who knows, maybe we'll luck out and his parents will have been married for thirty years."

Neither Annabelle nor Laura looked optimistic.

Mary struggled not to let their disappointment smother her hope like storm clouds on a sunny day. "We'll stick with the original plan." It was the only plan they had. "Tell me what's happening with Cupid's Couple?" She steered the conversation to a topic she hoped would remind her staff all was not lost yet.

"I met with them while they were having breakfast."

"Any complaints about our special Valentine's Day satellite programming?"

"Nothing logged at the front desk," Annabelle said.

Laura shrugged. "They didn't mention any problems to me. In fact, they both seemed happy. They're cute together."

Mary smiled, the news buoying her spirits for the first

time since Annabelle and Laura had walked through her door. "Let's keep focused on the goal. If we can get our Cupid's Couple to follow our script, perhaps the fact that they're similar in age to our new judge will work to our advantage."

"I suppose that's all we have." Annabelle conceded with a sigh. "I have a meeting with the judge for lunch. I'm going to suggest Cupid's Couple as the guests for his interview. What else is on the agenda for today?"

"Housekeeping's in the Warlord's Tower as we speak, leaving a surprise to encourage our young lovers to indulge themselves in some sex games. Laura, what have you got planned?"

"I assigned them a radio and suggested they explore the grounds. Apparently they like to ice-skate, so I sent them to the pond. I also told them about the bungalows. With your permission, Ms. J., I'd like to have one stocked. They seem to be the outdoorsy types and you never know what opportunities might arise while they're outside in this kind of weather. I'd like to be prepared."

Mary envisioned the river bungalows, gingerbread cottages that were so popular they booked solid from spring to fall. "Good idea."

"Not mine, really," she admitted with a smile. "I stole it from Dougray. Trapping Cupid's Couple in the elevator was a stroke of brilliance."

"He has hexed the whole place," Annabelle cautioned. "You know how…*enthusiastic* he can get. We have to keep our eyes on him to make sure we don't end up with a liability."

Mary smiled. Leave it to Annabelle to go straight to the financial heart of matters. That was one of the reasons that Mary had adored working with her for so many years—she kept everyone around her grounded in reality.

"Speaking of liability," Laura said, "Bruno's not going to poison Cupid's Couple with his herbal aphrodisiacs, is he? I certainly didn't see any results that his scheme was working today and it would be a shame if they ended up in the hospital with food allergies like our judge."

"Oh, please, Laura." Annabelle rolled her eyes in exasperation. "What results were you expecting to see? I hardly think such a nice couple would be playing touchy-feely inside Bruno's Place during the breakfast rush." Sinking back in the winged-back chair, she lifted a hand to her head. "But talk about liability. We might as well just close our doors if word gets around that we drug our guests."

"Not all our guests," Mary corrected. "Just Cupid's Couple. And besides, technically we're not drugging anyone. Bruno has made it clear that he cooks with herbal seasonings. Legally, we're off the hook."

"Ethically?"

"If Cupid's Couple falls in love and gets married, they'll thank us. No harm, no foul."

Annabelle exhaled heavily, driving home the point that they were on very edgy ground here.

"Admittedly, we're playing for high stakes," Mary said. "But everyone stands to win big here. WTA will have the best romantic getaway to tout for a year, and if we look good, they look good. We'll get the marketing push we need to establish ourselves and Cupid's Couple will live happily ever after. Just stay on your toes and keep your eyes open for opportunity."

Laura saluted. "Gotcha, boss lady."

A smile tugged at Mary's mouth, despite the fact that Annabelle's concerns were all too real. "Keep the faith. Falling Inn Bed, and Breakfast *is* the most romantic getaway. We just need to make sure we stand out from the other nominees."

And pray this whole scheme didn't blow up in their faces.
She didn't share that thought. "Anything else?"

Annabelle shook her head, apparently willing to lay aside
her worries for the moment. Laura, on the other hand, shot
to her feet excitedly.

"I'll go with the whole castaway theme and stock the
bungalow with some sexy games from Frieda's shop." She
paused in the doorway after Annabelle departed. "A whole
make-the-best-of-being-stranded routine. Very *Swiss Family
Robinson.*"

Mary forced a smile. "You do that."

And while Laura transformed a summer bungalow into
a love nest, Mary would try to find something positive in
this depressing turn of events.

Rising from behind her desk, she addressed the furry
group curled up and dozing in the corner. "Come on,
ladies."

Ears and noses twitched. Lipid eyes lifted curiously.

"I know you're tired of being cooped up. I am, too,"
she said. "How about a quick walk to the valet station?
I've got to see how the new parking arrangement is working out."

She didn't have to ask her ladies twice.

SAM SKATED the length of the pond, chucking across the
ice and practicing his stops and starts, while Maggie skated
in ladylike circles she called "figures."

The grounds of Falling Inn Bed, and Breakfast were everything the special events coordinator had claimed and
more. The superclub backed up to the park bordering the
Falls, and mist crowned the tops of the winter-stripped
trees.

Not only did the superclub's snow-laden grounds create
a peaceful winter idyll, with the steady rumble of the Falls

in the distance, but Sam could also appreciate the advantages of this prime location from a purely financial perspective.

Because Falling Inn Bed, and Breakfast had been built well over a century before, it had been grandfathered in when the state had assumed control of the undeveloped land bordering the Falls and sat on the proverbial gold mine. When he considered Bruno's announcement that all the superclub's supervisors were also stockholders, he couldn't help thinking that they'd made a very sound investment.

He'd made one, too, by coming here with Maggie. Slowing his pace, Sam watched her skate, body swaying fluidly as she traced imaginary figure eights over the pond.

She moved easily across the ice, a series of smooth motions, so graceful they appeared effortless. Sam knew better. Maggie had trained with a coach when she'd been younger, had taken dance lessons to augment that training and had even competed in some local competitions. She'd done extremely well—until her parents' divorce had brought a screeching halt to extracurricular activities for both Maggie and her mother.

He'd been pleased when she'd found skating again. Every year when he did her taxes and she bemoaned the hefty expense of skating, he reminded her that she would spend a comparable amount at any health spa. Of course, Maggie always replied with a threat to take up running, an inexpensive sport by comparison.

"Show me a triple axel." He skidded to a halt beside her, hockey blades digging into the rough surface of the pond and spraying ice in all directions.

She didn't flinch, just flashed him a dry glance from under the brim of her hat. "Only if you're looking to try sex with a cast, because I'll break my leg if I try a triple anything.''

"No casts, thank you. It would be a crime not to take advantage of that hot tub. Besides, you wanted to visit the Falls to see them iced over. We'll have to walk to get there.''

"We should go see them while we're out today.''

"Which means no broken bones." Sam glided along at her side, remembering back to his own eight weeks spent in a cast, and the miserable gyrations he'd been forced to perform with plastic bags and strapping tape just to take a shower.

The only thing that had made those eight weeks even bearable had been Maggie. She'd rallied the neighborhood gang into spending far more time playing kickball and riding their skateboards in front of Sam's house. When the gang couldn't be contained from riding off into the city streets in search of adventure, she'd curtailed her own activities to sit on his porch and play cards and board games with him.

"Show me something else, then," he said, the memory steeling his resolve to play for keeps. "Because the last time I saw you skate, you were flying across the ice like a goalie sliding for a save.''

"Sam!" Lashing out, Maggie thumped him playfully with a gloved fist on the arm, a thump he barely felt through the thickness of his jacket. "I only fell because you showed up.''

"Blame me, why don't you?" Then another thought occurred to him. "Or are you saying I distract you?''

Pointedly ignoring him, Maggie skated off in a huff. Sam caught up with her in two strokes, and when he did, he noticed the way her mouth and jaw were set in a defiant line.

"Fess up, Mags. Why did I make you fall?"

To his surprise, she didn't deny his charge, and he inhaled a fierce breath of icy air when she lifted that summergreen gaze and said simply, "Because ever since you agreed to come here with me, I haven't been able to stop thinking about sharing a romance-themed suite with you."

His chest seized up worse than when he'd been crosschecked during his last hockey game. He'd set out from the superclub today, planning to tackle step two, and it looked as though he'd had much more of Maggie's interest than he'd ever realized.

"Sharing a suite, Mags, or having sex?" he forced the question past his constricted throat.

Though her gaze never wavered, Maggie's cheeks above her scarf began to pinken, and since Sam knew that she talked sex with her patients, he could only surmise she blushed because he was right on the money.

"Sex might have crossed my mind…once or twice."

That rebellious look in those green eyes spoke of more than once or twice.

"I want more than sex. I want to make love to you."

The color in her cheeks deepened, but she held his gaze steadily. "I know. What I'm trying to figure out is why."

He forced himself to move past his emotional response to knowing she was attracted to him and focused instead on her willingness to admit it. This was definitely progress.

Looping his arm through hers, he pulled her close, anchored her to his side. "Is why really important right now?"

"It is," she admitted softly. "I don't want you to worry that I'll feel used once we get home."

"Will you?"

"Of course not." She shook her head vehemently, sending wisps of hair tumbling from beneath the rim of her hat.

"You're doing me the favor here. Trust me, Sam. I'm filling up the pages of my journal, and my eyes are opening big-time about how passion changes a relationship. Ever since you agreed to come here with me, I've been so preoccupied that I haven't been able to concentrate, or ice-skate, or—or *anything*. I'm actually glad we're finally here."

"Want to get it over with, do you?"

Maggie laughed, a sound that filled the wintry air, tinkling over the distant rumble of the Falls and making him want to pull her close and taste the sound on her lips. "Not over with it, *on* with it."

He'd known it and couldn't help feeling pleased that he'd not only anticipated her reaction, but had taken steps to circumvent rushing into things. "Then what happens?"

"I've given this a great deal of thought, you know. And I completely agree with you that we can't go back to the way we were before, but once we explore what's happening between us, I think it'll lose its mystery."

Making love would cure them of wanting to make love? The logic was so Maggie, he almost laughed, but she looked so earnest that he forced himself to keep a straight face. How could she not recognize what they shared was unique? No way would making love cure her. He wouldn't let it.

But remembering their earlier conversation, Sam had to face the fact that he might have overplayed his hand. He'd wanted to be a reliable influence in Maggie's life, not so predictable that she would think he was boring.

Was he? Her observations about his heavy workload were dead-on accurate. He'd never considered his schedule a problem before, but knew he would enjoy his off time a hell of a lot more if he could spend it with her.

If Maggie needed surprises, she'd get surprises. If Maggie thought he needed to make more time for fun, then he would make time for fun. But the only thing that sounded fun right now—

Skidding to a halt on the outside of his blades, he used their linked arms to pull her around, catching her when she stumbled against him to regain her balance.

She gasped. He silenced her with a kiss.

Proving that the chemistry between them was combustible, she balanced on her toe picks and sank into his embrace. Her chilled mouth melted against his, the warmest of invitations.

Cure her of wanting him? No way.

Curling her into the curve of his body, he sheltered her there, his impatience mounting in explosive degrees when she squirmed against him, trying to nuzzle even closer.

The irony, Sam thought, as his pulse kicked hard in response, his body primed and ready. How many men would have been thrilled with a woman who wanted a weekend of sex with no strings attached? If he was one of them, he could drag her back to the Warlord's Tower, strip away her clothes and warm her with his hands, his mouth and his tongue.

He wasn't. Maggie might want to lose herself to passion, but Sam wanted her to lose herself to love. Only then would he have the right to kiss her like this day after day.

If he didn't know better, he would say there was something in the water at Falling Inn Bed, and Breakfast. Slipping his hands beneath her scarf, he needed to touch her, to caress her soft skin, needed to remind himself that she was real and he'd be able to convince her to believe in them.

His gloves shielded him from any real contact, and Sam snarled a curse at the hindrance, though he knew their clothing was the barrier that kept him from tumbling her to the ground, to touch, to taste, to hear her cry out with wanting him.

Molding his mouth to hers, he forced hers to open wider with thrusts of his tongue. She responded in kind, her kiss as rewarding as it was challenging, setting his mouth on fire, his body, his imagination.

He wanted to feel her soft body unfold beneath him, spread her smooth thighs, feel her arch greedily toward him with a need only he could fill. He wanted to hear her cry out as he sank deep inside her.

Just the images made his breath hitch, made him anchor her closer, made his mouth impossibly demand even more. And suddenly, his gloved hands found their way beneath her coat, managed to burrow under her sweater, though he hadn't consciously meant to expose her to the cold. But he could almost feel her skin, almost feel her heat through his gloves.

"Sam?" she whispered against his lips, a warm burst of breath that crystallized on the freezing air.

She shivered. From cold or passion, he couldn't tell, but his entire body vibrated in reply. His thighs stiffened with hungry tension. His erection throbbed with raw need.

He answered her question with a savage growl against her lips. His heart pounded. The rush of blood rang in his ears. And something else, too. Some familiar sound on the fringes of his lust-fogged brain.

The sound was on top of them before Sam recognized it. *Barking.* But his senses were drugged with passion. Apparently Maggie's were too, because neither of them reacted quickly enough to avoid fifteen pounds of black-and-white boxer pup launching at them, catching him squarely in the crotch with all fours. Sam staggered back with a curse, before the dog rebounded back to the ice and sprang again.

In a mad yapping pack, two tiny black fur balls in pink sweaters shot toward their ankles, their ungainly attempts to stop on the ice almost comical. Sam might have laughed, had he not been so focused on shielding his crotch from the bulging-eyed jumping bean of a dog that kept lunging at him.

Maggie stumbled, trying to avoid harming the smoky-black fur balls with her sharp blades and Sam might have been able to steady her if a portly English bulldog hadn't chosen that exact moment to barrel into their feet like an oversize bowling ball.

Sam pitched backward, knowing he was going down, yet powerless to stop. Pulling Maggie against him, he tried to break her fall, without squashing a dog in the process. He landed flat on his back, and with a cry, Maggie crashed down on top of him, forcing the breath from his lungs with a whoosh.

He'd had no idea how close they'd edged to the rim of the pond during their kiss, until snow avalanched over their heads with a wet thump.

"Oh, oh! It's cold," she screamed, rolling off him and scrambling onto her knees.

Lunging toward her, Sam intended to help her stand, but liquid ice poured down the collar of his jacket and into his shirt, searing his skin with frigid fire. All heroic thoughts vanished. The only thing Sam could think of was cleaning out his own shirt before the snow melted.

Apparently the dogs escaped injury and thought Sam and Maggie scuttling around on the ice was an invitation to play. They descended in a yapping, tail-wagging pack of fur.

"Damn it," he growled, narrowly missing being French kissed by the crazed boxer.

Maggie laughed and Sam swiveled around to find her

fending off two of the tiniest poodles he'd ever seen. Her hat had come off in the fracas, leaving her hair a wild tangle around her head. Her scarf sat askew around her neck and shoulders and he couldn't remember ever seeing her look so beautiful.

Her green eyes sparkled. Her teeth gleamed white against her cheeks and her nose which had grown shiny red from the snow.

"Oh, aren't you just sweet," she cooed to the poodles, scratching them behind the ears in turn.

The boxer apparently decided Maggie was friendlier and scurried off to wrangle some attention for himself. Or herself. Sam had no intention of peeking to find out which.

The English bull crouched on its haunches beside him, regally surveying the scene. He definitely appeared the odd man out, given that he could have crushed one of the tiny poodles with a paw. Sam didn't think he could have moved quickly enough to catch the manic boxer.

"Aren't they cute?" Maggie beamed up at him, apparently unfazed to be sitting on a snowbank getting wet, and he knew she was getting wet because he was.

"Adorable."

Maggie frowned. "Oh, Sam. They just want to play."

He'd have rather been kissing her, but didn't get a chance to dwell on what he was missing when an approaching engine roared in the distance.

A snowmobile appeared over the rise, and a Scottish voice rang out, "Mugsy, Mickey, Tasha, Tia."

Sam stood, brushing off wet snow. Hands down, a dip in a snow bank curbed lust better than a cold shower any day.

Sam recognized the gray-haired man who disembarked from the snowmobile, as Dougray, whom Maggie would rather have died than let see her imprisoned naked in the shower stall.

"Tell me the wee beasties didn't harm you, Ms. James." An expression of horror etched his craggy face.

Given the laughing and yelping tangle that Maggie and the dogs made, Sam thought the question pointless.

"Oh, no, Dougray." She dodged a stroke from the boxer's greased-lightning tongue. "They're just visiting."

Dougray's gaze dipped to Sam's wet clothes and he frowned. "The wee beasties took off. Ms. J. will be fit to be tied, if she thinks they've been misbehaving."

"Who's Ms. J?" Sam asked, wondering what type of woman visited a romance superclub with four dogs.

"The general manager. The beasties live with her."

"Gray hair, serious expression and a uniform jacket?" Sam asked, remembering the woman in the lobby earlier.

"Och, no. That'd be Annabelle, the sales director. Ms. J. is the manager, laddie. She dinna wear a uniform."

Okay. Sam offered his hand to Maggie, who'd swiveled around and scrambled to her knees. She stood, then performed a little dance on her toe picks, while brushing snow and ice from her nicely rounded bottom.

Dougray politely averted his gaze. "Have you gone out to see the Falls yet?"

"Not yet. How far are they from here?"

"Follow the mist. The Falls are part frozen right now, so the mist isn't as heavy as in the summer, but you can still see it." Dougray pointed to the haze hovering above the forest of winter-bare branches. "Just follow the path over the crest and through the trees. Won't take long on the snowmobile."

"We can drive that into the park?"

"Aye, so long as you park the snowmobile before going up to the view point."

"Why don't we, Sam?" Maggie untied her scarf and wiped down her neck.

"We're soaking wet, for one thing." He glanced pointedly down at her snow-dampened jeans.

"We're already out, and I really want to see the Falls."

"We'll freeze. The Falls are all the way across the park."

"I have two spare snowsuits." Dougray slipped an all-weather rucksack from his shoulders.

Sam frowned. "You carry around spare snowsuits?"

"Gets chilly 'round here."

Sam continued to eye him dubiously, until Dougray finally gave them a sheepish grin.

"I was hoping you would do me the favor of taking the Arctic Cat back to the superclub," he admitted. "I've got to get the beasties back and they won't follow me on it."

"Of course we will." Maggie shot him a quelling glance that Sam recognized. He was supposed to keep his mouth shut. "We'll be fine in those snowsuits. The trip won't take long."

"Och, no. Not long at all," Dougray said.

Against his better judgment, Sam gave in, and within minutes, Dougray and the dogs took off. He and Maggie changed out of their skates and pulled on bulky snowsuits. He cranked up the snowmobile, and Maggie clambered on, wrapped her arms tightly around his waist in a position familiar from long ago.

His father had bought him a snowmobile for his tenth birthday, and during the ensuing years, he'd often taken Maggie for joyrides through the city's parks, or on rescue trips before the snowplows had cleared the streets.

The vibration of the powerful engine was familiar, the feel of Maggie pressed close as she sheltered herself from the raw wind behind his back, a sensation that made him gas the engine a little more, take the path over the snow a little faster.

She was right, Sam decided. He'd grown predictable. He didn't make much time for fun and found it unsurprising that the only fun he remembered having recently involved times he'd spent with Maggie. He wasn't sure if he should commend his single-mindedness or consider himself a hopeless case.

"Hang on," he said, gunning the engine and weaving a bold path through the trees.

Maggie laughed over the rush of wind, arms clutching tighter around his waist. Sam smiled.

His first view of Niagara Falls came after he and Maggie had parked the snowmobile and ascended to the observation point, to the sound of rushing water and Maggie's gasp when the Falls finally came into view.

The scene reminded Sam of a snow globe he'd brought Maggie from a business trip to Austria. White, pristine, unreal. The Falls, partially frozen, formed a collage of charging water, whiplash icicles, and icefalls that looked like giant snow-covered mushrooms. The gray sky hung low and heavy, an odd contrast to the sheer heights of the Falls, and the mist from the rushing water blurred the boundaries of water, snow and sky.

Maggie slipped her hand into his. "Wow. This is awesome."

"Yeah."

The scene brought to mind every cliché he'd ever heard about the beauty and power of nature, all fitting yet deeply inadequate. What struck Sam the most about the moment was that this awesome sight wouldn't have been nearly so impressive if not for Maggie standing at his side.

9

THE WARM CONFINES of the elevator did next to nothing to alleviate Maggie's cold. Clamping her jaw tight, she fought chattering teeth and tried to ignore the clammy dampness of wet denim clinging to her legs.

No luck. She was freezing.

"I—I—I'm bone cold. I h-have to t-take a hot shower."

Slipping an arm around her shoulders, Sam pulled her close, fitting her neatly against his chest. "How about a hot bath?"

Maggie assumed he was as frostbitten as she after that tumble into the snowbank. But the frigid trip to the Falls hadn't affected him as much as she'd thought. His teeth didn't chatter, for one thing. And the smoky gaze he raked over her was at polar opposites with the temperature, for another.

Excitement chased away some of her chill. "Are you saying you're ready to have sex?"

"No, that's not what I'm saying. I'm saying I'm ready to take the next step."

He pressed a light kiss to the top of her head, an inviting smile carving a dimple into his cheek and Maggie hoped this was the moment she'd been waiting for. An opportunity to wear down his defenses and get to the heart of whatever he was trying to prove. An opportunity to quench this desire that had completely transformed the way she felt about him.

And desire had altered her feelings. Though all the arguments that had kept her from ever seriously entertaining Sam as a lover were still solid in her mind, she felt excited and...*reckless,* as though she'd lived her life for this very moment, and now, she only had to enjoy it to the fullest.

Sam was entirely right—sex didn't have to mess up what they had together. They were adults and there was absolutely no reason they shouldn't get the tension out of their systems. Falling Inn Bed, and Breakfast was the perfect place to explore the sexual side of their relationship.

Sam withdrew his arm and stepped aside to let her exit, when without mishap, the elevator lifted them to the fifth floor. "You know what else would be perfect?"

"Hot cocoa?"

Judging by his smile, Maggie decided the ability to read minds was apparently another benefit to long-term relationships.

Well, it wasn't exactly mind reading, she admitted, as he worked the room key from a wet pocket molding his nicely muscled backside as they approached their suite. More like sharing a history together.

Sam's mother had been a stay-at-home mom, who'd always been available to warm them up with steaming mugs of cocoa when they'd been freezing cold and dripping wet after a day spent tobogganing or ice-skating or snowmobiling.

With a smile at the memory, Maggie watched Sam insert the key into the lock, then preceded him into the Warlord's Tower.

"Shall I call for room service?" she offered as Sam tugged her coat over her shoulders then hung it to dry on a pegged coatrack on the wall in the foyer.

His grimace left no question about his opinion of that

idea. "Why don't you run the tub while I go down and get some?"

Though she didn't like the idea of his traipsing back downstairs cold and wet, she refrained from argument. He clearly didn't mind and she didn't want any ill-timed interruptions when she planned to have him all to herself until they were due down at Bruno's Place for dinner. If she intended to quench her appetite for Sam, an appetite more ravenous than she could have imagined, she needed to get them moving.

Sam left, and Maggie headed straight to the bathroom to turn on the hot water full blast. Would she be able to convince him that they'd covered enough ground and the time was right to make love? Gazing down at the triangular hot tub with a multitude of jets and what appeared to be underwater lighting, Maggie decided Sam wouldn't have much of a choice. She fully intended to convince him, because relaxing in this tub together would be a complete waste if he only intended to talk.

Only after she'd wrangled with the tub's control panel, figuring out which button turned on the heater and discovering that those glass bubbles were indeed underwater mood lights, did Maggie notice the gift-wrapped package on the vanity.

A present from Sam.

Curious, she inspected the rectangular box, not finding a card with the package. Holding it up, she shook it, unsure if Sam had meant for her to open it without him.

The shuffling sound indicated a box filled with jars, and remembering the Treasure of the Sea bath items she'd admired down on the promenade, she decided to open it.

Sliding a finger into the neatly folded seam, she lifted the tape and peered at the bright graphics that revealed the box didn't contain the seashell jars she'd thought. Patience never having been one of her virtues, Maggie tore the wrapping away, hoping she wasn't spoiling a surprise with her haste.

Edible Finger Paints for Lovers.

She stared at the box, which depicted a colorful array of various fruits and spices, and giggled when she read the blurb. ''Turn your lover into a work of art with a sensual and colorful collection for creative lovers in twelve tasty flavors: cherry, lemon-lime, grape, blueberry, orange, banana, coconut, chocolate, espresso, cinnamon, marshmallow and peanut butter.

Had Sam arranged for this to be delivered while they'd been out sightseeing today? She knew he hadn't had time to shop on his own, unless, she supposed, he'd slipped out before she'd awakened this morning. Had the shops even been open that early?

Maggie didn't know, or care. In her hands she held the instrument of his downfall. Obviously he was feeling creative and she fully intended to oblige him.

Kneeling on the side of the tub, she slipped the jars of finger paints out of the box and stacked them on the tub's ledge between the candles. Candles. Where had Sam put that lighter?

Feeling breathless and slightly wicked, she leaped to her feet, tossing the empty box on the counter, and searched the vanity drawers. Jackpot. She found a long-stemmed disposable lighter in the top drawer.

After lighting the candles, Maggie flipped off the track lighting above the vanity. Candlelit darkness mingled with the Valentine's red-and-white glow from the tub's underwater lighting to create a very romantic effect.

Aware of the time and wanting Sam to walk in on a scene set for seduction, Maggie quickly brushed her teeth, fastened her hair on top of her head with a clip and then peeled away her snow-damp clothing. Her jeans proved defiant and by the time she'd wrestled them off and hung them over a towel rack to dry, she was freezing again, despite the steam filling the bathroom.

Or maybe excitement made her tremble?

Either way, she exhaled a very contented sigh as she stepped into the tub and slipped into the hot water. Closing her eyes, she let the heat seep into her frozen bones, easing her chill but not the exhilaration vibrating deep inside her. In any minute, Sam would return and walk through the door....

Opening her eyes, she surveyed the stacks of finger paints, wondered how bold she dared to be.

Very.

Choosing one, she unscrewed the top and swiped a glob of the goo onto a fingertip. She touched a bit to her tongue, surprised to find it smooth and pleasant tasting, even mingled with the minty aftertaste of her toothpaste.

What would Sam think? Would he be surprised by her daring? She hoped he'd be pleased and decided there was a lot be said for feeling comfortable in a long-term relationship, because she wouldn't have even considered hopping naked into a bathtub, slathered in edible body paints, to surprise any man but Sam.

Painting the white goo around one nipple, she created a masterpiece that resembled the top of a soft-serve ice-cream cone. With a smile touching her lips, Maggie examined the effect, shivered with an unfamiliar thrill, then painted her other breast to match.

Leaning her head back on the padded rim of the tub, she arched her back to keep her breasts above the water, tried to calm the thready pace of her pulse and waited for Sam.

She didn't have to wait long.

"I'm back, Mags," he called out, voice growing louder

as he approached the bathroom. "I put the Do Not Disturb sign out."

"Good idea."

When he saw her, he stopped in the middle of the bathroom and stared, eyes widening. Her heart came to a similar halt, a crazy jumble of anticipation and uncertainty and hopefulness.

"I know you like marshmallows with your cocoa."

Her sexy declaration echoed in the steam-soaked quiet as though she'd shouted it into a canyon, and for a breathless instant, she thought Sam might actually drop the foam cups.

But he transformed from Sam her best friend into Sam her almost-lover in the time it took for her heart to jerk hard once and jump-start into breakneck speed.

A slow smile curved his lips, and the glint in his smoky eyes assured her she'd been right about his preferences. The appreciation in his expression made Maggie feel more beautiful than she'd ever felt in her life.

It was his manner of bold intent that made her shiver as he strode toward her, pulling the lid from one of the cups and setting the other on the tub's ledge.

His gaze caught hers above the rim of his cup and she savored the promise of the moment, thrilled by the unexpected depth of this man whom she'd thought she'd known. While she might have known him as a friend, she'd never, ever imagined he would be such a bold lover.

After taking a healthy swig of cocoa, he reached forward to swirl a fingertip through the marshmallow goo on her breast.

Just one simple, seductive touch, and her body reacted greedily. Her breath snagged in her throat, and her nipple peaked, straining toward his touch. Pleasure cascaded through her, a rolling wave that tumbled like a current of a deep-running river toward that sensitive place between her thighs.

Sam's gaze revealed just how much he enjoyed her reaction, and promised that she hadn't seen anything yet. When he lifted his finger to his lips and sucked the marshmallow goo from its tip in a suggestive motion, Maggie simply melted inside, every ounce of her provocative intentions and willpower and restraint just flowing into a puddle of sensation deep in her womb.

Sam withdrew his finger from his mouth, a long, slow pull that brought to mind another similarly shaped body part. "Cocoa wouldn't taste right without marshmallows. Some things were just meant to be together."

His inference to their relationship was unmistakable, but Maggie couldn't find her voice to reply, even if she had known what to say. She just sat there, watching as he took another swig, then set the cup on the ledge beside hers.

A foamy mustache haloed his mouth, contrasted intriguingly with the shadow of a beard stubbornly reappearing along his chiseled jaw. His expression was alight with promise as he descended toward her breast, cocoa-covered lips slightly parted.

Maggie arched upward to meet him, fascinated by the anticipation building inside her by the sight of his dark head lowering over her pale skin. A gasp slipped out when his lips locked onto her breast, a sound of utmost surprise, though she'd fully known what he intended.

Perhaps that sound wasn't surprise at all, but wonder at the way he gently drew the peak into his mouth and sucked with a long, hot pull. A motion that suggested the rhythm of sex, of what his body would feel like gliding in and out of hers. Maybe it was amazement at the sensations streaming through her and her own heated thoughts, or the need to spear her fingers into his inky black hair to make sure he didn't stop.

Stopping didn't seem to be on Sam's mind as he flicked his tongue across her nipple then darted out to lick more marshmallow from her skin. Maggie leaned her head back against the tub's padded rim and closed her eyes. She wanted to analyze her incredible reaction, but the very idea of thinking was a joke. Each lavish stroke of his tongue made her thoughts scatter like a current breaking into rapids.

When he shifted his attentions to her other breast and his strong hands joined the game, Maggie gave up on anything but focusing on the feel of his strong fingers and teasing kisses on her skin. He nibbled along the curve of one breast and continued up her neck, warm erotic bites that made tension mount inside, until she squirmed on the hot tub seat.

"Your turn." His whisper blew gently against her ear, made her shiver.

"Mmm."

That pleasure-drenched sound was all she could manage. She had no idea what he was talking about and didn't feel like directing her energy away from the tingly warmth flooding her senses to figure it out.

Fortunately, she didn't have to. Lifting her cup from the ledge, Sam uncapped it and handed it to her. The cup weighed heavily in her limp hand, and she gripped it tighter, bracing an elbow on the edge of the tub for support.

"Drink. It'll warm you up," he suggested.

"Oh, I'm quite warm already, thank you."

Judging by his smile, Sam was very pleased with both himself and her response to him. He stood, and Maggie sipped her cocoa, watching him unlace his hiking boots and then toe them off one by one.

"What's in here? Cinnamon?"

"I think so. Bruno and his spices strike again." He stripped the sweatshirt over his head in a perfunctory motion, revealing his impressively broad back and wide straight shoulders that made the spicy warm cocoa taste even more decadent in her mouth.

He'd always been an attractive man, Maggie knew, but why hadn't she ever noticed before how neatly his broad back veed to a waist kept nicely trim by playing hockey?

If she thought hard enough, she could remember all the way back to the days before his chest had filled out and sprouted those velvety thick swirls of dark hair that nestled in each hollow and ridge of his chest. So why had she never before appreciated just how attractive he was?

Because she'd never owned up to her fantasies about him?

This was definitely another of those questions she must give some thought—when thinking was possible again, which was definitely not now as she happily feasted on the sight of his bared upper body and the muscles flexing and rippling as he flung his sweatshirt onto the vanity.

She wanted to see him with an urgency that made her tingling breasts tingle even harder. And he seemed quite content to be seen. He gave a wriggle of his hips, and Maggie stared, riveted by the sight of his erection springing free from the tangle of denim and cotton.

If she'd had any doubts about Sam's reaction to their newfound intimacy, the sight of him so hard and eager for her would have quickly put any questions to rest.

She barely noticed the pants sliding down his muscled thighs or when he kicked them away, because suddenly he moved toward her, all rock-hard power and rippling sinew, perfectly at ease with his nakedness in a way that was uniquely male.

She swallowed hard as he climbed into the tub, sitting

directly across from her, his legs tangling with hers in the hot water. She felt every inch of the crisp hair layering the firm muscles of the legs he pressed against her. Every inch as he shifted around, nestling her right foot into the space between his thighs. If she stretched her toes out just a bit, she would surely touch…

"Pass my cup, please."

His request was so *normal,* but there was nothing normal about the glint in his eyes. She reached for his cup, almost splashing cocoa into the water when her hand trembled with excitement, and he eyed her with the calm superiority of a man who knew he had the upper hand.

Sam accepted the cup, leaned back with a sigh, and took a sip, while beneath the water his big toe traced a lazy circle on her hip. "So, here we are, Mags, naked together in a hot tub. Did you ever imagine this?"

She shook her head, unable to force out a reply. Only in her fantasies had she ever imagined such a scenario, feeling that she wanted nothing more than to feel his hands and his mouth on her again. But even her fantasies had never prepared her for the intimacy of his solid legs twined through hers.

"I have."

After clicking on the jets, he trailed his toes over her hip and down the length of her thigh. His touch made those tingles inside strike up a big band beat.

"This feels so good." He mirrored her thoughts exactly, and though she wasn't sure whether he referred to the jets or to touching her, there was no denying both felt wonderful.

"Mm-hmm."

She obliged when he urged her thighs apart with his foot, gasping when bubbles jetted under her bottom and whooshed right between her legs.

"Oh!" The exclamation slipped from her lips, forced her to rise up from the seat a few inches.

"Are the jets too forceful?" Sam held his hand poised over the control panel.

Maggie lowered herself, inch by tantalizing inch, aroused by the steady, but gentle caress of the jets along her skin. Some of her surprise must have revealed itself on her expression, because Sam settled back with a smile.

"No, they're...interesting."

"Interesting?"

"Arousing."

And they were. The rhythmic pulsing was just forceful enough to part the sensitive skin between her thighs, creating a very titillating friction.

"Looks like fun."

"You really should try this." She rocked her hips to coax the spray along her skin, swallowing back a moan as bubbles massaged that steadily mounting ache.

Sam didn't need to be convinced. He scooted along the bench, repositioning himself in front of a jet. His eyes widened. Maggie giggled as arousal softened the edges of his expression and made her melt inside.

As if she needed more arousing. Her bottom already clenched tight in fluttering bursts, yearning for a bolder touch. All she could do was stare at Sam, marveling that she felt this way, for him, a man she'd only fantasized about late at night, so needy, and excited, and breathless.

He must have been similarly affected, because she read his intent in his eyes, even before he clamped a hand around her wrist, pulled her off her seat, and dragged her toward him. Their bodies met in the middle of the tub. The feel of his satin-slick erection against her abdomen came as a shock, but she had no chance to dwell on anything other than the feel of his hard body branding hers.

The water rose almost to her breasts, and the combination of pulsing hot water and cool steamy air served to create a host of new sensations that spurred her to slip her arms around him and run her hands over the firm curves of his backside.

"I never noticed you had such nice biscuits, Masters."

His hands traveled a similar path over her bottom, sending her nerve endings into an uproar in their wake. "There are a lot of things you've never noticed about me, James. While I, on the other hand, have noticed everything about you."

"Everything?"

There was something so potent about his admission that Maggie felt an unfamiliar hesitancy squelching the audacious response that formed on her lips.

"Everything." He emphasized his words by squeezing her buttocks playfully, which served to grind his hard male length deeper against her.

Anticipation made her feel hot and weak and shaky. Sam must have noticed because he arched back slightly, letting her drape full-bodied against him, while he tipped her chin up and searched her face.

"I've noticed everything about you, Mags. Now I want to become more intimately acquainted."

The purposeful gleam in his bedroom eyes promised just how good intimacy with him would be. Maggie ran her hands lightly along his waist and up his back, making Sam shiver.

"Intimately acquainted sounds very good."

His gaze flicked to the jars of finger paints stacked neatly between the flickering candles. He traced his hands along the curve of her neck, then over her shoulders and down her arms, eliciting a responding shiver with his touch. "How can I possibly improve upon nature here?"

"Glad you approve."

"Beyond approve, Mags. Praise. Laud. I can't possibly improve upon nature with my limited skill."

While he contemplated the finger paints, Maggie contemplated the effect of the candlelight on his face. The flames flickered when he held a jar to the light, cast shadows on his chisel-cut profile that made him seem all at once impossibly handsome and powerfully unfamiliar.

"Grape?" He set the jar back down. "No. It'll clash with your hair. What about cherry?"

"You wish." The brash statement just popped out of her mouth, and the instant it did, Maggie wished she could take the reference to her virginity back.

He arched a dark brow, and the skepticism she saw in his expression made her blush.

"Disappointed?" She shielded awkwardness behind a demand.

He ran a fingertip along her cheek, a gentle caress that contrasted sharply with the hot swell of his erection against her tummy. "I'd be lying if I said that hadn't been a fantasy of mine once upon a time. But that was when I was young and impressionable. Truth is, I like you exactly the way you are, and I wouldn't change a thing about how you got to be this way."

Casually, as though his admission was no more than an offhand remark that wasn't making her heart melt and her insides tremble, he picked up yet another jar, cracked the lid, and sniffed the contents. "Chocolate. That's it. Although I wouldn't mind a Maggie who tasted like fruit punch…."

A smile completed his statement, and Maggie watched as he sluiced a fingertip through the rich dark goo, forced herself to ask, "Once upon a time? Just how long have you been fantasizing about having sex with me, Sam? You said Fall Harvest.''

He didn't answer, and had they not been pressed skin to skin, Maggie would have thought he hadn't heard her. The chiseled lines of his face revealed nothing more than an intense concentration on her breasts, and when he dolloped chocolate paint onto a nipple, Maggie gripped his hips to steady herself.

She thought about pushing him for an answer, but the simple truth was, she wasn't certain she wanted to hear it. Not now when he was using those magnificent hands to paint her breasts in a decadent glaze of rich chocolate. Not when he was nibbling at the chocolate with intimate flicks of his tongue and raising goose bumps along her skin.

Not as his touches made her breasts burn so hot she couldn't stop from pressing into his palms, yearning for more than caresses from his paint-slick hands and teasing mouth.

How could she think about anything except the way he stood naked and imposing before her, just waiting for her eager fingers to explore him? The underwater lights haloed his body in a colorful glow, made his water-soaked chest gleam, the crisp spattering of hair nestled in those sculpted ridges glisten. He looked so sexy that dealing with this incredible moment seemed much, much smarter than trying to make sense of the past.

Reaching for a jar, Maggie twisted the lid, thrilled at the anticipation in his expression, the way his entire body went rigid when she slathered a glob of…strawberry, she thought, onto his chest.

With fingers trembling from excitement, she smoothed the satiny paint into the rigid muscles and valleys, pleased with the glossy effect. When she swirled strawberry around his nipple and tugged playfully at the tight peak, he mimicked the motion on her breast, sending a shower of heat through her.

Though they knelt, he towered above her, his gaze alight with challenge, and Maggie had never been one to back away from a challenge. Dipping her head toward him, she stroked her tongue over his nipple in one long lick. Definitely strawberry.

A shock ran through Sam, and his erection jumped, his breath catching raggedly, his chest heaving. A smile curved Maggie's lips as she drew his nipple into her mouth and pulled hard, amazed by the raspy feel of his chest hairs, the way the tight little bud rolled over her tongue.

She nipped him lightly with her teeth and his ragged groan came hoarse, and so very, very satisfying.

But Maggie didn't have long to revel in her triumph before Sam issued another taunt of his own, which involved more paint, still chocolate, she thought, though she couldn't be sure. To find out she would have to focus her gaze in the candlelight, and even the thought required too much effort when his hands blazed a hot path down her ribs over her hips, to that oh-so-sensitive place where her pelvis met the top of her thigh.

Clinging to him, she gasped as his fingers threaded through the curls offering only a bogus veil of protection against his exploration. The velvet-rough pads of his fingers rounded her woman's mound, sought that intimate gathering of nerve endings with paint-slick strokes.

Maggie moaned, knees dissolving into liquid beneath her, but it didn't matter, because suddenly Sam locked his arm around her waist, anchored her, and then his mouth found hers. She could taste the chocolate on his lips, the way it mingled with the strawberry on hers and then they tangled tongues. Running her hands along his wet skin, she explored each hollow and ridge of his beautiful body, arched against that exquisite pressure he applied between her legs.

She'd never felt this way before, as though she might fly apart like a wave breaking against a cliff, and when Sam stroked her sex, slipping his fingers gently inside, just enough to separate her responsive skin and intimately caress her, Maggie sagged against him, boneless, powerless to resist the riot of sensation building inside her.

Her mouth clung to his, and she sighed, a feeble sound that he caught with a demanding kiss.

"Not yet, Maggie, my dear," he whispered huskily against her lips, his hands latching around her waist.

Lifting her out of the tub, he propped her up on the edge, spraying water all around them. She rocked backward, was forced to anchor her hands behind her to remain upright as her entire body heaved with a coil of relief and anticipation and desire that was so intense it was almost painful.

Her eyes fluttered closed, only to fly open again when he clamped his hands on her knees and spread her legs wide.

"Oh…Sam!"

Her moan sounded strangled and raw above the bubbling of the hot tub jets, a sound that Sam plainly found amusing because he couldn't contain his smile when he said, "I was interrupted last night."

The idea of protesting swept through her mind, a fleeting thought that couldn't possibly be taken seriously when she was dissolving, simply melting beneath Sam's powerful touch. Why on earth would she deny herself this incredible experience?

Maggie couldn't come up with a thing, and when Sam smiled wickedly and held up another jar of paint, she gave up trying.

"Cherry."

She wanted to reply with some witty rejoinder about fruity Kool-Aid mustaches that didn't wear off for days, but she grew sweltering and light-headed as he painted the folds of her most sensitive skin with gentle curls of his fingers. She couldn't manage more than to stare at the top of his dark head when he lowered his face between her thighs.

For all of a disbelieving second, Maggie held her breath, tentative, unsure, until the first devilish stroke of his tongue made her suck in a ragged breath.

This was passion, Maggie realized. Passion the way it should be. Passion the way she'd never experienced it before. A total possession, a feeling of wanting, and yearning, and trusting herself to be possessed.

As Sam's clever tongue tempted and teased, and his wicked fingers stroked and ignited, Maggie marveled at how Sam, her friend, had transformed into a skilled lover, sweeping her away on a riptide of sensation that bordered cataclysmic.

She wanted to be devoured, knew somewhere deep inside that this shattering experience wouldn't even be possible with anyone but him. She had never trusted enough to give so completely, to let pleasure roll in on her like waves, until, without any hesitancy or pride, she arched into his touch, sought fulfillment, gave a broken sob when she got caught in the upsurge of a rushing orgasm.

And as Maggie's body burst with an explosion of sensation, she only had one desperate thought. How could they ever go back to being only friends, when passion with him was like this?

10

SINKING BACK into the tub, Sam pulled Maggie off the ledge and into his arms. He cradled her against his chest, fitted her head comfortably on his shoulder and stroked her damp hair as the jets bubbled around them, a steady, soothing sound that filled the steam-soaked quiet.

Pressed close as they were, Sam could feel her thundering heart gradually slow its rhythm, but unfortunately, his own conflicted thoughts didn't follow a similar path. He'd done exactly what he'd intended, but watching Maggie come apart in his arms hadn't left him feeling satisfied. Relieved that he'd been right about the attraction between them—yes. Sexually frustrated—absolutely. But triumphant—hardly.

Sam pressed a kiss to the top of her head, inhaled the scent of orange blossoms. Sharing the day together, realizing he'd been shielding himself from life behind his work because everything else seemed lacking when he couldn't share it with Maggie only proved just how much was on the line.

He'd invested everything in this weekend. What would he have left if he lost the gamble?

"So, do you still think making love will cure us of wanting to make more?" he asked, needing to hear her voice right now.

When Maggie lifted her gaze to his, beautiful green eyes still glazed with desire, not only did Sam's blood surge with appreciation, but that uncomfortable lump of emotion nesting in the middle of his chest swelled annoyingly larger.

"I'd planned to seduce you, until you couldn't resist making love to me." Her laugh sounded more hysterical than amused, revealing that she wasn't nearly as unaffected as she tried to appear.

Hooking his ankle around hers, he tugged her closer, trapped her legs between his. "I knew what you were doing."

"And what's that?"

"Engaging me in a power struggle."

"If I'd have tried that hard to seduce you, I would have."

Her expression was pure Maggie daring, and Sam saw right through it. She was as rattled as he, only much less inclined to admit it. Maybe that was what was needed here. Some truth.

He ran his hand over her hair. "Even if you dress up like *I Dream of Jeannie,* I won't make love to you until we're ready."

Although he'd controlled his voice, his emotions must have been plainly visible. He could see them reflected in Maggie's expression, and if she'd somehow missed them in his kisses and his touches, she was staring the truth full in the face now.

Sam knew that whoever had coined the cliché "a deer caught in headlights" had admirably summed up the expression. Panic leaped to life in her eyes. Sliding out of his arms, she retreated across the tub.

He knew just how easy it would have been for her to laugh, to segue past the moment with some joke or other lighthearted comment, but to Sam's amazement, she didn't.

With the shelter of distance between them, she asked,

"This is about more than making love to me, isn't it, Sam?"

He'd avoided answering her questions before, used fore-play as a diversion, but now... "Do you want me to be honest?"

Still, he gave her an out. Not only because it was habit, but because Sam knew if Maggie ran from the truth he'd have nothing left to hope for.

She held his gaze with eyes that had lost their impassioned glaze and glinted wistfully instead, and that damned lump in his chest grew bigger, making it tough to breathe. "I've been a coward and you deserve so much better. Please be honest."

He inhaled deeply, forcing a grin that felt so tight he expected his face to crack. The truth would change everything between them. Forever. "Suffice to say, this weekend isn't only about making love to you. It's about loving you."

His admission hung in the air between them, sounding so pitifully inadequate for the strength of what he felt inside that Sam shut his eyes to dispel a sudden wild sense of desperation. What if he couldn't make Maggie understand?

He heard the water swirl as though she were moving and then her fingers caressed his cheek. They trembled slightly, and he opened his eyes to find the glint in her gaze growing brighter.

"You never told me—"

"I did. You weren't interested. I figured it was because you weren't ready and chose to wait until you were."

Maybe knowing that he'd made that choice willingly would erase the stricken expression from her face.

It didn't. Her hand froze.

"Oh, Sam. I thought it was just a phase you went through, not something serious."

He lifted his hand to cover hers and drew them away

from his face. "I'm always serious when it comes to you, Mags. You said so yourself, remember? You said I was boring."

She stared down at their clasped hands, and shook her head as though trying to throw off a daze. "I didn't mean...I never said you were boring."

"You did."

"No. I didn't. I said you work too much and don't make enough time to have fun."

Lifting her hand to his mouth, he brushed his lips across her knuckles. "My mistake, then."

She frowned. Tugging her hand from his, she motioned toward a seat. "Come sit down. I need you to hold me."

For once she wasn't escaping behind laughter, and she apparently didn't intend to let him, either. Sam clicked off the jets and gathered her into his arms.

Her long silken curves unfolded against him, and he marveled at the effect she had on him. He'd just opened his heart, yet his pulse still raced double-time. If Maggie had any idea how much he wanted her, how close he'd come more than once to abandoning his plan and making love to her, he didn't think she'd be suggesting they sit here in this tub any longer.

"Let me get this straight," she said. "You haven't just been thinking us about having sex since Fall Harvest, but about a romance, too?"

"Not exactly. I've been thinking about romance with you ever since we kissed during the first rehearsal for *Carousel.* I only tried to convince you to give us a shot as a couple during Fall Harvest." No need to tell her about his first unsuccessful high school attempt. She'd feel less pressure believing he'd temporarily lost his mind. So would he.

"Oh. So you won't make love to me now because...?"

Several of the candles had burned low on their holders, and Sam contemplated the candlelit silence, the feel of Maggie stretched against him, her wet skin as smooth as hot satin.

Honesty.

Here's hoping Maggie truly wanted an honest answer. Sitting up, he helped Maggie shift around until she sat across his lap, her smooth bottom curled against him, his arm locked around her so she couldn't get away. He idly ran his fingers along the curve of her waist, light, easy contact that kept the intimacy alive between them.

The chocolate paint had washed away, and her breasts beckoned pale, inviting. He forced his gaze to her face, to the thin sheen of perspiration on her skin, the wispy damp curls that clung to her forehead and cheeks. She was so beautiful with her vibrant green eyes and golden freckles. Everything he'd ever imagined the perfect woman to be.

In that moment, he wanted nothing more than to make love to her, to give her the experience she wanted and make the most of their time at Falling Inn Bed, and Breakfast without a thought for what would come after.

If she ran screaming, he would only have himself to blame for missing his one shot to be her lover. But his gut told him to hold out for the prize, and Sam always listened to his gut.

Tightening his grip, he scooted her up until his erection nudged the soft skin between her thighs, escalating his own sweet agony and branding her in some strangely primeval way.

She let out a gasp, her breasts swaying gently as her chest heaved, and it took every ounce of his control not to lean forward and clamp his mouth around one of those exquisite peaks.

"I won't make love to you until you're willing to commit. I want forever, Mags, or at least a shot at it."

Her face transformed into a frozen mask, her eyes wide, her mouth forming a pale-pink O. But she didn't pull away, and Sam considered that a very good sign.

"I want you to let me into your heart all the way. I won't be another one of your dates that you leave in six weeks because you're afraid."

Maggie winced. Sam felt the shiver travel the length of her slim body, and she suddenly looked pale, vulnerable. He smiled, hoping to ease the bite of his words.

"I won't make love to you, because I care too much," he said softly. "I love you, Maggie. I have ever since I figured out what love was, and I can't handle making love to you if I'm going to get the boot because I've gotten too close. You have to let me help you believe there's nothing to be afraid of."

With his fingers gripping her waist, he gave her a shake, wanting to erase that wounded look from her face, loving her because of it. She hadn't tried to get away, hadn't denied his claims, she'd just listened, giving him a chance to prove his case even though the truth plainly hurt.

"If I thought for one instant that you weren't attracted to me or that we didn't stand a chance together, I'd back off. But that's not what's happening here. You want me, Mags. You know it. I know it. You just need to accept it."

His words hung between them, an accusation that emphasized their closeness, the intimacy of his hands still gripping her so tightly around the waist, he left faint marks on her skin.

Sam consciously loosened his grip, stroked away the marks, unsure whether to expect a slap in the face or a kiss. Emotions took on a whole new meaning with Maggie. His future rested on this moment, on Maggie's response, and he watched her, needing to know if he stood a chance or if she'd cut him down, because she controlled everything that mattered to him.

Then, slowly, amazingly, with the silence broken only by their shallow breaths and the snap of a guttering candle, Maggie's response built in her gaze, a richness of emotion that finally let Sam breathe past the lump in his chest.

"You're much too good to me, Sam," she said so softly, he had to strain to hear. "You always are."

It was exactly what he needed. He grinned stupidly, and when he opened his mouth to reply, his voice came out sounding absurdly light in contrast to the power of the moment.

"That's because I think you're the best."

Apparently that was exactly what Maggie didn't need to hear, because tears gathered in her incredible eyes, and she inhaled a breath that was more like a string of broken sobs.

Flinging her arms around his neck, she pressed her cheek against his, crushed her breasts to his chest, and for an instant his hands remained in midair in surprise. But only for an instant. The sound of her sobs breaking softly against his ear brought him back, and he wrapped his arms around her, stroked the creamy length of her back, the smooth curve of her neck, the soft cloud of her hair.

"Oh, Mags."

These weren't heartbroken tears, but overwhelmed tears, and overwhelmed tears were okay, because he actually had a chance to hope. He was so filled with the moment that he buried his face in her hair, inhaled the scent of orange blossoms, and smiled.

Sam wasn't sure how much time passed before Maggie drew away, but a few more candles had melted down when he decided he wouldn't mind spending the rest of his life

holding her like this, even if it meant turning into a water-
logged prune.

She sat up and swiped at her eyes. "I'm sorry."

"I didn't mean to make you cry, or worry, either."

"I'm not crying," she insisted, though more tears rolled
down her cheeks and splashed into the water between them.
"And what do you mean by worried? You don't worry
me."

It was a lie. He knew it. He knew she knew he knew it.
The bravado in her voice was pure Maggie, and suddenly
they were back on familiar turf. Sam knew what she
needed. Before today, he might have let her escape without
confronting the truth, but now... "Oh, I don't worry you,
do I?"

Lifting her chin a notch, she shook her head and stubbornly held her ground, managing to look both haughty and
affronted, despite the tears still glistening on her cheeks.

"Oh," Sam said, raising his hands to her breasts to test
their soft weight. "So, when I do this, you don't wonder
why you've never suspected how good it could be between
us?"

He brushed his thumbs across their tips, the friction causing them to harden into tight little buds. Maggie emitted a
low sultry moan and closed her eyes.

"When I do this, you don't worry that I'm going to get
past the distance you keep between your emotions and your
dates?"

He plucked at the tips, rolling them between his thumbs
and his forefingers, the blood surging to his crotch as he
watched Maggie arch into his touch, her mouth opening
slightly as a sigh slipped from those luscious lips.

"When I do this, you don't worry that you just might
like it so much that you don't want to ever let me go?"

Leaning forward, he stroked his tongue over one tight

nipple, then the other, felt her reply in the pulse of her sweet sex against the length of his erection. She latched her hands onto his shoulders as though afraid she might fall.

"So tell me again, Mags, about how I don't make you worry."

"Tell you? Tell you what?" she emitted in a strangled squeak. "When you do that, I can't breathe, let alone talk."

Sam laughed, so filled with pleasure, that he could only kiss her. An eager, satisfied, hungry kiss that she met stroke for stroke with her tongue, and when they broke apart, she gazed up at him with such incredible warmth glowing in her beautiful eyes that Sam's heart stumbled over a beat.

"So now I know."

"So now you know."

Her entire body seemed to relax, her mouth softened into a thoughtful smile. "I don't know how I feel yet, Sam. This is way too much for me to take in all at once. But I do know that I respect how you feel and wouldn't dream of agreeing to anything until I figure out what I feel inside and what I want."

He inclined his head, appreciating her honesty. His happiness rested in her worthy hands, and now Sam only had to wait, and take advantage of any and all opportunities to convince her that what they had together was right.

"And I won't push you to make love until you're ready, either. I'm getting a crash course in how passion affects long-term relationships without consummation, anyway. You've proven that there's much more to sex than intercourse."

"Yes, there is," he agreed, the look of contentment softening her features making him feel the ridiculous urge to pound his chest in triumph.

"I may not know how I feel about all this yet or what

I'm going to do, but one thing I do know is that we've got something incredible going on here and at the moment, one of us is very, very satisfied and one of us isn't.''

Skimming her hands along the outsides of his thighs and up his hips, she slipped from his lap and smiled sexily. ''So, hop up on that ledge, Sam, and pass me the jar of peanut butter. I've been wondering what it would taste like ever since I first saw you without your glasses.''

Maggie didn't have to ask twice.

EVERY SWALLOW of the chateaubriand went down in a tasteless lump, and only slightly more appealing was the rich burgundy with which Maggie chased each bite. At least that was wet.

She couldn't lay the blame on the food, though, not when all the other diners appeared to be very content with the fare. Table upon table of couples dined, clinked glasses and silverware, and whispered intimately over candlelight.

Rather, she was the trouble. She wasn't a worthy judge of anyone's cuisine tonight, having left her appetite somewhere between the Warlord's Tower and the entrance of Bruno's Place.

Sam didn't appear to be suffering the same affliction. In fact, he seemed to have worked up quite an appetite during their afternoon activities in the hot tub.

She watched him slice the tender cut of steak, looking very contented with a tiny smile playing at the corners of his mouth, a smile that had been there ever since she'd sampled the edible peanut butter finger paint and he'd released an impressive amount of sexual tension.

Just the memory of his throaty growls as she'd coaxed him to climax made Maggie tremble inside, made the mouthful of wine she'd sipped stall in her throat. Swallowing hard, she allowed the sensation to pass before she choked.

Shouldn't she feel content? After all, she'd come to Falling Inn Bed, and Breakfast seeking an understanding of how passion affected long-term relationships. Even though she hadn't spent any time at all observing other couples, her eyes were opening. Sam had responded to her sexual attention in a way that had simply blown her mind.

He loved her.

If Maggie expected the world to stop revolving because of his admission, she'd been wrong. He was just as he always was—a pleasant dinner companion, who enjoyed his meal with relish and was solicitous of her wants, a man too damned handsome with his gray bedroom eyes and satisfied little smirk.

He loved her.

He inquired about her meal, drank his wine and smiled as though ultimately pleased to be spending time with her. Admitting he loved her hadn't diminished him in the least, hadn't weakened him in her eyes.

Why had she thought it would?

Setting the wineglass back on the table, Maggie pondered that shocking thought. What was wrong with her? She was a relationship therapist, for goodness sake. How had she avoided dealing with her own relationship issues for so long?

All the old adages she'd ever heard about the plumber's pipes being clogged or the hairdresser needing a haircut sprang to mind, along with the time-tested advice to clean up one's own house before worrying about a neighbor's.

Looked like it was time to push up her sleeves and begin some serious spring-cleaning.

"So what inspired you to buy finger paints?" Sam asked.

That question snapped Maggie from her self-analysis. "You didn't send them?"

He shook his head, his slow smile driving a dimple into his cheek. "No complaints here, though."

"I don't understand. The package was gift-wrapped and everything. I just assumed it was a Valentine from you."

"You haven't gotten mine yet, and I'm reserving the right to give it to you when I decide it's time. Maybe not on Valentine's Day, but definitely some time during our stay."

Maggie wondered what he could have possibly gotten her that would make him sound so mysterious, but Sam dropped his fork and sliced a narrowed gaze around the restaurant.

"The superclub."

With a frown, Maggie set down her wineglass. "You think they left us the finger paints?"

"It's almost Valentine's Day, and this is Falling Inn Bed, and Breakfast, with the most attentive staff on the planet."

"That's for sure. But I didn't read anything in the brochures about the staff conspiring to get us to make love."

"That's what this place is all about." A seductive glint lit Sam's eyes. "That's why you brought me here, remember?"

"I remember."

"You just don't seem too happy about it." He dropped his gaze to her plate. "Are you sure everything tastes okay? You've barely touched anything."

"It's delicious."

He arched a dark brow, but Maggie refused to spoil his meal because she had some unpleasant facts to face about her life. "I've got so much buzzing around in my brain I'm distracted."

"Think talking might help?"

It was so Sam to worry about what would make her feel better that tears prickled at the backs of her lids. Maggie blinked hard. What was it about this wonderful, kind man that frightened her so much?

She didn't have an answer and wasn't sure she should try to figure it out with him. With her emotions so close to the surface, she may say something unguarded that might hurt him.

He sipped his wine, clearly content to give her his undivided attention until she made that decision, even though his meal grew cold in the process.

"What's wrong with me, Sam? Now that I know how you feel, it's so obvious. Everything about you and our friendship just proves it. Why have I been so afraid to see it?"

"You're the analyst, Mags. What do you think?"

"That my powers of denial are pretty amazing."

He chuckled, and just the sight of his mouth curving in an easy smile, the sheen of wine still on his lips, made Maggie remember the way he'd feasted on her breasts earlier, the way he'd nibbled his way up her thighs and brought her to fulfillment. She wanted Sam so badly that she clamped her thighs tight beneath the tablecloth to ease the wild pulsing that started when she remembered his mouth on her.

"Yeah," Sam said. "I'd have to agree with you there."

Retrieving her knife and fork, Maggie sliced another bite of meat, praying Sam would return his attention to his food and give her a chance to collect herself.

"I know you don't intend to eat that, so I'm guessing that talking is making you nervous."

Nervous? Now it was Maggie's turn to laugh, and she set her fork back on the edge of her plate. "I don't want your meal to get stone cold."

"Fair enough." He speared his steak and sliced through it with gusto. "You talk. I'll eat."

Maggie drew a deep breath, as collected as she'd ever be tonight. "You told me you don't think I have a balanced viewpoint on relationships, but I'm not sure it's just that."

He chewed thoughtfully and swallowed. "Think it might have to do with watching your parents' marriage come unglued?"

"You have a knack for this."

"I don't know a damned thing about relationships, except about those between people and their money." He wiped his mouth with his napkin and smiled. "But I do know you, Maggie, and I remember how tough it was when your parents broke up."

She sipped her wine, the taste of which had surprisingly improved, and thought about the devastating aftermath divorce had had on her family.

"It wasn't the lifestyle changes that were the problem," she said. "Although they definitely required adjustment."

A big adjustment, Maggie remembered. Losing her mother to a job had come as a blow. Maggie had relied upon her to play chauffeur and be available to talk, and generally put her family's needs first.

"Mom going back to work was rough, but when I think back, it was really the emotional aftermath that strikes me as being the hardest. I didn't care about sacrificing my skating coach and piano lessons, or not getting to go with my friends to cheerleading camp. But the emotional adjustments…"

Her mother had spent two years in a depression so deep that dragging her out of bed each morning to get ready for work had been a traumatic ordeal, resulting in Maggie developing daily bouts with hives that cropped up between the time she got off the school bus and walked up the steps to her house.

"Losing Dad was tough, too."

"Well, you already know my spin on him," Sam said, and Maggie noticed he'd stopped eating again. "Seeing you reminds your father that he let you and your mom down."

"I forgave him a long time ago. None of us is perfect."

"But he hasn't forgiven himself, Mags. You couldn't make him see that then. I don't think you ever will."

"I know."

"I'm just sorry he hasn't been there for you." Reaching across the table, Sam caught her hand, his fingers slipping through hers, warm, strong and comforting. "You deserved a father, no matter what his flaws. And having a man around as an example wouldn't have hurt any, either. You might have a clue about what's normal in a relationship."

"Sam!"

"Face it, Mags, you expect all men to leave."

"Many men do."

"Many but not all. Because of your work, you see a surplus of those who do. And you can't count those poor Joes you've dated, because not a one ever stood a chance."

She opened her mouth to argue, but then shut it again.

Sam squeezed her hand. "I'm still here."

"Yes, you are," she said softly, squeezing back. He couldn't possibly have any idea how grateful she was.

"Excuse me," a familiar voice said.

Maggie and Sam glanced up to find Laura, the special events coordinator, with a cheery smile on her face.

Sam didn't release Maggie's hand. "Hi, Laura. We skated."

"I heard. I also heard you met Ms. J.'s menagerie."

"They were adorable," Maggie said.

Laura nodded appreciatively. "Ms. J. certainly thinks so. She lives on the property, so they've become our mascots around here. And she, incidentally, is the reason I'm interrupting your meal." Whipping out a business card from her jacket pocket, Laura set it on the table where they both could read it. "We've got a photojournalist from the Worldwide Travel Association staying with us right now, and he's asked to interview a few of our guests. Ms. J. suggested you, if you'd be willing to talk with him."

Maggie glanced down at the business card. Tyler Tripp, Photojournalist. "What does he want to interview us about?"

"The Worldwide Travel Association nominated us for their Most Romantic Getaway award." Laura smiled, looked excited. "It's a big deal in the industry, and Mr. Tripp is here to judge how romantic we are. He'll ask you questions about your stay, about how the staff is treating you, things like that."

"The staff is certainly award-winning." Sam caught Maggie's gaze, silently inquiring if she was interested. "When would he want to do the interview?"

"At your convenience." Laura inclined her head toward a table near the window, where the man Maggie recognized as the one who'd checked in earlier to an honor guard of superclub employees, ate alone. "If you're willing, I'll send him over after your meal and you can work out a time."

Maggie twined her fingers through his, a silent signal. "I'm game if you are."

Sam picked up the photojournalist's business card and dropped it into his jacket pocket. "Send him over, Laura."

"Thank you so much." She did a funny sort of hop-skip, looked genuinely delighted. "Oh, and I wanted to tell you to go up to the roof tonight after dark. We have an observation deck, and if it's a clear night, you might be able to catch some of the Valentine's Day light show at the Falls.''

"We'll check it out." Sam watched Laura depart, weaving through the tables toward the front of the restaurant. "Now we know why he got the royal treatment today." Sam squeezed her hand. "I'm not surprised this place is up for an award."

"We should come up with some nice things to say."

"I've got a few choice words about their satellite lineup. And a staff that has the knack for interrupting at the worst possible moments."

Maggie remembered being rescued from the shower stall and couldn't bring herself to complain.

"But I've got loads of good things to say about their hot tub and those gift-wrapped packages they leave around. And we could probably launch into an amusing tale about that—that *thing* hanging on the bedroom wall."

"The Bungee Swing."

"Except the photojournalist will probably want to know if we've tried it. I don't want my clients reading that interview. If I deny using it, they'll think I'm a wimp, and if I say we have, I'll never stop hearing sex jokes."

Maggie dissolved into a fit of giggles. Cracking a grin, Sam withdrew his hand, picked up his fork and speared her steak.

"I'd better take a few bites of this before the chef shows up and thinks something's wrong. We'll never get rid of him."

Amused, Maggie reached for her wineglass. She just couldn't imagine life without Sam. She loved spending time with him. She always had. His dry humor always spurred her to prove that life wasn't nearly as black-and-white as he made it out to be, challenged her to loosen him up and make him have fun.

And when she did think about life without him... This afternoon had changed everything. The security she'd always felt in their friendship had suddenly been ripped away. When she thought about him getting tired of waiting and moving on with his life, while leaving her to date her guys du jour and remember the incredible sex they'd once had...

Sex? They hadn't even had sex.

Maggie swallowed hard, her fingers suddenly clammy around the stem of her wineglass. She'd been incoherent with passion today, because of foreplay. Incredible foreplay that had left her pretending Sam's admission hadn't shattered her, that being in his arms hadn't felt completely and utterly right.

But it had. So totally right.

And if this turmoil was her response to *foreplay*...Maggie had better figure out what was wrong with her, and quickly. Sam wouldn't make love until she decided what she wanted. She understood. She'd never ask him to change the boundaries he'd set for himself, nor would she risk hurting him.

But Maggie also didn't trust those boundaries, or her ability to adhere to them. Not when she wanted Sam so badly that just holding his hand and listening to his wry jokes sparked a fire inside her.

The passion between them was hotter than anything she'd ever known before, and when he touched her, she lost all ability to think. Maggie couldn't promise that she wouldn't get caught up in the moment, or that Sam wouldn't, either, for that matter. Tonight they'd be in that big bed together....

Making love until she figured out whether or not she was capable of commitment wasn't fair to Sam and she never wanted to hurt him. For once, she needed to think of what was best for him and that meant protecting both of them from this incredible attraction they shared.

But how? Distracted, Maggie forced herself to look around the busy restaurant. She gazed at the photojournalist, who sat at his table drinking coffee and reading a newspaper, looked beyond him to the promenade through the window.

And then inspiration struck. An inspiration for an even better Valentine than the upgrade to Sam's prized hockey puck that she'd stolen from his mantel and called in favors with a patient to have autographed by his favorite professional player.

"Why don't you order dessert, Sam? I'm running to the ladies' room."

"Dessert? You barely touched your dinner."

"All of a sudden I've got a craving for something sweet."

He eyed her skeptically, but she only smiled and made her way toward the rest rooms. As soon as she was beyond Sam's view, Maggie doubled back and headed out of the restaurant.

The perfect Valentine, indeed.

11

ALTHOUGH LAURA had termed Falling Inn Bed, and Breakfast's nomination for an industry award "a big deal," Sam hadn't fully appreciated how big a deal until meeting with the long-haired, earringed photojournalist from the Worldwide Travel Association.

According to Tyler Tripp, the Most Romantic Getaway award was one of the highest industry honors and one accompanied with a generous marketing package that typically resulted in a tremendous growth of earnings for the winning property.

They'd agreed to meet with Tyler Tripp for an interview in the afternoon the following day. On Valentine's Day, to be precise, which had made Laura coin the phrase "Cupid's Couple," when she'd suggested photographing Sam and Maggie in front of the decorated topiary in the front lobby.

Sam didn't mind doing his bit to help Falling Inn Bed, and Breakfast win the award. A well-deserved award, in his opinion, since the superclub was certainly proving to be the most romantic getaway for him and Maggie.

And never more so than when they returned to their suite after a trip to the rooftop to check out the distant light show over the Falls.

Someone had visited the Warlord's Tower during their absence and erected a Valentine topiary that appeared to be a one-tiered replica of the lobby display. They returned to find twinkling red lights reflecting off the Warlord's armor and moonlight spilling through stained glass illuminating the suite.

Maggie gasped. "Isn't it lovely?"

Sam nodded.

Romantic ballads played softly on the stereo system, and he watched as Maggie swept toward that crazy topiary, shrugging out of her coat and dropping it onto a chair along the way. She looked so beautiful cast in shadow and twinkling lights that Sam decided Cupid must have nailed him with another arrow tonight.

With a graceful arm, she reached out to touch an ornament, examined it closely. "Look, these are the same erotic ornaments decorating the tree downstairs."

"Erotic?"

"Oh, honestly, Sam." Glancing over her shoulder, she rolled her eyes at him. "You really didn't notice the ornaments on the topiary downstairs?"

He shrugged, unwilling to admit that he'd only had eyes for her the last few times he'd been in the superclub's lobby. "Maybe I will order another pair of glasses. These contacts don't seem to be working, after all, do they?"

She chuckled, and the soft sound lured Sam to her side, to contemplate the ornaments she found so interesting.

A quick inspection revealed enough erotic poses to make his pulse jump hard. Maggie's nearness combined with the memory of the magic she'd performed with her mouth and hands on him earlier were a powerful combination.

"I want to do this to you." He pointed to an ornament of a man with his erection buried between the woman's breasts—and held it up for her inspection. "Will you let me, Maggie?"

She tilted her head back, gazed up at him with excitement flushing her cheeks. "I'd be delighted."

Without conscious thought, Sam slipped his arms around

her, pulled her against him, every drop of blood heading south at the feel of her slim curves crushed against him and the thought of burying his suddenly pounding flesh between those soft breasts.

"Oh, Maggie." His mouth sought hers, met the hunger in her kiss with a hope unlike any he'd known before, the hope that Maggie would let him lead the way into the future, *their* future.

Her fingers twined into his hair, drawing him deeper into their kiss. And when she arched that sweet body against his, standing up on tiptoe to grind his erection into the welcoming softness between her legs, Sam knew that touching her this way only tempted fate. But foreplay was all he had right now. He'd take what he could get and hope like hell he could control himself when the time came.

"This is pretty incredible," she whispered breathlessly against his lips. "And you always knew it would be?"

Heart racing, Sam traced the outline of her warm velvet lips with his own. "Yes."

Her mouth slowly slipped away, and she turned in his arms, as though she needed to think about his answer and couldn't bear to watch him while she did. And they stood there, admiring the topiary, lost in their thoughts, sharing a companionable silence that only two people who knew each other well could share.

"I wonder if all the other romance-themed suites are so unique?" Maggie finally said, switching to a safer topic.

Sam squelched his disappointment, reminded himself that she stood in his arms. A very good sign, which meant he was still in the running. Step four of laying a strong relationship foundation was support, and he'd promised to be here for her until she was ready to take on her demons. "I wouldn't be surprised, if the Warlord's Tower is any indication."

"Perhaps we can come back in spring. I'd love to see the Falls then."

"I'd love to see the Sultan's Seraglio."

"I'll just bet you would." He could hear the smile in her voice. "*I Dream of Jeannie.* Who'd have guessed?"

Maggie might have, had she ever seriously considered him as more than a friend, but Sam didn't say that, knowing he'd already made incredible strides toward proving how much potential they had together. He had to invest wisely here, and pushing Maggie at this point wasn't a sound strategy.

Not when he could seduce her, instead.

Which doubled back to step three—intimacy. Cupid decided just then to grant Sam's fondest wish, when the music segued into a song they'd recently danced to at a friend's wedding. Suddenly eager for seduction, to feel her warm against him, Sam swung her around in his arms, caught her hand in his, and dipped her low over his arm.

Maggie went fluidly with the motion, gasping as her hair tumbled out behind her and her breasts arched invitingly toward his face. He nipped at the irresistible swell through the thickness of her sweater and she moaned in reply.

"Dance with me, Mags."

She giggled as he pulled her back up and into his arms, melted against him as he led her across the lush carpet in steps that loosely resembled a waltz.

"We haven't danced together since Kimberly and Peter's wedding." She followed his movements easily, and the way she brushed her thighs against his drove him wild.

"You looked good enough to eat in that clingy gown. I thought I might explode and you weren't even teasing me then."

Maggie tipped her head back and eyed him imperiously

down the length of her delicate nose. "I'm not teasing you now."

"Right," he growled as she gave another quick thrust of her belly against his erection. He decided right then that it was time to test his ability to resist her. "It's getting late and there just happens to be a big bed in the next room."

He waltzed her in that direction.

"But I'm not tired at all."

Sam scowled. "I wonder if eating tiramisu and drinking espresso at eight o'clock at night has something to do with it?"

"I suppose it might have."

"Might have? I could put big bucks into a soft market and still earn on that one."

"As usual, you've got stocks on the brain."

"Trust me. Work is the furthest thing from my mind."

He emphasized his statement by resting his head on top of hers and discouraging further conversation. She melted against him, her curves molding against him, her cheek resting lightly against his shoulder.

"I have an idea," Maggie said. "Why don't we exchange Valentines?"

"Let me think." He dipped her low again, this time nipping at the cashmere-covered belly stretching temptingly before him. "Because it's not Valentine's Day?"

"It's close enough."

Not nearly close enough, Sam decided. Close enough would be lying stretched out on the bed, naked. "I'm not giving you my real Valentine yet. It's not time." And it wouldn't be until he and Maggie made love, with a promise between them.

"That's okay. I'll save my big one until tomorrow. I just want to give you one. It's sort of a last-minute inspiration."

For Maggie, last-minute was normal, so for her to admit

to spontaneity was enough to make Sam cringe, especially when he noticed her suggestive—and decidedly smug—expression.

Whirling her away from him, he smiled when her hair whipped around her, thrilled to hear her laughter. "Okay, Mags. Let's exchange Valentines."

Breathless, she came to a sudden stop. "I'll be back."

With that, she sailed into the bedroom, and when he heard the bathroom door slam, his pulse started to slug through his veins in anticipation of her "last-minute inspiration."

If nothing else, anticipation was half the fun, Sam decided, while retrieving one of his gifts from his garment bag and placing it under the topiary, christening it as a sort of Valentine's Day tree. As an afterthought, he set the Do Not Disturb on the door and was about to strip out of his clothes, when Maggie called out, "I'm coming. Go sit down."

Excitement made her voice sound breathy and high-pitched, and Sam found his own tension mounting as he obliged.

Last-minute? For Maggie this was a scary thought.

Sam wasn't sure what he expected. Lingerie maybe, knowing Lyn had swapped Maggie's pajamas for the kind of sexy outfits that made his tongue tangle in his mouth. Or maybe a surprise that had nothing to do with sex at all.

What Sam didn't expect was for Maggie to emerge from the bedroom, wrapped in the comforter from the bed. Her gorgeous curves covered from chin to toe. She'd piled her hair on top of her head in a haphazard style held by a bright-purple clip.

"Wow, Mags. You look gorgeous," he said with a laugh, not sure whether this was her Valentine or not, but knowing that playing it safe was his best bet.

Sinking to her knees beside him, she freed an arm from the tangle of quilt, giving Sam a glimpse of a pale breast in the process. Things were getting better by the second.

He couldn't miss her flushed cheeks, her eyes alight with excitement. Her gaze dropped to the package he'd placed under the Valentine's tree, and she exhaled a sigh that sounded strangely like relief.

"Can I open mine first? Do you mind?"

Smiling, Sam handed her the package. "Happy Valentine's."

She hurriedly tore off the wrapping and flung it aside before pulling off the lid and lifting out the furry gray slippers with an expression of rapture.

"Oh, Rocky the Squirrel slippers! I love him, Sam. I was hoping you would give me these." She tugged them onto her feet one-handed, then rose to her knees and pressed a kiss to his cheek.

"I'm predictable."

"You're charming."

"I'm boring."

"You're not," she said emphatically, her smile fading when she caught his gaze. "And when it gets right down to it, don't you think I'm flighty enough for the two of us? I mean, one of us has to be grounded, right?"

That she thought of them in terms of "us" and "we" was enough to make Sam's mouth go dry. Was this a step toward commitment? He didn't get a chance to ponder the thought because Maggie propelled herself up, lifted the hem of her makeshift gown to show off the two identical grinning squirrels on her feet.

"I'd say they work. What do you think?"

The slippers looked odd paired with the quilt, but again Sam didn't get a chance to reply, because she'd already sailed toward the stereo and cranked up the volume.

"Are you ready for my gift?"

He didn't see a gift, but he smiled gamely anyway. "As I'll ever be."

Raising her brows as if to say, "You just wait and see what I've got for you," she strode over to the windows. Moonlight bathed her in a multihued glow, and when she turned her back to him and started to sway with the music, Sam's erection gave such a hard throb he winced.

With her hips circling gently beneath the fall of thick quilt, she raised a hand and unfastened the clip binding her hair. Before the silky waves had even tumbled over her shoulders, Sam realized what Maggie had planned.

A striptease.

His mind seized up, just froze. This was a fantasy in 3-D, and he sat riveted, half disbelieving, half convinced this was a dream. But if this was a dream, he hoped, more than he'd ever hoped for anything before, that he wouldn't wake up.

Shards of colored moonlight flashed over her like light from a disco ball as she moved with graceful motions, inching the quilt down her shoulders, past the length of her arms, hips spiraling as she uncovered a red satin nightgown with dramatic slits in the fabric that revealed more than it concealed.

Thank you, Lyn.

Sam's breath came in broken gasps by the time the quilt fell in a puddle around her Rocky slippers. She kicked it aside, one Rocky the Squirrel head bobbing as the hem caught on his faux-leather pilot's cap, striking Sam with the unusual sight she made, an intriguing combination of seduction and innocence and Valentine cheer.

Maggie cast a coy glance over her shoulder to make sure her audience was paying close attention.

He was. He was paying such close attention that he was

forced to unfasten his slacks before doing permanent damage.

With a sidelong glance and a smile, she watched him unzip his fly and then slowly swiveled around to reveal the thin satin tie holding her nightgown together. Well, sort of together. The gap reached straight down to her navel and exposed every creamy inch of smooth skin in between. Slits shot up to her hips, gifting him with tantalizing glimpses of her pale thighs as she moved seductively, drove him crazy.

Tugging at the silk bow with slim fingers, Maggie coaxed the silk from the loops, let the fabric part to reveal those incredible breasts, smooth skin swaying gently, deep-pink nipples beckoning, revealing her own excitement.

The slow tempo of the music faded, transitioning into a more upbeat sound. The title of the song was buried in some numbed part of his brain, but he had the vague thought that he'd never enjoyed it more than when hearing it played to the motion of Maggie's enticing breasts as she shrugged the nightgown down her arms, leaving her whole upper body bared to his gaze.

Her eyes had grown glassy with desire, and he knew she was as aroused as he, wondered what she'd do if he tugged that nightgown right off her body. Would she resist if he dragged her down to the floor, sank his body into hers and made hard fast love to her with nothing on but those ridiculous slippers?

Valiant thoughts, when in reality Sam couldn't move. If he did, if he shifted just one fraction of an inch, he'd explode.

A faint whoosh of satin that he actually imagined more than heard above the music and the nightgown slipped down her waist, over her hips, down the length of her long, long legs....

His gaze shot back up to her hips and the familiar red leather apparatus that resided there. It took a full minute for him to register what he was actually seeing.

The chastity belt from the store on the promenade rested lazily around her hips, dipping between those sweet thighs.

"Happy Valentine's Day."

Surprise dulled the desperate edge of his lust. "Jeez, Mags. I don't believe you bought that."

"I didn't. No time. I asked Laura to have it sent up before we came back from dinner."

He winced at the thought of the superclub's staff sharing this Valentine, but he didn't get a chance to think much when Maggie sidled up to him, the chastity belt level with his nose. Every drop of Sam's blood plummeted straight to his crotch.

"Oh, look," she said excitedly, reaching for his hand and guiding it to the top of the belt. "Another Valentine."

Their gazes collided, his surprised, hers bold with an underlying touch of uncertainty he found irresistible. She sucked in the smooth curve of her belly, and Sam obliged her by slipping his hand inside and retrieving a small white envelope.

Sinking down beside him, she motioned for him to open the gift, and with fingers that shook slightly, he lifted the flap to reveal a tiny golden key.

"For that," he ground out past constricted vocal chords.

She nodded and lifted the key the out. "Now put this where we can't get to it, and let's go to bed. We can have all the fun we want without having to worry about crossing the line."

So that's what this was all about. Maggie didn't want to hurt him. She respected him enough to accept his boundaries and cared enough to help ensure they stuck to them.

Her actions demonstrated step four's support in a way that humbled Sam.

Catching her hand, he plucked the key from her fingers and pressed a kiss to her palm. She smiled softly, an expression that told him she understood how touched he was without words.

And he was more deeply touched than he'd ever been in his life, because in her gaze he recognized how Maggie felt about him. Even if she didn't yet. That crazy leather apparatus riding low on her hips proved just how much she loved him.

"So this is going to keep us from crossing the line, hmm?"

Maggie shook her head and the trust he saw in her gaze urged him to find out just how much fun they could have. Making a great show of dropping the key into his pocket, he reached toward her, slipped a hand between her thighs.

She gasped, grabbing his shoulders as she arched backward, her wide gaze searching his, questioning, softening when he fingered the supple leather strap that nestled between the tender folds of her flesh.

"All the fun we want, huh?"

He tested the leather strap, found to his pleasure that it shifted easily to allow him to fondle her. He wouldn't be able to make love to her, but he could definitely play to his heart's content and bring her to fulfillment.

Stroking the tip of one finger along her moist depths, he thrilled to watch her expression glaze with desire.

"Yeah, Mags, this will work nicely."

"Mmmm." She watched him through half-closed lids and arched into his touch, driving his finger in deeper.

He caressed her slick skin, marveled at the expression of dazed satisfaction that made her eyes greener, her gold-tipped lashes brighter, her full lips pinker.

Yes, this'll work out very well.

Dropping a kiss to those pouty lips, he pulled his finger away, smiled when she issued a discontented sigh.

"Let's go to bed, Valentine."

Shaking her head as though to shrug off a daze, she spun around, rising up on her knees to give him such an incredible shot of her firmly rounded bottom with the thin leather strip wedged between those sweet cheeks that he almost pulled her down beside him. He watched with eager interest as she searched the big white blooms that made up the Valentine topiary until she found what she sought. With a smile, she held out the erotic ornament he'd pointed out earlier and dangled it between them.

Sam's gaze dropped to the ceramic sculpture of the man cradling his erection between his lady's breasts, and his heart skipped a few beats, then kicked into overdrive.

Before he could think of a worthy reply, she was on her feet and across the room, plucking the red plume from the knight's helm.

"Come on, warlord." She gifted him with an inviting smile and extended her hand. "Let the games begin."

The games?

Sam wasn't about to ask questions, when all he could think about was getting her into the warlord's bed. She gasped when he grabbed her wrist and hoisted himself up. He scooped her into his arms, the Rocky the Squirrel heads on her slippers bobbing wildly as he lifted her against him.

He set her down in the middle of the bed. Maggie placed the erotic ornament and the plume on the night table, then lay back and arched her back, a pose designed to drive him wild. It did. Her hair tumbled over the pillow and around her shoulders like a red-gold cloud, a sexy halo that drew his gaze to her bared breasts and slim curves. To that outrageous faux-medieval belt fastened seductively around her hips.

"Will you join me?" She patted the bed. "I've got a very special Valentine planned."

Sam could barely draw a breath. Judging by the light dancing in Maggie's eyes, she had some crazy idea in mind, and since whatever she had planned involved them in a bed, he didn't intend to put up any resistance.

Propping a knee on the edge of the mattress, he immediately caught the flavor of her game when she caught him by the belt loop and pulled him down beside her.

In one stunning motion of flashing thighs and quivering breasts, she straddled him, the erect peaks of her rosy nipples hovering just above his mouth. But before he lifted his head off the pillow to catch one with his lips, Maggie stopped him.

"You've been calling all the shots since we got here, so I've decided it's high time for the warlord to relinquish some of his control."

Sam had read about role-playing and submission somewhere in the superclub's promotional material, but he couldn't remember exactly what, when Maggie brushed her nipple against his mouth and said huskily, "Are you game, *milord?*"

"I'm game."

"Good."

Maggie urged him to sit up as she divested him of his sweater, and when he made the move to help, to speed the process along, she only brushed his hands away.

"Let me." She anchored him against the bed by sitting squarely on his crotch.

His erection thickened in pace with each button she unfastened, straining against constricting denim in a noble attempt at liberation. Maggie ground her hips into his in a move that told him she was aware of his predicament, but didn't intend to be rushed. She bent low over her task, and he stared at the top of her head and wished she'd speed things up.

Her sweet orange blossom scent assaulted his senses, filled his mind with thoughts of unlocking the chastity belt and stop playing games right now. The warlord had been waiting most of his adult life to make love to Maggie and he wouldn't be able to wait any longer if she kept up this agonizing pace.

But Maggie only tugged the shirt from his waistband and slipped it away. Scooting off him, she started the whole slow process over again with his jeans, and by the time she'd discarded them in a heap on the floor, he was breathing like an Olympic sprinter, his erection standing as proudly as the torch.

Her gaze locked onto his, and he couldn't miss the delight in her beautiful face as she ran a fingertip along the length of his hot skin. Sam shuddered, the last game they'd played with peanut butter finger paint still vivid in his mind.

A smile tugged at the corners of her mouth. "I'd say you're rising to the occasion."

He managed to rise even higher as she shimmied her hands up his shaft, then abandoned him to reach for the plume on the night table. Sam barely had time to register what she intended before the feathery tip sashayed in light circles over his chest, tracing each muscle and sending sparks like Fourth of July fireworks erupting along his skin.

"Do you like how this feels?"

"Yes." He ground the word out.

She traced the plume down his stomach, then in tantalizing sweeps over his hips. Sam groaned. Maggie replied by forcing his thighs apart with her knees to tickle the sensitive skin beneath his scrotum.

He bucked unceremoniously in response. She smiled knowingly and dipped low over him, her bare breasts hovering just above his erection, practically scorching him with their heat. His muscles turned to molten lava and a languor filled him, his mind suddenly crowded with the image of that erotic ornament and Maggie fulfilling his fondest desire.

He reached for her breasts, barely had their silken weight cupped in his palms before she arched back and pulled them away.

"No touching," she whispered breathily. "Not unless I give you permission. Okay?"

She coaxed his promise with the plume, circling the tip of his shaft in a spiral, then proving she wouldn't take no for an answer as she turned the feather into an instrument of erotic torture. Sam had no choice but to nod his agreement, because his blood pounded so hard he couldn't form words to reply.

When Maggie rose above him, all slim curves and pale skin, and dropped the plume on the bed beside her, Sam exhaled sharply, a sound of mingled relief and disappointment. But he wasn't disappointed for long, because suddenly she was straddling him again, trapping him in the hot vice of her velvet thighs. His breath caught, a painful barrage of air that almost choked him, when she rocked her hips and the heat of her sex began a slow, swirling assault on his senses.

He ached to pull her against him, to feel every inch of her naked body draped over him, a warm, welcome weight. Burying his hands beneath the pillows, Sam fought the urge to touch her. This was Maggie's game. She wanted to make the warlord lose control with her own brand of sensual torture and she was close to getting her wish.

She slid down the length of his body, and he tried not

to thrust as the satin weight of her breasts pillowed his erection, but his hands suddenly reappeared without his consciously willing it.

"I didn't say you could touch me," Maggie warned in a sexy whisper, her teeth nipping the tender skin of his nipple and stopping him.

Surrender.

Sam let his hands drop to his sides, aching to touch her, but unwilling to spoil the fantasy of the moment. Here was a side of Maggie he'd only dreamed existed. And when she lay against him, cradled his erection in the fullness of her breasts, rode him with stunning strokes of her upper body, Sam could only close his eyes and enjoy the ride.

"Trust me," she said, her warm breath bursting against his skin in a breathy gust as she licked the top of his erection, and the sound of her voice, deep with desire, lifted him toward the top of this fantasy.

Sam's eyes shot open, drank in the sight of her arching above him, red-gold waves tumbling over his stomach, her gleaming breasts controlling him completely. A triumphant smile touched her luscious lips, and his blood gathered in one powerful surge that threw him right over the edge.

MAGGIE AWOKE on Valentine's Day to a heavy snowfall that shimmered over Falling Inn Bed, and Breakfast and the grounds like a layer of seven-minute icing, untouched by any presence save an artistic stroke from nature's paintbrush.

Gazing through the magnificent windows of the Warlord's Tower, sheltered and warm, she awakened Sam to share the beautiful sight, and they exchanged their Valentines, lying naked beneath the topiary. Even though Sam had held back her "real" Valentine, as he called it, Maggie wouldn't have changed a minute of this incredible morning.

He'd loved his autographed hockey puck, just as she'd known he would, but had been shocked that she'd stolen the puck right off his mantel without him noticing.

He couldn't blame that oversight on his new contacts, she thought contentedly, which left Maggie to wonder how a man so incredibly oblivious to things around him could be so insightful when it came to her.

He'd sensed how passion would be between them, while she'd been surprised by the depth of her reaction to him. The most remarkable part of all was that sometime during the night, as she'd discovered Sam as a lover, she realized that he amazed her, a man she thought she'd known well was actually a man she'd barely scratched the surface of.

He'd revealed so many things about himself in bed.... He had a fondness for featherlight kisses along his back and neck, and she could make him shiver with her mouth pressed to his skin. He was also what Maggie called a "bun man," because no matter where they'd squirmed on the bed or what explorations they'd indulged in, Sam would always end up with his strong hands sinking into her bottom.

Experiencing the way he'd cherished her body—and that was the only way Maggie could describe it—had left her awed by both his skill and the obvious depth of his feelings.

While Sam might be oblivious to things like missing hockey pucks, by comparison Maggie had to be out-and-out blind to have missed that he loved her, when his feelings were evident in his every gesture, his every word, his every touch.

Knowing this, she no longer had trouble imagining why a visit to Falling Inn Bed, and Breakfast had had such a profound effect on Anna and George Weatherby. Not only was Maggie going to write down her discoveries in her idea journal, she was going to suggest Angie and Raymond pay a visit. Lyn and Charles, too.

Because it wasn't just passion that worked wonders at creating closeness between a couple, it was feeling loved that held all the magic.

And she'd felt loved. All night long. More loved than she'd ever felt before. Becoming intimate with Sam, the man she'd fantasized about and held as her ideal for so many years, had forced her eyes open about how she felt about him, too.

By the time they'd made their way down to the lobby to meet Tyler Tripp for the interview, Maggie knew that the unfamiliar sensation swelling inside her chest every time she looked at Sam meant that her feelings for him ran a whole lot deeper than she'd ever imagined.

To her astonishment, the realization didn't frighten her. Amazed her, yes. She'd always taken pride in her self-awareness, when it seemed she had an incredible capacity for self-denial. Thrilled her, too. If this excitement she felt was part and parcel of long-term relationships, she had definitely been missing out on something incredible.

But frighten her, no. Knowing that her feelings for Sam ran so much deeper than she'd imagined only left her to worry about whether she was actually capable of commitment.

How could she trust her ability to commit to him, when she'd lied to herself for so long?

Maggie had no answer, but she did ponder the question from Bruno's Place, where she sat at a table by the window overlooking the lobby, sipping espresso and watching Sam talk with WTA's photojournalist.

He looked so at ease sitting in a winged chair, legs spread, black hair glinting in the light thrown by the cut-crystal chandelier. He gestured occasionally to make a point, and as Maggie watched him, she realized that she was seeing the side of Sam that had made him so successful in his work. He had a caring and confident manner that easily encouraged people to trust him with their money.

And with their hearts.

The thought caused her to set the cup down on its saucer with a clatter. Did she love Sam? Well, of course she loved him, but did she love him as more than a friend? Was this crazy balloon of emotion in her chest—the feeling that she might explode with excitement and happiness by just sitting here watching him—love?

Did she trust herself not to hurt him?

Her track record was so abysmal. The only thing she knew with any certainty was that Sam had said he'd help her and she could take that to the bank.

"Your turn, Mags." His voice came out of nowhere, and Maggie glanced up to find him sitting down across from her.

She'd been so preoccupied with her thoughts that she'd completely missed him leaving the photojournalist, even though she'd been staring directly at them.

"How was it?" She forced herself to sound calm, when she felt anything but.

"I liked him. He was professional. He didn't ask anything cheesy, so I don't think we'll have to worry about misrepresentation. I did ask him to send us a draft of his article before it goes to print, though. Just as a precaution."

"He didn't mind?"

"No, he even offered to send us copies of all the photos he takes to repay us for our trouble."

"That's nice." Maggie took one last sip of espresso to fortify her and stood.

"Speaking of nice." Sam caught her hand before she had a chance to move away. He brought it to his lips. "I said very nice things about you."

His breath gusted warmly across her palm, a soft, sultry

burst that reminded Maggie she wore no panties beneath her skirt and tights, only the chastity belt.

Which had definitely served its purpose last night. While she and Sam hadn't made love, they'd brought new meaning to the term *foreplay*. The glint in his bedroom eyes told her he still rode that particular high, and to her profound exasperation, she felt a responding heat creeping into her cheeks.

"I'll say nice things about you, too." Maggie took off, hoping to find safe ground away from him and that lethal gaze.

Unfortunately, there was nothing safe about her interview with Tyler Tripp. Though she agreed with Sam's assessment of the photojournalist—he was easy to talk to and professional—their conversation proved dangerous to her peace of mind.

Sam had apparently explained the complexities of their relationship, and Tyler Tripp was very interested in how Falling Inn Bed, and Breakfast and their self-proclaimed ability to put romance into any relationship, was helping Maggie's transition from friendship with Sam to romance.

She could only reply honestly and hope the man censored raw content from his article. "It would be hard not to think of romance around here. This place is incredible. It's like reality doesn't exist, and the only important thing is being together and in love."

"What do you think specifically creates that impression?"

Maggie chuckled. "What doesn't? Have you looked closely at that Valentine's display?"

Tyler shook his head, making the thick silver hoops in his ears dangle, and Maggie leaped to her feet and motioned for him to follow her to the towering topiary.

"Take a close look," she suggested.

Tyler Tripp did, and Maggie nodded in satisfaction when his brows shot halfway up his forehead.

"This is exactly what I'm talking about. The romance around here is subtle, but it's everywhere. I think the su-perclub and the staff have done an incredible job of playing to the senses in the food, the furnishings, the themed suites—in everything. Even the television. I can't help *not* thinking about romance and sex."

"Well said." Tyler smiled in a way that made him seem artistically satisfied. "So, Maggie James, do you think Fall-ing Inn Bed, and Breakfast is helping you fall in love?"

Here it was, the million-dollar question.

She'd wondered if Sam was a man with a need to con-trol, only to discover that he'd been clever enough to use seduction to show her what she'd been too blind to see for herself. He'd loved her enough to wait while she sorted out her issues.

That sensation in her chest mushroomed until Maggie could barely force an answer out. "Given the wonderful man I came here with, I can hardly help falling in love."

Tyler beamed. "May I quote you?"

She glanced toward Bruno's Place, glimpsed Sam flip-ping the pages of the paper—looking for the business sec-tion, no doubt—and was filled with a warm feeling of con-tentment…. "Yes."

Maggie's warm satisfaction didn't last beyond their first round of smiles in front of the Valentine topiary.

Tyler buzzed around the lobby, moving furniture and creating a scene that depicted the charming, homey sort of atmosphere he was looking for. He sat Maggie and Sam on the floor between the topiary and the fireplace and Maggie wondered if he would zoom in on the erotic ornaments in any of his shots.

"All right, smile," he instructed them. "Come on, you

can do better than that for your first Valentine's Day together as an official-couple portrait.''

Official couple.

What if their first-ever official Valentine's photo was actually their last? What if learning to commit wasn't something she could overcome with Sam's help? After all, her
father had never learned. Could she honestly sit by while
another woman took pictures with Sam on Valentine's Day,
woke up with him every morning, shared his life, his love
and maybe even made babies with him?

Could she honestly be content to play Auntie Mags,
knowing that she might have had it all, if she'd only had
a little confidence in herself and some faith in Sam?

No, no, no!

Maggie wasn't going to make the same choices her father
had. She would tackle this issue head-on with Sam's help,
because she didn't want a future without him, didn't even
want to speculate on how empty that future would be.

12

"I'M NOT like my father."

Sam heard Maggie's declaration and came to an abrupt halt in the foyer, hand poised on the still-open door. Glancing at her, the back of her head to be precise, he watched her sweep into the Warlord's Tower, agitation fueling her quick strides.

He closed the door, noticing absently on his way into the suite that housekeeping had already visited in their brief absence. Did they lurk in the hallways, waiting for guests to leave their rooms?

"Who said you were like your dad?" he asked, catching up to her where she paced the floor in the nook in front of the windows. "I mean, you do have his coloring, the green eyes and the hair, maybe, but that's about all—"

"I'm not talking about resembling him, but acting like him. Being afraid to commit." She heaved a huge sigh, mortification and disbelief written over her expressive features as clearly as if the words had been spray-painted on her forehead. "I've always hated what he did, to us, to *himself,* every time he ran away, but I've been doing the same thing, except I've tried not to disappoint anyone by never letting anyone get close." She shrugged helplessly. "Or at least I thought I had."

"Oh." Sam knew she referred to him and half sat on the arm of a chair. He had to admit that though he hadn't drawn the parallel before, her evaluation made sense. "This is your professional opinion?"

"As professional as I can get, given that I'm analyzing myself." Cracking a strained grin, she continued to pace, launching into a breathless examination of why she'd been shying away from commitment and avoiding dealing with the truth.

Sam watched, wondering what had brought on this epiphany when he'd come out of the interview unfazed by comparison.

Just about the time he'd thought he was actually making headway at pulling together all the threads of her disjointed tirade, Maggie said, "And that's why I couldn't see that I loved you. You were already so important to me and I couldn't fathom needing you any more than I already did. I've compared every man I've ever dated to you. In my mind you were the ideal man, so no one ever stood a chance. But I couldn't go for the real thing because I was afraid I'd mess things up between us...."

She loved him?

He shook his head to clear it, blinked, and stared hard at Maggie. Had she just admitted that she loved him? He couldn't confirm this incredible revelation, because she hadn't stopped talking to draw a breath yet. Her mouth still moved, but he couldn't seem to focus on what she was saying.

"Did you just say you loved me?" he asked, raising his voice above her chatter.

She stopped abruptly and stared at him blankly. "What?"

"Did you just say you loved me?"

Confusion gathered in her expression like clouds bunching up before a summer storm and she frowned as though mentally backtracking to remember what she'd said.

Sam's heart started to race.

Suddenly, her frown melted away, and she lifted that beautiful green gaze to his. "Yes, Sam. I love you. I thought you already knew that. I mean, you're the one who told me—"

"Yeah, well, knowing it and hearing you admit it are two different things." Was that strangled-sounding voice his?

She smiled. "I've always known that I loved you as my very dearest friend, but I really love you so much more."

He could only gape, hearing the words he'd always hoped to hear tied his tongue in knots.

Maggie's smile grew wider. "I love you, Sam."

"So what brought this on?" he finally managed to croak out.

"Tyler Tripp and his first-Valentine's-as-an-official-couple portrait." She tossed up her hands and shook her head, as though blocking out some image only she could see. "Sitting under that crazy topiary and realizing that if I keep running, some other woman may take my place."

"There's no other woman, Mags. There never has been."

She eyed him dubiously. "Right."

"Well, no other woman who came close to my heart. I decided a long time ago to wait for you, and I'm a patient man."

"Beyond patient." She launched herself into his arms with such force that he slipped right off the chair's arm and into the seat. But not before he'd locked his arms around her waist and brought her with him, feeling every inch of those supple curves against him in all the right places.

"Does this mean you're willing to give long-term a shot?"

"I'm willing to take the first step," she said gravely. "I

can't promise next week. I have to take each day as it comes."

"A twelve-step program for recovering commitmentpho-bics?"

She pulled back and glowered at him. "Don't you dare make fun of me. I don't know if I have the knack for this, or if I'll ever get it. And I couldn't live with myself if I hurt you."

"You won't hurt me."

"I don't trust myself."

The anguish in her face told him how true that was, and for the first time in memory, Sam wasn't sure how best to help her.

"I'm only asking for a shot, Mags." He wanted forever, but he would travel there one step at a time if that's what Maggie needed to learn to trust herself. Step four—support.

"You'll need to help me."

Winding his arms around her waist, he locked her against him, his body surging in response to her nearness. He could feel the indentation of that crazy leather belt beneath her skirt and physically shivered at how much she was willing to do to ensure he didn't get hurt. He dipped his face to taste those shapely lips. "I can be very helpful."

Their mouths met, eager yet tentative, the awareness that this kiss marked the start of the next step, together, almost palpable between them.

"But, Sam, what if I can't do this?"

Uncertainty made her voice throaty and low, and Sam wanted to tell her that he believed in her, even if she was unsure of herself. But he chose to encourage her instead. He'd add his own step to building a strong relationship. Step six—faith.

"Mags, you've never failed at anything you ever put your mind to, and together we can do anything. We always could. Think about how strong our friendship is and how good we are as lovers...." He let his words trail off as he traced her luscious mouth with his, but suddenly she reared back, breaking their connection, almost toppling off his lap in the process.

"The key!"

"What?"

"The key to this chastity belt," she repeated.

"What about it?" Sam wasn't following her, but he couldn't miss how her eyes suddenly widened in horror.

"Proving that I can handle commitment may take a while, and I don't plan to wear this indefinitely." She plucked at the red leather. "Do I have to prove myself before we can make love?"

Sam hadn't really given any thought to the criteria for making love beyond Maggie understanding how deeply he felt and her acknowledging that she had to stop running. Step three was intimacy, and perhaps they needed to backtrack there to assuage Maggie's doubts. "I'm willing to take a day at a time, too."

"It'll mean taking a chance, even knowing I might never conquer this. I won't promise what I'm not sure I can deliver."

"I know."

"Are you sure you're willing to trust me?"

Her eyes fluttered closed, gold-flecked lashes trembling slightly against her cheeks. Her chest rose and fell, as though she were having difficulty breathing. Sam thrilled with a surge of pure male pride to know that the thought of making love to him inspired such enthusiasm.

More than he'd ever before wanted anything in his life, Sam wanted to make love to Maggie. "I trust you, Mags."

Her eyes flew open and she exhaled a sigh of unmistakable satisfaction. Then she lifted her hands to flank his jaw and tugged his face toward hers. She planted a moist kiss on his mouth. "I'm so excited."

"Me, too." He chuckled, caught up in her excitement. "It's my turn with the warlord's feather."

"It's a plume, Sam. Warlords don't wear feathers. Are you sure you wouldn't rather try the Bungee Swing?"

"The warlord's not really in the mood for sexual calisthenics," he said with a dry smile. "What did you do with the key after you showered?"

"I put it back in your pocket. I'll get it."

Slipping off his lap, she rose in a fluid motion that held him riveted and crossed the room, curls bouncing lightly, backside swaying gently, and Sam felt as if Cupid had come through big-time by piercing Maggie with a love arrow in exactly the right spot. This was one Valentine's Day he'd never forget.

He watched her search through one pocket of his slacks, then another, pulling out the linings and frowning a frown he didn't like the looks of. "What's wrong?"

"Did you take the key out of your pocket?"

"No."

"That's odd, then, because it's not here. It must have fallen out." Sinking to her knees, Maggie scooted around, searching behind the chair, under the edge of the carpet and behind the ornamental screen, while Sam indulged himself in the view of her nicely shaped backside.

"Sam, I can't find it," she finally announced, sitting back on her haunches and fixing him with a puzzled stare.

"Let me help you look." He pushed himself to his feet.

"I'm telling you, it's not here."

He sank down beside her, quickly confirming Maggie's evaluation of the situation. The key was nowhere to be found.

"Did it come with a spare key?"

She shook her head. "No, just the one I gave to you."

"Well, it must be here somewhere. Maybe it fell into the chair." Removing the cushion, he searched the grooves in the upholstery. No luck. "Maybe one of us accidentally kicked it under something."

Maggie gasped. "You don't think that housekeeping… Oh, Sam, what if they vacuumed it up?"

"Don't panic. We'll just go down to the shop and get another. That lock is generic. There's bound to be another chastity belt down there with a key to fit."

Shooting to her feet, she glared down at him. "Honestly, we were just down there. Didn't you notice the shops all closed early for Valentine's Day?" Without giving him a chance to reply, she said, "I'm not asking anyone to open the shop, so everyone knows I'm stuck in this thing."

"Let me see." Sam motioned for Maggie to lift her skirt. "There's a way to get it off. Maybe I can pick the lock."

Schooling his expression so Maggie couldn't accuse him of not taking the situation seriously, he nevertheless enjoyed the view as she hiked her skirt, revealing a long thigh and the sleek curve of her hip beneath wool tights.

Running a finger into the gap between the belt and her skin, Sam found the adjustable leather belt locked too snugly to even contemplate forcing her out of it. Whoever had designed the damned thing must have had an engineering degree.

"The leather's too thick for scissors, but I can get through it with a pair of cutters."

"Did you happen to pack a pair in your suitcase?" Her voice rose hysterically. "Because I'm not dialing 19 and explaining this predicament to Dougray and Bruno won't let me starve long enough for it to fall off by itself."

Remembering the way Maggie had stood in the shower until she'd turned blue prompted Sam not to argue. "All right, don't freak. We won't call for help. Let's just look around some more. It's got to be around here.''

Despite a frenzied search, the key didn't turn up. Sam finally called down to housekeeping to ask if they'd turned up a missing key while cleaning the suite, but to no avail. The key appeared to have vanished.

They were long past coming up with alternate Plan B, but Maggie stubbornly wouldn't hear of calling maintenance. Sam tried a different tactic.

''That thing isn't supposed to be worn long-term is it? I mean how are you supposed to...*you know?*'' Sam tried to sound casual yet still urge her to deal with reality.

Maggie's scowl didn't hide her blush, and he knew she'd gotten the gist of his concerns about using the bathroom. The way she'd been pumping espresso all morning...

''As you well know, it moves around a bit,'' she snapped. ''I'll manage.''

''What if we try to find a pair of cutters ourselves?'' He couldn't think of anything else to do and wasn't about to let Maggie remain trapped in a chastity belt out of pride, when he could be making love to her, instead. ''I remember passing the maintenance building on our way to the pond yesterday.''

''That's a great idea,'' she cried, heading toward the coatrack to grab their coats.

Sam certainly hoped so.

''Ms. J! YOU SHOULDN'T be in your office today. Not only is it Valentine's Day, it's your birthday.''

''Come in, Laura. Doesn't appear as though anyone will be going anywhere today.'' Mary turned away from where she stood gazing out the window of her office, an office she'd chosen largely because of its view of the grounds that were now blanketed with a pristine layer of newly fallen snow.

Mary smiled, realizing Laura wasn't alone. "Hello, Annabelle. I might say the same about the two of you. It's also Sunday. Shouldn't you be at home with your families?"

"With the WTA judge and Cupid's Couple meeting for their interview?" Laura asked in a voice that held a note of horror. "I took a room last night, thank heavens, because the roads aren't cleared yet. I'd have never made it in."

"You, too, Annabelle?" Mary already suspected the answer.

"Duty called," she said.

Mary motioned for them to sit, while she circled the desk and settled in her chair.

"You're staying for Ms. J's birthday party, aren't you, Annabelle?" Laura slid into the chair in front of the desk. "Bruno said he'd be ready around three."

"Of course. I wouldn't miss Mary's party."

Laura appeared relieved, and Mary held back a smile, realizing that Laura, as the newest addition to the staff, hadn't yet realized that her birthday-Valentine's party was a tradition Bruno had begun many years ago.

Annabelle apparently realized this, too, because she extracted something from a pocket. "See, I've brought my gift." She held up a tiny golden key and the disbelief on Laura's face suggested there was some unseen significance to the gift.

"What does it unlock?" Mary asked.

"Ohmigosh!" Laura rocketed from her chair and bounced excitedly on tiptoe, before bracing both hands on the desk and staring at Mary. "Remember what I had sent up to Cupid's Couple's room last night? That's the key."

"The only key?"

They both turned to stare at Annabelle, who dangled the key triumphantly and smiled in confirmation.

Mary cleared her throat to take command of vocal chords that had suddenly tightened like violin strings. "Tell me you didn't have housekeeping pilfer that from the Warlord's Tower."

Annabelle met her gaze smugly. "Well, you've been allowing the rest of the staff to take such liberties—"

"Only because I was counting on you to keep your head and steer us clear of liability."

"Of course." Annabelle cocked her head defiantly, giving her steely gray curls a decided shake. "Would you believe that key was lying on the carpet in plain sight? Must have slipped out of our boy's pocket when he threw his pants over the chair."

"You went into the suite with the housekeepers?"

"Had to have witnesses to avoid liability, didn't I?"

Mary just stared, momentarily taken aback at Annabelle's uncharacteristic daring, and Laura stepped into the breach, allowing her a much needed moment to collect her thoughts.

"I thought the whole point of our game was to encourage Cupid's Couple to fall in love. If they can't have sex because you've taken their key, how are they supposed to do that?"

Annabelle patted her hand. "Trust me, Laura. I'm creating a demand. When you told me Ms. James bought a chastity belt as a Valentine for her young man... Well, clearly we don't want anything keeping Cupid's Couple from having sex, and if that's what's going on between them...they need a push."

She turned back to Mary. "I checked with Natasha in the lingerie shop and she told me they manufacture the chastity belts with treated leather, which means Cupid's

Couple won't be able to cut it off with regular scissors. Dougray promised to let us know when they contact him for a tool to do the job. Sort of ups the stakes, wouldn't you say?''

She waggled her brows suggestively and Mary would have said something—she wasn't exactly sure what yet— had Bruno not chosen that exact moment to burst through the doorway.

''Dougray just radioed in that he caught Cupid's Couple sneaking around in the maintenance building.''

''What did I tell you?'' Annabelle said.

''Did they ask him for a pair of leather cutters?'' To Mary's surprise, she managed to make her voice work.

Bruno shook his head. ''No, and they won't find a pair lying around either. Dougray has hidden his tools.''

Mary knew by Bruno's sober expression that this wasn't all the news, and she was equally positive she didn't want to hear the rest. ''What else?''

''He told Cupid's Couple there was a hardware store at the north end of the park that might be open on Sundays.''

''There's no hardware store—''

''But there's a bungalow with an unlocked door and all the provisions they'll need to spend a cozy night together,'' Laura said, clearly grasping the purpose of this turn of events.

''But what about their little problem?'' Mary pointed to Annabelle's key and the pertinent fact that everyone seemed to have forgotten. ''Cupid's Couple won't be enjoying tonight or any other night unless Dougray gives them a pair of cutters.''

''He left a pair in the bungalow,'' Annabelle said. ''See, it's all coming together, Mary. No need to worry.''

''Dougray sent Cupid's Couple out into this storm and you don't think we should worry?''

Annabelle waved the key. "Opportunity knocked."

From anyone else on her staff, Mary might have expected such derring-do, but not Annabelle. "Tell me, how is Cupid's Couple getting into town? No, let me guess," she added dryly, finally understanding the game. "You took their key, and Dougray replaced it with the key to a snowmobile."

At Annabelle's nod, Mary asked, "What guarantee do we have they'll actually make it to the bungalow and not unintentionally head into the park, get lost, and freeze to death?"

"Don't worry," Annabelle said. "Dougray took care of the snowmobile. They won't get far enough to get into trouble."

Don't worry? "What did he do, fix it with a tracking device so they'll be sure to head in the right direction?"

Mary could tell by Annabelle's smug smile that she was thoroughly enjoying the commotion. "No, but they'll head in the right direction. There's a storm out and they're not idiots. And you have to admit they must want to make love awfully bad to go out in this weather."

"That's true, Ms. J.," Laura agreed. "None of us expected Ms. James to have me send up that chastity belt last night. It wasn't exactly what we were hoping for."

"No, it wasn't what we were hoping for." Mary had hoped for Cupid's Couple's avowals of everlasting devotion and a wedding booking, not room theft, conspiracy or jeopardizing the guests' safety in inclement weather.

How had their plan gone so grievously off course?

Everyone stared expectantly, and Mary massaged her temples, trying to curb the ache blooming there. She had *not* envisioned spending her birthday with a staff that had run amok. At best, Falling Inn Bed, and Breakfast would lose its reputation. At worst, she and her staff would wind up in prison. No doubt she'd share a cell with Annabelle, who'd surely lost her mind.

"They do have a radio, don't they?" she asked.

Laura smiled. "I issued them one yesterday."

"But we don't intend to answer it unless they're in real trouble," Annabelle added.

Mary had the sinking feeling that the only people in danger of real trouble today were the general manager of Falling Inn Bed, and Breakfast, and her out-of-control staff.

13

"WHAT'S WRONG, SAM?" Maggie asked, when the snow-mobile ground to a halt on the forest path. "Why are you stopping?"

"I'm not stopping. This is." He pounded a gloved fist on the windshield and exhaled a breath that burst from his lips as an icy vapor. "I don't believe this. We're out of gas."

Out of gas, *here,* in the middle of a frosty nowhere? "But Dougray said—"

"Yeah, well, Dougray was mistaken."

Maggie glanced over his shoulder, scanned the instrument panel. "But the gas gauge reads half a tank."

"It's stuck then, because we're out of gas."

Sam had owned a snowmobile and if he said the gas gauge was stuck, Maggie wasn't going to argue. She scrambled off the seat, wishing she could smooth her skirt inside her snowsuit, immediately uneasy when she sank ankle-deep in the snow.

The trail they followed wound narrowly through the forest, beneath trees that formed a skeletal arch above them. The spiky branches were snow-laden and shadowed against the stormy, late-afternoon sky, and Maggie worried that when darkness fell, it would fall quickly. "Maybe this wasn't such a hot idea. Maybe we should have waited until morning."

Although the idea had seemed very hot a short while

ago. But perhaps that had been because returning to the superclub after failing to find a pair of cutters in the maintenance building had been unthinkable. She wouldn't have been able to make love to Sam, or to shower…but to venture out in a storm so late in the day? What had she been thinking?

She hadn't been. As usual, Maggie had acted on impulse, taken Sam along for the ride, and it seemed as if Mother Nature wanted to reiterate how dangerous impulsiveness could be, because snow flurries started to drift through the forest overhang.

Sam glanced up, caught a huge flake on his eyelash that made him blink. "If life only had a rewind button, right?" Searching beneath the hem of his down jacket, he unfastened the radio from his belt loop. "I thought the superclub was crazy to assign us this. Shows you what I know."

He turned a knob, and the radio beeped and crackled. "Mayday. Mayday. This is Sam Masters from the Warlord's Tower. I've got a problem."

He held the radio transmitter to his ear and waited for a reply. And waited. He depressed the transmit button again. "Is anyone there?"

More silence.

Sam clicked the radio on and off again, switched channels. "Didn't Dougray say channel one?"

Maggie nodded.

"Then I don't understand. The radio seems to be working. I'll try another channel."

But they got no response from channels two, three, four, five or six, either. Without a word, Sam refastened the radio on his belt loop and was scowling hard by the time he caught Maggie's gaze.

"The elevator, the shower stall, a snowmobile with no

gas and now a radio that doesn't work. I'd say Falling Inn Bed, and Breakfast needs a new maintenance supervisor.''

Maggie didn't argue. Now that the radio wasn't hissing and spitting static, the silence of the snow-muted forest seemed downright spooky. ''Should we head back?''

Climbing off the snowmobile, Sam glanced around, the expression on his face making Maggie even more apprehensive. She hadn't seen him this edgy since her sophomore year in high school when that stupid jock from a rival school had tried to maneuver her into his back seat after a football game, despite Maggie's having declined his invitation in no uncertain terms.

Sam had broken the jock's nose, gotten suspended and sworn he'd do it again if anyone ever tried to force Maggie to do anything she didn't want to do. He'd been her knight in shining armor all along—even though she hadn't been ready to admit it.

''I'm not sure if we're farther from the superclub than we are the town,'' he finally said, ''but either way, it's going to get dark soon.''

''We've been riding for a while.''

''I know.'' He glanced down the trail, brow furrowing in concentration. ''Didn't Laura mention something about bungalows around here?''

Maggie peered into the gloomy jumble of stark trunks and twisted undergrowth, grateful Sam was using his brain while all she could manage was visions of them frozen solid with icicles dangling from their noses like Jack Nicholson in *The Shining*. ''You're right. On the north end of the park. Do you think we pass them on our way into town?''

''Let's walk ahead and see. We can't be too far, because I hear the river.''

Maggie smiled gamely, linked her arm through his, and

tried to curb the anxiety that had her drawing parallels between Falling Inn Bed, and Breakfast and Stephen King's Overlook Hotel. Thankfully, she wasn't tested too hard, when only five minutes later, they emerged in a clearing, where a cluster of quaint bungalows nestled in a half moon along the riverbank.

"I don't think I've ever been happier to see civilization in my life."

Sam arched a dark brow, clearly questioning her interpretation of civilization. They'd both been reared in Baltimore proper, so this cluster of vacation cabins barely qualified as a street corner, let alone civilization.

"I bet they're great in the summer," she said defensively.

"They're shelter now. *If* I don't have to break a window to get in one."

With brisk movements, he headed toward the bungalow closest to the trail and began rattling windows to find access. Maggie headed toward the front porch, intending to help, and as she passed the door, she gave the handle a quick turn, just in case.

Unlocked.

With a gasp of delight, she pushed the door open and stepped inside. In contrast to the snow-covered landscape outside, the bungalow looked like a summertime Eden with light airy furnishings and walls of paned windows. The ceiling and floors were painted wood beams and the pots of silk palms and tropical flowers added to the gazebolike atmosphere.

A fireplace should have seemed out of place among the wicker and cast-iron furnishings, yet the whitewashed stone and gold-filigreed screen seemed perfect for chasing away the damp chill after a summer storm…or a blizzard.

Through a wall of many-paned French doors, the back

half of the bungalow opened onto a courtyard that Maggie was certain would bloom with flowers during the summertime. Right now, though, the flower beds, the hanging planters and the birdbath all sat blanketed beneath a thick layer of snow.

Sam clambered through the doorway, his nose red and a sheepish grin on his face, and stomped the snow from his boots. "Guess I should have tried the door first. Good thing I didn't break a window."

"Today's my lucky day."

"What about the phone?" He glanced at a nearby stand that Maggie hadn't even noticed.

"Didn't try it."

Sam obliged, replacing the receiver in the cradle almost as quickly as he'd picked it up. "It's dead. I suppose they turn the service off until the spring."

"Well, at least we won't freeze to death until someone notices we're missing."

Sam inclined his head, but looked pained as he gazed around. "That's something I suppose, but do we actually want to stay here? This place lacks the Neanderthal atmosphere of the Warlord's Tower."

"I think it's charming."

"I think that's the point, Mags." His dimple flashed. "No self-respecting male would ever choose to stay here, which means they've designed it exclusively to appeal to women who lure their men here with promises of sex."

"Sam!" Maggie laughed, rubbing her arms to chase away the chill. "Well, I suppose I did exactly that. Unfortunately, I won't be delivering on my promise any time soon." She cast a meaningful glance down to where the chastity belt resided beneath her skirt and let out a dramatic sigh.

"Don't be so sure. Do you see what I see on the table?"

Following his gaze, she let out a gasp. "Is that what I think it is?"

"Sure as hell is." He covered the distance to the table in two powerful strides. "A toolbox."

"You don't think there might actually be a pair of cutters in there, do you?"

Sam was already opening the lid. "Dougray said he couldn't find his and look what we have here. A pair of cutters."

Maggie crossed her fingers. "Will they work?"

"They should."

She'd barely had a chance to whoop with relief, when Sam gazed suspiciously down at the toolbox as though another thought had occurred to him.

"How convenient that there just happens to be a toolbox in this bungalow with the exact pair of cutters we need. Does this strike you as fishy?"

"What are you saying?"

"I'm not sure."

"That would mean that Dougray sent us out into the storm, knowing we'd wind up here." Maggie shrugged. "How could he know that? Better yet, why would he do that?"

"I don't know." Sam held up the cutters and eyed them dubiously. "This just seems awfully opportune."

"I can't even go there." The thought of Falling Inn Bed, and Breakfast's staff knowing she was trapped inside a Valentine red chastity belt was just too much to handle.

"It's a coincidence, Sam. No hotel in the world is going to assume the liability of forcing guests out in a storm like this. It's absurd. Dougray was probably in here making repairs, then left his toolbox and forgot to lock the door."

Sam regarded her thoughtfully for a moment before nodding. "Yeah. You're probably right. Talk about luck though, huh? Let me see about turning on the heat or start-ing a fire to warm this place up, and then, Maggie my dear, I'd say it's high time we disposed of my Valentine.''

His expression sent a tingle shooting straight to her toes, and Maggie headed down the hall, calling back, "I'll go look for the thermostat.''

Not only was the central heat and air unit in good work-ing order, but combined with the fire Sam fueled in the fireplace, they were quickly on their way to making the bungalow habitable enough to strip off their snow gear. Very habitable, Maggie thought, when she found a linen closet stuffed full of warm blankets. Dragging them into the living room, she created a nest on the floor in front of the fire. "I wonder why a summer cottage would store all these blankets?''

"I'm not complaining, as cold as I am.'' Sam cast the blankets a frowning glance before moving to the telephone desk. "Look what else I found.'' He held up a Do Not Disturb sign.

"Do you really think we'll need that out here?''

"Knowing this place, I'm not willing to take the chance.''

Opening the door, he let in a gust of frigid air that made Maggie cringe closer to the fire and hung the sign on the doorknob. He slammed the door shut and threw the hotel latch. "We shouldn't get any surprise visitors now.''

"Only crazy people would be out in weather like this.''

"That includes us.'' Sam strode toward her with slow, purposeful strides, his hunger as visible as the sheen of snow on the landscape outside. "Because I'm crazy about you.''

Scooping the cutters off the table as he passed, he held them up and said, "Warm enough to take off that skirt yet, Mags?''

He stood there, tall, dark and oh-so-commanding. The promise in those gray bedroom eyes warmed her in a way no fire ever could. Maggie's breath caught in swift reply.

Sam must have found his answer in her expression, because before she could utter a word, he scooped her into his arms and brought her hard against his chest. With one hand he placed the cutters on the mantel, then grasped her chin and tipped her head back to stare into her face. "I like it when you can't catch your breath. It means I arouse you."

Maggie was aroused, from the top of her head down to the tips of her toes, aroused with wanting to know how it would feel to have him pressed deep inside her. Her breathing broke from her lips, a little faster, a little threadier.

"See." A smile curved his lips as he brushed them against her forehead. "When you're aroused, your skin gets all hot and sexy, and I just have to kiss you."

The way he traced lazy circles along her temple and cheek sent spirals of eager sensation straight to her womb. She moaned, a tiny, yielding sound that evoked a smoldering gaze from Sam as he reared his head back and gazed into her face.

He clearly knew how his kisses affected her and he was very pleased with the result. His mouth came down on hers, and she met his kiss eagerly, with a demand of her own.

Love me, Sam.

The thought swelled in her mind, a yearning to explore everything he offered, a willingness to follow him into the uncharted terrain of long-term and commitments and just possibly a forever she'd never believed possible.

Pressing eagerly into his touch, Maggie let her hands roam freely into the cool thickness of his hair, urging him closer and deepening their kiss, testing her newfound freedom, a privilege to touch him that was suddenly hers.

She stroked her fingers down his neck, exploring the supple cords of muscle there, then over the sweater-covered width of his shoulders, their broad strength so suddenly unknown, yet inviting…speaking through touch, telling him how much she trusted him to lead the way.

Sam understood. With one arm locked around her waist, he braced her against him, steadied her when her knees grew liquid and she doubted her ability to stand. But his other hand…his other hand traveled a path similar to hers.

With exquisite precision, he traced the shell of her ear, then the curve of her jaw, his touch light, unhurried, as though he, too, were just now realizing that he'd earned the right to touch her and intended to make the most of the freedom.

Smoothing his strong hand down her neck, he caressed each inch of her exposed skin, his tongue tangling with hers, his kiss mirroring his growing hunger, and hers.

Maggie was so hot, so ready. Arching against him, she felt every pleasure point melt against the hard strength of his body in exactly all the right places.

Yet, amazingly, Sam was in no hurry, even after his long wait. Patient, he'd said, and she knew he had been. Far more patient than most men ever would have been.

Now was his moment to explore his fantasy. Maggie inhaled deeply to calm her excitement, to transform urgency into appreciation, to enjoy the taste of his mouth on hers, to revel in the knowledge that *she* was this incredible man's fantasy.

Their time had finally come, and she reached deep into her memory to measure the moment against those intensely private fantasies she'd harbored in the late night through the years. And found fantasy paled beside the reality of Sam's desire.

No dreams could compare with the strength of his hands as he sought more intimate contact beneath her sweater. Maggie shivered when his cool fingertips brushed her skin and she sighed when his mouth broke away.

With his broad, muscled body, he crowded her down into the blankets, urged her to spread out before him, poised for his inspection. As he sat back on his haunches, Maggie trembled with the intensity of the moment, and waited.

His breath came hard. His gaze smoldered with need. But it was the expression on his face, as though she, and the image she presented, were living up to be everything he had ever dreamed about, that made her insides melt.

His mouth curved slowly into a satisfied smile, a look as inviting and intimate as a kiss, and Maggie smiled back.

"I want you," she said, a purr of a sound.

"I know."

She thrilled at the throaty assurance in his voice, a sound of such conviction that she finally understood the power of what it meant to be wanted. Sam wanted her, and his desire had empowered him and guided her to this incredible moment.

With swift, sure motions, he stripped the sweater over her head. Her bra followed and she was left bared from the waist up, feeling decadent and erotic as his smoky gaze traveled over her, and her nipples peaked into tiny knots, strained toward the approval she saw deep in his eyes. A lush appreciation of what she offered. An earnest promise to love her and make love to her and take her places she'd never gone before.

A ripple of sensation shimmered inside her, heated her blood until it coursed through her in a scorching rush.

When he unfastened the zipper of her skirt, brushed the

parted fabric over the chastity belt and down her hips, she slipped her hands from his shoulders, intent upon helping him free her from the tangle of wool tights and leather constraints, but he only brushed aside her hands.

"Please, let me."

The throaty roughness of his voice suggested that undressing her was another of his fantasies, and Maggie let him, knowing that she'd never felt so assured of her femininity as she did right now, knowing she was Sam's fantasy.

His love was apparent in the almost reverent way he pulled the boots from her feet, stripped the wool tights down her legs, pressed his hot mouth into that responsive curve of her ankle. His every touch sparked her longing, ignited needs she'd never known needed satisfying, made her quiver and yearn and want....

"Here," he whispered, his mouth a rough-velvet caress across her skin.

"What?"

"Orange blossom perfume." Glancing at her sexily from above her ankle, he brushed his lips over her skin again, didn't release her gaze. "You dab perfume down here, too, don't you?"

She could only nod in reply, amazed that he would notice something so simple about her, that he cared to explore even the most subtle nuances of her personality.

A light touch on her knee and her legs parted, and his finger trailed up her thigh with silken precision to the juncture of her thigh.

"And here, too."

Before she had a chance to reply, his dark head descended, and a sound suspiciously like a growl emitted from the region between her knees. The last thing Maggie saw was the satisfied smile that touched Sam's lips before she closed her eyes, rested her head back in the blankets, and sighed deeply as he nibbled his way up her thighs.

The balmy bursts of his breath against her skin mimicked her own shallow breathing. The combination of heat from the fire and Sam's warm mouth left her woozy and giddy and gasping.

Somehow he managed to find every nerve, every pulse beat as he explored the juncture of her thighs. He laughed at the chastity belt still shielding her, brushed aside the strip of leather as though it were completely unworthy of notice and not the insurmountable obstacle it had been a short while ago.

His fingers grazed her skin and, bared to his gaze, Maggie couldn't force her eyes open. Not when her skin felt so sensitive. Not when she couldn't control the way her thighs trembled involuntarily in response to his touch. Not when she gasped a sound of utter delight as his fingers curled into the moist folds, finding that private little knot of nerves.

She arched upward in amazed delight, opening her eyes. For all of one jerky heartbeat, she stared at the top of his dark head, at his broad shoulders bracing her legs apart, as he began to tease and to tempt.

He handled her with exquisite care and such knowledge-able precision until she was drowning in rolling waves of sensation that made her grow moist with anticipation. Maggie could only abandon herself to his skilled touch, marveling that this was Sam, *Sam*, who was making her insides melt, making her heart drum wildly, forcing her thighs even wider and thrusting deeper and lifting her toward the promise of such incredible pleasure.

Suddenly he was arching above her, all broad shoulders and male power, and Maggie had never wanted so much as she did as when he bent his head low over her breasts, his mouth tasting, exploring and chasing away all thoughts of long-term relationships and commitment on a rush of need.

Whatever lay ahead, she'd finally know him completely as a lover. She wouldn't think beyond this moment. Wouldn't think beyond exploring the most wonderful relationship she'd ever known, with the most wonderful man. She'd focus only on the here and now, on the strength of Sam's hand as he lifted her breast to his mouth, the hot velvet swirl of his tongue, the playful tug of his teeth on the rigid crest and the answering throb deep in her womb.

With his dark head bent low over her and his mouth drawing deeply on her nipple, he stroked the creamy folds of her sex, proved how much he would cherish her, how eager he was to lead them into the future. Maggie could only hold him close, tempted to her very depths with each luscious stroke of his tongue, feeling the stubble on his jaw abrade her skin with an intimacy she yearned to make a part of their forever.

She wanted Sam. Wanted to coax pleasured groans from his lips and to please him as thoroughly as he was pleasing her. When his mouth drew away and somehow, the cutters appeared in his hand, though for the life of her, Maggie didn't remember him grabbing them, she laughed in sheer excitement at what the significance of those cutters meant.

"Finally."

"Finally," he repeated, sliding his finger from between her legs and fastening his hand over the curve of a buttock, guiding her. "Lift up."

She did as he asked, rising off the blankets, allowing him the freedom of both hands to lift the leather away from one hip…*snip,* then the other…*snip,* before Maggie's Valentine fell from her bottom like the peel from a ripe tangerine.

Damaged red leather quickly disappeared from view and

the heavy cutters skittered across the wood plank floor. The clatter faded into a silence heavy with expectation, their ragged breaths the only sounds above the snapping of the fire.

Sam's even white teeth flashed in a wicked grin as he grabbed her behind the knees, urging them upward, spreading her before him, open, vulnerable.

"Finally."

She heard only laughing relief in his voice as he leaned over her to press a kiss to her newly liberated sex.

Maggie came up off the blankets.

"Sensitive?"

"Yes." The word came out a strangled gasp.

"I suppose that shouldn't come as a surprise with that leather strip rubbing against you for close to twenty-four hours. Are you sore-sensitive or aroused-sensitive?"

His gaze on her most intimate parts sent a gush of hot desire through her that answered that question with blinding certainty. "Definitely aroused."

"Good."

Instead of touching her, Sam stood, leaving Maggie trying not to envision what a sight she must make, lying sprawled naked on the blankets, knees up and parted. The fire's glow made her prickle hotly, from her nipples to that sensitive place between her thighs that kept drawing Sam's gaze.

A wave of molten sensation made her ache to feel Sam inside her, and Maggie could lay there no longer, had a few of her own fantasies to fulfill. Scooting around, she drew up onto her knees, forced back a wave of self-consciousness as her breasts jiggled with her movements and earned Sam's undivided attention.

She tugged at the hem of his sweater and urged him down on his knees beside her. "Do you mind?"

His grin flashed, dazzling against his skin, but Maggie recognized the surprise in his gaze and suspected that his fantasies about her must have been very one-sided. Suddenly she wanted to turn the tables, to convince him that he hadn't been the only one enjoying seduction fantasies.

She caught the hem of his sweater and shirt with both hands. "I've got something to confess, Sam."

"A confession, Mags? What do—"

She muffled his reply by tugging the sweater and shirt over his head, revealing the silk-brushed muscles of his chest to her inspection. He dragged his arms from the sleeves, but she teased him by taking her time peeling the fabric over his face.

Somehow it seemed easier to confess her own fantasies without being held accountable by his smoky gaze, but she couldn't resist arching against him, brushing her stiff nipples against his powerful chest, melting inside when she felt his erection swell inside his jeans in reply.

"Once upon a time," she began in a sultry voice, bunching the fabric beneath his jaw when he tried to pull it from her grasp. "When I was very young and very intrigued by sex, I had this dream about making out with this guy I knew. It was pretty innocuous really, we French kissed, he slipped his hands up under my shirt and bra and touched my breasts. But my response to that dream, Sam. I'd never felt like that before. All those raging teenage hormones…"

Maggie leaned against him, pressed her breasts sexily into his chest, bare skin against bare skin, crisp hairs gently abrading her nipples and bringing back the magic of that first sexual awareness with an intensity that made her ache.

Sam stiffened, his back ramrod straight, fusing their bodies closer, though from arousal or near suffocation, Maggie didn't know. But the vigor of his growing erection convinced her he wasn't in any immediate danger of asphyxiation.

"When I woke up the next morning and remembered my dream, I was mortified. Somehow the daylight tarnished what seemed so completely wonderful in the dark, but the next night... Guess what, Sam? The next night when I crawled into bed, I found I couldn't get that dream out of my head. My imagination had run wild, thinking about all the delicious, completely forbidden things I could do in my fantasies." She loosened her grip, biting back a grin when Sam ripped the shirts from his head so fiercely his hair stood on end. "...*with you.*"

His gaze blazed, his expression so intense that she felt riveted to the spot, completely naked and vulnerable as he searched her face, and—Maggie breathed again—found the truth.

Her hands shook as she slipped her fingers into the waistband of his jeans, avoided the potent combination of wonder and power in his expression as she worked loose the button. "I've never admitted this to a soul, but as I grew up, so did my fantasies. They were all mine. Intensely private, reserved only for very late at night. I couldn't even think about them any other time, because I—I just couldn't. Then I'd have had to address the emotions behind them, and it was so much safer, and pleasurable, to imagine you as my knight in shining armor. Then in the daytime, when I saw you, I wasn't accountable for anything I'd imagined at night."

His zipper parted beneath her fingers, the metallic clicking so subtle over their breathing, the hiss of the flames, yet so symbolic that her sex pounded, hot and moist and eager.

Easing the fabric down his hips, she settled them on his thighs, freed his erection from the soft cotton bind of his briefs. It sprang forward, rock-hard and oh-so-proud, and Maggie caressed the hot length of it, shivered when it jolted against her palm.

"I used to imagine myself touching you." She circled her fingers around him and gave a sleek tug.

Sam groaned, and she lifted her gaze to his, unable to fight back the need to lighten the force of the moment, of his expression, to shift the balance of power so she didn't feel so incredibly vulnerable, so exposed, as she forged ahead with the admission that she intended as a gift for his belief in her.

"I'd imagine you were a knight who'd rode in to save me from an evil villain, and then I'd thank you by stripping off your armor and *white cotton briefs,* right in the middle of the sunny battlefield, and sink down on my knees and suck you off."

Maggie bowed over his shaft, hair tangling in the jeans bunched around his thighs as she swirled her tongue around the thick head and drew his hot length into her mouth.

Sam's growl was unlike anything that she'd ever heard before, so much more than need. It was the sound of pleasure and appreciation and triumph. His voice rasped like gravel, when he said, "Oh, Maggie."

Suddenly his fingers speared into her hair, not rough enough to hurt, but so possessively that Maggie moaned in reply. Her breasts grew heavy and eager for his touch. Her sex pulsed, ached to feel him inside her.

She sucked on him, drawing him deeper into her mouth, then releasing him only enough to swirl her tongue lightly along his length. She thrilled when his hips bucked sharply and he issued another hard growl.

Shoving the jeans and briefs down his thighs, Maggie didn't have a chance to protest when he arched his hips and slipped from her mouth, his fingers still gripping her head tightly and tipping her face to his.

The urgency in his expression made Maggie gulp back the lump of emotion that rose in her throat, a crazy knot of longing and excitement and sheer appreciation for this man who'd wanted her so much that he'd not only been willing to wait, but had also been willing to help her find her way.

He sank down onto the blankets and yanked off the last of his clothing, sprawled before her unabashedly naked and undeniably aroused. Passion made him a much loved stranger. She didn't know all the subtleties of his lean body yet, how his muscles flexed with his movements, the way he moved powerfully, unhampered by his nakedness as he gathered her against him.

But Maggie knew the expression on his face, the chiseled planes and angles creating a familiar whole, an eagerness she thrilled to see.

An eagerness to love her.

Sam rolled on top of her, strong upper body obstructing her view of the firelight, the bungalow and anything except the muscled cords of his neck and those broad, broad shoulders. His knee urged her legs apart and he thrust his heated length between the cradle of her thighs.

His eyes fluttered closed as he teased her moist opening with his hardness, and Maggie gasped, suddenly unable to think about anything except that they were pressed skin to skin, steely male heat branding trembling feminine softness, the firelight glazing them both in warmth.

His body was so hard and strong, and he pressed inside her only the barest inch or two, but enough to hint at the strength of his yearning, enough to tempt her beyond all reason.

"I love you, Maggie." The love in his gray eyes told her that he'd never meant anything more in his life.

She brushed her knuckles along his jaw, savored the rough-soft feel of his skin, and when she spoke, her voice snagged on a sound that was very much a sigh. "I love you, Sam."

It must have been exactly what he needed to hear, because his mouth caught hers, and she could taste the smile on his lips. Pure delight at knowing she'd pleased him was Maggie's last thought before she lost herself in the way the fire heated her bare skin, the way Sam's hands stoked the fire inside her.

She wanted this man with more clarity than she'd ever wanted anything before in her life. This was right. No matter what she had to face to earn the privilege, she would face, because she wanted her future to be one with Sam's hands on her eager body, his lips stoking her desire to life.

Unable to resist touching him, Maggie slipped her hands between them, stroked the base of his erection, and gently coaxed his hardness against her. To show him how willing she was. To delight at his answering groan. He thrust into her palm, inching that wide head inside her even more, stretching her, teasing her, tempting her.

His eyes half-closed, he moved against her with short stabs that gave her the control, but she quickly found that privilege a double-edged sword. She ached to feel him inside her, but couldn't maneuver herself any closer.

But Sam knew what she wanted, and with a groan, he obliged, brushing her hand away, shifting her leg around him, positioning himself against her. His gaze captured hers as he thrust inside her, one long upward stroke that stole her breath with the intensity of his entry.

And then he began to move, sliding and stroking, steel into velvet, heat into heat, dazzling Maggie beyond comprehension that anything could feel this right, this gratifying, this completely and utterly good.

She clung to him as he pushed into her with ever increasing strength, each thrust mounting her pleasure into a blinding need, until she could only touch him, urge him on, follow him as he guided her into a position that applied pressure exactly where she needed it the most.

Somehow, as though she'd waited her whole life for this moment, she looked into Sam's eyes, saw his love, saw their future, and knew she'd waited forever to be in his arms.

When her orgasm surged, Maggie eagerly met it, helpless to do more than sink her fingers into Sam's hips to urge him deeper, meet him stroke for stroke and cry out his name when the waves broke over her.

Then she heard him gasp, felt his shudder, his low groan of satisfaction. He pulsed hard with his own climax, added his pleasure to hers, left her awed by the sensations stealing through her, and they strained together, thrusting again and again at slowing intervals, their bodies revealing the love they were too overcome to speak aloud.

TOO WEAK to open her eyes, Maggie clung to Sam, her naked body twined around his so closely she felt like a twist tie nestled in the pile of blankets. They were still joined, locked tight hip to hip, because amazingly, he was not nearly as depleted as she would have thought he'd be.

The fire crackled, punctuated only by the broken sounds of their breathing, casting her in its heat, though she would still be warm had the flames gone to ash in the grate, her entire body glowing from the feel of Sam inside her.

Overwhelmed by the conflicting urges to laugh and sob hysterically, Maggie managed to force out a strained whisper. "Our sex isn't normal, Sam."

"Normal?" He laughed, the sound just as raw and overwhelmed as she felt. "If this was normal, I don't think either of us will live to see forty."

She cracked an eyelid, saw his profile etched in the firelight, his own eyes closed, his face so familiar, so dear that her conflict dwindled away. She chuckled, even as tears prickled the backs of her lids.

"I mean it *really* isn't normal, Sam." Maggie blinked furiously. "This *really* isn't normal."

"Way beyond normal."

Locking his leg around hers, he anchored her against him and gave one strong heave to pull the blankets over them. The marvelous friction of the movement made Maggie gasp and instinctively grind her hips against his.

He groaned. She sighed. They slipped back into an awed silence, clinging to each other, hearts still thundering. Maggie was awestruck by the power of her orgasm, the force of the weakness now claiming her body and her mind, and the sheer enormity of how incredible she and Sam were together.

His thoughts must have been running a similar course, because he sounded just as amazed when he said, "I can't believe you've been fantasizing about me. And I thought I was the only one suffering from unrequited lust in the house."

Maggie snuggled closer with a sigh, pleased she'd found the courage to take the first step toward emotional honesty and commitment by admitting the truth to him.

"You know we have to explore this fantasy thing, Mags," he said. "I want to know your deepest, darkest fantasies."

"Hoping to find *I Dream of Jeannie* in there somewhere?"

"I've got that one covered." He gave a throaty chuckle

that quickly lapsed into thoughtful silence as he brushed a kiss on the top of her head. "And now we'll have a chance to try it. Step five has been the best."

"What are you talking about?"

"Step five—commitment." At her look of obvious confusion, he explained, "You know, your dissertation. You wrote about the five steps of building a strong relationship."

"You read my dissertation?"

"While you were pilfering my hockey puck, I was helping myself to your old schoolwork in the basement. I figured the steps to building a solid relationship would have to work if you'd written them."

His arms tightened around her and Maggie nestled her cheek against his shoulder, marveling at how perfect her head fit in the crook of his neck. "So you've been checking off each step on what...your list of things to do?"

"No. My list of things to do to seduce Maggie."

Pressing a kiss to his neck, her tears stung harder now, forcing her to blink wildly to stave them off. He'd put so much effort into helping her see the truth. "Thank you."

"You're welcome."

When Sam opened his eyes, the love in his warm gaze pitched Maggie right over the edge. Tears won out, slipping down her cheeks, and Sam knew, he *knew,* with just a glance, that they were happy tears, because he thumbed them away with a smile.

The tenderness in his expression made Maggie sob even harder, as though now that she'd opened her eyes, barriers no longer existed, either between them or around her heart.

"So what happens now?" She hiccupped.

He looked thoughtful. "I give you my Valentine."

Suddenly he slipped out of her arms and was flashing

her a striking glimpse of his bare buns and flexing thighs as he propelled to his feet to retrieve his jacket from a chair.

She wanted to object to his leaving, to the sudden emptiness she felt, but had only managed a disgruntled whimper before he was back, sinking to his knees, digging into a pocket.

She propped herself up on an elbow, intrigued. "You've been carrying my Valentine around while we've been looking for a pair of cutters. When were you planning to give it to me?"

"I hadn't exactly planned on—"

"You hadn't exactly planned, Sam?" Maggie sat up, incredulously. "Are you telling me you're being impulsive?"

He arched a skeptical brow. "Not exactly. I've been carrying this around ever since I got to the superclub. I wanted to make sure I had it when the time was right."

The idea of him carrying around any gift, waiting for the right time, touched Maggie so deeply that she reached out to caress his cheek. "You're so good to me, you know."

"I try to be," he said earnestly. "And I want to spend my life being good to you." He withdrew a small box from inside his jacket, a box that looked suspiciously like a ring-size jeweler's box.

Every ounce of blood seemed to drain from her head in a whoosh, and she only stared, wide-eyed, as he flipped open the box to reveal an exquisite heart-shaped diamond on a platinum band, a ring that looked familiar, a ring she might have been able to place had his next words not stunned her so completely.

"Marry me, Maggie."

Capturing her gaze with dove-gray eyes that shone with emotion, Sam lifted the ring from the box and held it up to her.

Maggie stared at it as though seeing an engagement ring

for the first time. "But…how can I…I mean…" She sputtered, vainly trying to quell her racing heart, to shut out the voice inside, telling her to say yes and get this man's ring on her finger before she took another breath.

With effort, she finally managed to articulate the obvious question. "But I don't even know if I can commit."

Sam smiled as though he'd known exactly what she was going to say. "Do you like making love with me?"

She managed a lame nod, not quite sure where he was going with this, when she didn't see that it mattered in the face of the obvious problem before them.

"Do you like the thought of a waking up tomorrow morning without me?"

She shook her head emphatically.

"What about the idea of me taking family pictures with another woman beneath a Valentine's topiary?"

"No." The denial burst from her lips practically of its own accord, making Sam smile.

"Do you trust me, Mags?"

"You know I do."

He brushed an errant curl from her temple. "Then trust me now. I've added a new step. Step number six—faith. I believe in you, because I know you and I know what you're capable of." His voice was a rough-velvet whisper, his expression so completely sincere, when he said, "I trust that you love me, and because you do, you'll want to be with me not only today, but tomorrow, and the day after that."

"What if—"

"I believe in you, Mags. That's enough for me. I can't promise you we won't have rough times, because that's part of love and commitment, too, but I'll be here for you when we do. When you don't believe in yourself, I'll believe in you, and I already know you'll return the favor. Let it be enough."

The enormity of what he said hit her. She remembered her five steps of building a strong relationship, too. Step number four—support. By asking her to marry him, Sam was promising to stand by her side as she learned to face her fears about step number five—commitment. And with step six, he wanted her to trust his judgment, even though she didn't trust her own.

And Maggie had always turned to him when she needed help. Sam had never steered her wrong. Why should now be any different? Why should they waste any more precious time, when they could tackle this obstacle together and enjoy the incredible love they'd found?

Maggie couldn't come up with a single reason.

"Oh, Sam."

Launching herself against him, she wrapped her arms around his neck, tears welling in her eyes when he wrapped his arms around her. The kiss he planted on her lips took her by such surprise that Maggie didn't have a chance to react before he slipped the ring on her finger.

With a misty gaze, she stared down at the heart-shaped diamond, a perfect stone that was neither too tiny, nor pretentiously large, and the shiver inside had nothing to do with foreboding or fear, and everything to do with excitement.

Then it hit her. "This was your mom's ring."

A frown creased his brow. "You don't mind, do you? I want you to have it, and I know she would, too."

She gazed down at the ring, amazed by how easily it rested on her finger, fascinated by how her hand fitted so perfectly within his. "Are you sure? I mean, your *mom's*, Sam…"

He thumbed the ring, a simple gesture that told her he was very sure. "Mom helped me make the decision to wait for you, Maggie. She would have wanted you to have it. She thought of you as a daughter.''

''She knew?''

''Even before I did.'' Sam smiled. ''She said she'd known ever since we first moved to the neighborhood and you took me around to meet your friends, then threatened to pop Tommy Tepper's bike tires if he didn't stop making fun of my glasses.''

''I remember.'' Maggie laughed, laughter soggy with tears. ''But what did that have to do with her knowing how you felt about me?''

''Apparently, when I explained what you did, I also told her that when I grew up and got married, I'd marry someone just like you. I don't remember saying that, of course, but she also said that whenever I set my mind to something…'' He buried his face in her hair, inhaled deeply. ''Behind your ears.''

''What?''

''You put that orange blossom perfume behind your right ear, but not your left. Am I right?''

''Yes, but—''

She never got to finish her question because he was pulling her back into the blankets, kissing her with abandon. ''So what do you say, Mags?'' he whispered against her lips. ''Marry me?''

Propping up on his elbows above her, he slipped his fingers between hers, trapped her beneath the heavy warmth of his body. His grip pressed the slender band into her finger, an unfamiliar band that felt so very right. ''How can you resist? I mean, we've still got to try out that Bungee Swing.''

Who could possibly resist a ride in the Bungee Swing?

''I love you, Sam. I want to marry you.''

His whoop of excitement made Maggie laugh aloud, and

the sheer enthusiasm of his kiss brought to mind the Weatherbys and how they hadn't been able to keep their hands off of each other.

She finally had something to share with Angie and Raymond, something to help them find the excitement they'd misplaced over the years and get their relationship back on track again.

And as Maggie arched up to meet Sam's kisses, she decided that maybe, just maybe, when a couple knew each other very well, loved each other enough, and were committed to share life's ups and downs, that perhaps sex could cure everything else, after all.

Epilogue

JAMES-MASTERS Wedding, Falls Ballroom

Mary gazed at the marquis in Falling Inn Bed, and Breakfast's lobby before slipping inside the Falls Ballroom to take an inconspicuous seat at the back of the room.

The ballroom accommodated up to a hundred guests and it appeared the room was close to full occupancy. Just this morning, Annabelle had informed her she'd booked rooms to accommodate guests from as far away as Florida and Oklahoma.

Cupid's Couple had quite a turnout, Mary decided. To those who cared about the bride and groom, distance seemed only a minor obstacle. Then again, what could be better than having a romantic excuse to visit Niagara Falls in the spring?

Not only would Cupid's Couple's guests get to enjoy the magic of the Falls, they were in for an incredible celebration. The staff of Falling Inn Bed, and Breakfast had quite a reception planned, because they'd taken Cupid's Couple's nuptials as a personal triumph.

As well they should, Mary decided, watching the happy couple gaze dreamily at each other as the bride met her groom beneath a flower-filled arch. While her staff may not have been solely responsible for bringing about these events, they had certainly lent a hand. The hand-delivered wedding invitations that had arrived addressed to each of her staff only proved that Cupid's Couple had assigned them all some credit.

A job well done, Mary thought proudly. The bride wore an exquisitely simple gown of white satin that needed no more ornament than the color in her cheeks, the sparkle in her eyes, and the wild roses that formed a crown on her head.

The groom looked resplendent in his tux, but what struck her the most about him was the adoration on his face when he gazed down at his bride.

Mary sighed. *Ah, love…* and they would have plenty of time to explore that wonderful emotion over the next week in the Sultan's Seraglio, where they'd booked their honeymoon. She made a mental note to line up some sexy wedding gifts for housekeeping to plant whenever the newlyweds left their suite. *If* they ever left their suite.

When the justice announced Cupid's Couple husband and wife, the new Mr. and Mrs. Samuel Masters kissed to an uproarious round of applause and an explosion of camera flashes from none other than WTA's photojournalist, Tyler Tripp.

While Mary and her staff had originally feared the photojournalist's youth and inexperience against the panel's older judges, they hadn't counted on Tyler Tripp's sheer creative genius. His artistic slant on Cupid's Couple's path to love had not only earned them the Most Romantic Getaway award, but had also gotten him noticed by some prestigious journalism committee that would be publicizing his work internationally and providing even more press for the superclub.

Falling Inn Bed, and Breakfast had won the marketing package and secured their existence through the next offseason. Cupid's Couple was taking their first step toward a happily-ever-after, and not one of her staff had landed in prison.

Yes, Mary decided, dipping her wand into a decorative bottle and blowing a stream of bubbles into the newlyweds' path, it looked as though everyone had shared in the good luck that came from being born on the day when Cupid flew around with his quiver filled with golden arrows.

The Cities
New York, Houston, Seattle

The Singles
Dating dropouts
Chelsea Brockway, Gwen Kempner, Kate Talavera

The Solution—THE SKIRT!

Can a skirt really act as a man magnet? These three
hopeful heroines are dying to find out! But once
they do, how will they know if the men of their
dreams really want *them*...or if the guys are just
making love under the influence?

Find out in...

Temptation #860—*MOONSTRUCK IN MANHATTAN*
by Cara Summers, December 2001

Temptation #864—*TEMPTED IN TEXAS*
by Heather MacAllister, January 2002

Temptation #868—*SEDUCED IN SEATTLE*
by Kristin Gabriel, February 2002

It's a dating
wasteland out there!

This Mother's Day
Give Your Mom
❀ A Royal Treat ❀

Win a fabulous one-week vacation in
Puerto Rico for you and your mother at
the luxurious Inter-Continental San Juan
Resort & Casino. The prize includes round
trip airfare for two, breakfast daily and a
mother and daughter day of beauty
at the beachfront hotel's spa.

INTER·CONTINENTAL
San Juan
RESORT & CASINO

Here's all you have to do:

Tell us in 100 words or less how your
mother helped with the romance in your
life. It may be a story about your engagement,
wedding or those boyfriends when you were
a teenager or any other romantic advice
from your mother. The entry will be judged
based on its originality, emotionally
compelling nature and sincerity.
See official rules on following page.

Send your entry to:
Mother's Day Contest

In Canada	**In U.S.A.**
P.O. Box 637	P.O. Box 9076
Fort Erie, Ontario	3010 Walden Ave.
L2A 5X3	Buffalo, NY
	14269-9076

Or enter online at www.eHarlequin.com

All entries must be postmarked by April 1, 2002.
Winner will be announced May 1, 2002. Contest open to
Canadian and U.S. residents who are 18 years of age and older.
No purchase necessary to enter. Void where prohibited.

PRROY

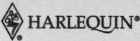